Desiderium

Desiderium

Julie Furxhi

First edition.
ISBN 979-8-9885924-1-9 (paperback)
ISBN 979-8-9885924-2-6 (ebook)

Fiction: Historical, Women's, 20th Century

For Zemra ime, and the women who fought,
and fight, with their mind, body, and heart.

Author's Note

This is a work of fiction. All incidents and dialogue, and all characters with the exception of some well-known historical and public figures, are products of the author's imagination and are not to be construed as real. Some characters were heavily inspired by real people, women in particular. Against all odds, they fought with their lives against larger, merciless, well-armed powers.

Please see Further Reading for resources used by the author.

Pronunciation note
'xh' is spoken like the 'j' sound in English.
'c' as in "Bac" is spoken like a 'ts' sound in English.
'y' as in the name Ymer is spoken like a 'u' sound in English.
'j' as in the name Fejzi, is spoken like a 'y' sound, as in 'yellow,' in English.

Dita Arbani's Family Tree

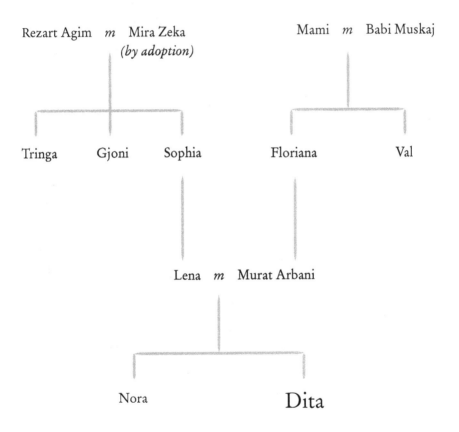

Rezart Agim *m* Mira Zeka
(by adoption)

Mami *m* Babi Muskaj

Tringa   Gjoni   Sophia

Floriana   Val

Lena *m* Murat Arbani

Nora   Dita

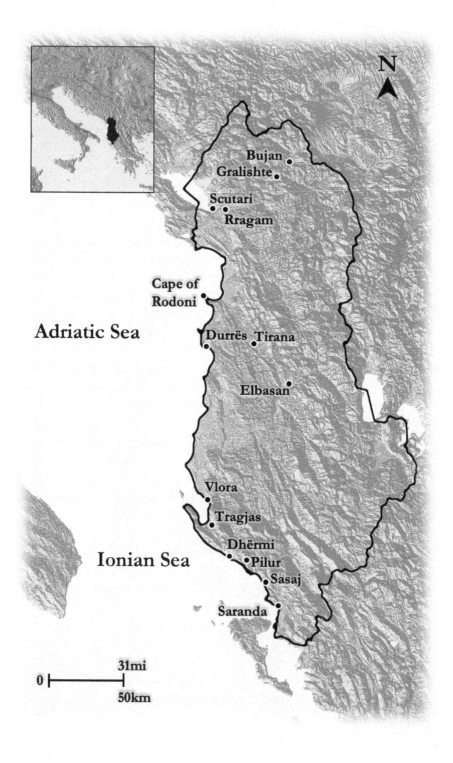

N

Bujan
Gralishte

Scutari
Rragam

Cape of
Rodoni

Adriatic Sea

Durrës Tirana

Elbasan

Vlora

Tragjas

Dhërmi
Pilur
Sasaj

Ionian Sea

Saranda

31mi

0

50km

Mira Zeka

The story my mother, may she rest in peace, told me when I was not yet eight years old, went something like this:

There was once a widow with nine sons and one daughter. The daughter came of marrying age, and a man who lived far away asked for her hand. All the brothers save one, Constantin, refused to give their blessing to the arrangement. Her mother hated the idea of her only daughter living so far away and feared she would never see her again. Constantin convinced his brothers they should agree to the man's proposal. He promised their mother he would bring his sister back to visit in the future.

The time came for the brothers to go to war. All nine sons kissed their mother goodbye and went far away to battle.

All nine died on the field.

Then came a day when the mother really wanted her daughter to come home and visit for a while. True to his word, Constantin rose from his grave and found his sister. After a long journey by horse, they arrived at their childhood home.

'Go and knock on the door, I'll put the horse in its stable,' said Constantin, the faithful brother.

So, despite the late hour, the daughter knocked on the door of her mother's house.

'Who's there?'

'It's me, Mother, open the door.'

'Who are you? My daughter is far away and all my sons are dead. Leave me alone!'

'Constantin brought me on his horse. Mother, open the door.'

The mother opened the door to her daughter, and they both died instantly."

It wasn't the dead daughter or the dead mother that terrified me. It was the idea of a body moving, talking, *being*, without a heartbeat. That was the night my crippling fear of ghosts began.

Unfortunately, one night in early May, I woke with sweat soaking my down pillow and nightclothes.

In my sleep, the vague form of a body, bathed in a blue fog, was coming toward me. It started at the top of a hill, between trees, and came closer to me. But it stopped twenty yards away, like there was a glass wall between us. Then, as if on a loop, the nightmare began again with the figure at the top of the hill. Again and again.

I reached for my headscarf and wiped the back of my neck. I breathed in and out, in and out, and squinted to find something familiar. I made out the shine of the sword hanging over the front door. Behind me, the last embers of the cook fire glowed in its place. The moonlight poured onto the sheep hides covering my shaking legs. I focused on brushing the coarse hair.

My pounding heart began to simmer. I noticed my brothers' breathing and my father's low, gargled snore. Edging as close as possible to the cool stone wall, I looked for the moon, half-lit yet fully proud, through the drafty window.

"Not again," I whispered to the night and closed my eyes.

*

I rose with the village roosters' first crows. The remnants of the nightmare followed me like an impatient child. It sat with its chin perched on the edge of my bed, with big, round eyes, while I changed out of my nightclothes into an undershirt, black woolen pants, overshirt, and stockings. I wiggled my feet into my *opinga* and I wound my heavy braid into a bun at the base of my neck. I started up the fire with a handful of twigs and kindling kept in a box that had been to the left of the fireplace ever since I could remember. The nightmare's presence toddled and waited behind me as I set yesterday's cornbread on the table. I pulled the cheese out of the whey and placed it on a plate, with the feeling that an extra set of eyes was watching me. I heard my family stir and get dressed.

When Bac came to the common area for breakfast, he acknowledged me with a head nod. My father led by example and expectation, choosing to save his words for when they were imperative. His peppered mustache hid his mouth. Every muscle in his body was used to doing the right thing by his family and tribe.

Genti, lean and serious, and Deda, thicker and the more talkative of my two brothers, managed "Good morning" with deep voices not yet awake. They left the house to pull up the day's water at the village well.

The absence of my eldest three brothers, Nikoll, Veli, and Luan, sat like a yoke on our shoulders. We had received confirmation that Luan was killed last year in battle. Nikolli and Veli were missing in action, officially. At first, my father had disapproved when they joined a wild campaign against the Ottoman Empire. Now, I think his heart ached too much to judge. But he wasn't about to let anyone see that.

Bac finished his breakfast in three bites and set the coffee to brew over the fire. "Genti, Deda, you'll need to check the boundary walls and fences today. We'll have an early supper and go to the meeting tonight." He looked at me. "You too, *Shpirt.*"

A shock rippled through me. Me, a woman, to attend a meeting of the tribal leaders.

My father had never remarried, and, although he spoke to me more gently than he did my five brothers, in every other way he treated me like another son. He taught me how to stick a lamb for Easter, how to fish, and the basics of sheep shearing. Two years ago, when I turned seventeen, he took me trapping. Every other woman my age was married or betrothed. I believe my father pushed societal norms more than he knew. Or maybe he knew precisely.

The shadow of the nightmare waited for me by the door, ready to start the day by my side. I checked that the house was in decent order while I tied on my waistband and tucked in my knife. The small bucket of old coal I kept near the fire caught my eye. Occasionally, I saved pieces that would be good for sketching out on the boulders while with our herd. I grabbed two, rough and fragile, and tucked them into a pocket.

My brothers and Bac had already left and wouldn't return until mid-afternoon for lunch. I shut the door and shuffled down the stairs to our animals' pens on the first floor of our house. I concentrated doubly hard on tasks requiring no effort—an extra ear scratch to the pig, checking the chickens, opening the sheep gate—in hopes that by will alone I could push the ghostly remains to the forest. Anywhere I wasn't.

The sheep were reluctant to move. I couldn't blame them: the sun shone gloriously, warming me through and through. I leaned over the fence and bounced my foot on the bottom rung, thinking about the meeting. I didn't see my place, my reason for being there. It would be a conference of the tribal heads, relaying information and reconsidering tactics to rout the Ottomans once and for all.

"Oy! Mira!" I spun around and my eyes landed on Gjergji, a young man about fifteen years old and engaged to a girl in the next village north. What I didn't see was the obstinate shape of my nightmare. It vanished in the open air. In the open air, where so many other nightmare ghosts must exist. Everyone we knew had lost someone or two. Hell, Widow Ramize had lost five to date.

"Morning!" He proudly held up a string of fish. "Good catch today! You've got to get some!"

"Morning!" I replied. "Thank you, I'll try later. Going to the meeting tonight, so I may run out of daylight."

"Well, well! A trade, then?" He tucked a thumb into his vest. "I'll catch some for you and you'll tell me about the meeting?"

"More than fair, thank you. Say hello to your family. Good day!" I called the sheep and led them to one of our pastures northeast of town.

I had yet to go beyond the mountains, these steep, steely mountains. Traveling for trade, a marriage to another tribe, or war were the only excuses to leave them. On this quintessential May morning, the mountains' faces shimmered and sparkled, like a knife's edge catching the sun.

I sat on my favorite west-facing rock. From here, I could see the town below and the valley shaped by the Valbona River, flowing north to south. This was my perch, for in front of me lay a smooth stone, my natural canvas, barely rising out of the earth.

I suppose I could have drawn the puffy clouds drifting downriver. I could have done a portrait of a sheep and the serenity in their dense eyes. Instead, I began to shape Luan, my middle brother. My throat tightened at the thought of him. His face took form by highlighting the shadows—eyebrows, jawbone, thin yet round nose, and that unkempt hair.

Growing up, Luan took me under his wing. He was a great storyteller. His narrations of talking animals and legendary warriors held me rapt. He must have gotten that skill from Mother. I understood Deda, closest in age to me, was trying to fill in the hole Luan left, but he couldn't tell stories the same way. With an air of urgency, like the split second before a spark catches, Deda instead spent time explaining the whys and hows, so that my traps, my aim, and my own intelligence of the world would improve.

For all the taxes we've paid to the Empire, all the men we've had to give over to their army, we've received nothing in return. That was one of Deda's lessons. The Sultan would not be sated until he also dominated Europe. We were too proud, too stubborn, and too hurt, to be ruled for another year. Legends of fighting against the Ottomans were already centuries old.

Next to Luan, I drew what my memory knew of my mother, Bujan's esteemed embroiderer and matchmaker. I darkened the stone's crevices further, smudging with my thumb to create a generic headscarf I assume she wore. It upset me to not know how she looked in absolute detail. A single tear fell from my cheek to her, and for a moment, her head shone in the sunlight.

The four of us walked side by side to Rinaj's house at the other end of town. His was built of stone and mortared with rain-colored river sand, same as everyone's. We could hear passionate voices through the open, and small, windows. The best way to harvest plums and the arguments of war were discussed at the same intensity and carried on the same breeze.

When my father opened the door, there was a brief, audible pause. My father, considered a brother by everyone inside, entered first. Everyone stared. Rather, they stared at me. The silence, save for Rinaj's halting tune on the two-stringed *çifteli*, almost said aloud: *A girl. Mira. He brought Mira. How … Well, yes, of course he did. He's Lef Zeka.*

Most of the men wore white wool pants with thick black detail coursing down the sides of their legs; others wore solid black pants. Rinaj continued to play an upbeat tune. I recognized a few men from other tribes, because their waistbands were different. Where there weren't men standing, there were men sitting, and where there weren't men, there were wide stumps as tables for bottles and glasses of *raki*.

The space around the fireplace, smaller than ours, remained unoccupied. The fire had run out. Stern, mustached, beaten but not broken men stood shoulder to shoulder around the periphery, more than enough heat to warm a room in late spring.

Bac went straight to Lleshi on our left. Lleshi was a neighbor with one foot and fewer teeth than most. Lleshi shuffled his weight to stand and greet my father: handshake while holding each other's elbows, then kiss, right cheek, left cheek, then pat one hand on top of the other with vigor.

I put out my hand. Lleshi looked at it, then at my eyes. He smiled an infectious smile and shook my hand quickly. And so it went, greeting every single man.

Lastly, standing in the middle of the tense room, was a man half a head shorter than me. His cheekbones were high and distinct. His dark hair splayed madly from under his woolen *plis*.

"Rezart!" said my father, greeting him like a long-lost friend. "Good to see you. I've brought my daughter, Mira, and two of my sons, you know, Genti and Deda."

My heart, my hands, my words of greeting, everything in me stumbled. Rezart Agim, living hero of the cause. Deda had mentioned him more than once. As deft with words as with weapons and, miraculously, alive. I lowered my eyes to see my hand shake his. When I looked up, I saw he had been aptly named, for in his eyes I saw a ray of fire, *a golden ray*. I saw an unnerving and unique alertness, like a wild animal hearing a branch snap.

In the time it took me to clear my throat, he was already greeting my brothers. Lleshi scooted over for my father and me to sit on the bench under the front windows. Genti and Deda found friends standing by the door. The man I sat next to reached in front of me to give my father a glass.

Rezart held up a glass of *raki*. "Brothers!" Rinaj stopped playing.

"Sons of Mic Sokoli!" Men cheered loudly and clinked their glasses with their neighbors' at the mention of our own local hero. Rezart's voice commanded their attention. "Brothers, I have recently returned from Scutari. If you have been before, I tell you, you would not recognize it now. The market has been torched. The mayor's building is a pitiful hospital, truly little more than a gathering of starving bodies."

Grunts and tongues clicked, making a *tsk* sound around the room.

"The foreign press is scarce, meaning neither London nor Paris will come to our aid. Women are begging for a cup of maize to boil for their children."

I wasn't prepared for this; Deda had kept more details from me than I realized.

"I do not exaggerate when I call them barbarians. They are soulless, killing without reason or regard. Without a fight."

The code among our tribes could be summed up in one word: honor. It comes with nuances, as all things worth fighting for do. Honor to respect, honor to keep, honor to avenge. I learned very young, be it by blood revenge or simple hospitality, honor is above even love.

"They are burning every home in their way, Muslim or not." He took a deep breath and looked around the room. "They are *impaling* men, then taking what little food there may be from the mouths of children!" His nostrils flared. A few men added the worst curse words as commentary.

"I have seen it, I swear to you on my life," Rezart said quietly and placed his hand across his chest.

The images he had quickly conjured tore at my naïveté. Deep in my bones, my very marrow began to seethe. My toes began to stir, eager to run, knives out. Then, in a flash, I saw in my mind's eye the ghost of Luan, bound, bloodied, and forced to walk past burning villages. I felt cold with fury.

"They are coming." He waited. He looked Lleshi in the eyes. He looked at me. "It will be a matter of months, or less, before you can smell the fires and hear their razing. We must do more. Now!"

Rezart smoothed his mustache and continued. "Their disadvantage, the mountains, is our advantage."

The mountains created an order mirrored in our own code. They stood as tangible protection for those who knew the cliffs and caves, but treacherous for any outsider.

"Now, in the summer, we will take out each camp, one by one." He set down his glass. "Not in a large formation, because"—a singular dimple appeared when he smiled, as he opened his hands out to the room—"as you can see, we are not a large formation." A couple of chuckles quickly settled, with an edge of bitterness.

"You are here because you are ready. Because you want our land to be *ours* and only ours. Yes?" Rezart reached forward with his upper body. His fists clenched.

"Yes!" My father's voice startled me. I did not see the anger I had anticipated. Instead, he was full of hope.

"Lef!" Rezart pointed at Bac. "Gather four other men. Can you leave the day after tomorrow for Berishe, due south? Stay in the trees, above the road, of course. Ambush at night. When you get as far as Berishe, return and we will know that direction is clear."

My father agreed.

"Rinaj." Rezart's voice was even now, like a quiet spot in the Valbona River. It was as if he was reciting the plans he had formed in his head.

Rinaj set down his *çifteli* and stood.

"My good man, will you take three men on the west side of the river toward Scutari?"

Rinaj nodded. Others stirred, raising their chins in the air, eager to also be called to such a worthy task. I hoped Rinaj was as good with a gun as the *çifteli*.

Rezart organized two other groups, along the main road and one west of us. He himself would go a bit farther north to gather more men, and come back through Bujan. His idea was that all the men would then travel together as a formidable group, head for Scutari, and reclaim it as Albanian, free from the Sultan.

The meeting ended with another round of shaking of hands and clapping of backs. Lleshi shook my hand. I managed a quick look at Rezart before I crossed the threshold into the breezy evening.

I laid a fish from Gjergji's catch on the iron grill over a low fire. There was no denying the excitement tingling in my hands, a wild agitation coming to life from the inside out. Genti and Deda sat cross-legged on either side of me. Their backs rounded and they kept their gazes low, avoiding both me and Bac.

"Why did you take me to the meeting, Bac?"

He threw another fish on the grill. "I've been a fool for too long. It's time you knew more. To know who took your brothers."

The steam from the fish burned my mouth. Its meat was light and fresh.

"He's right, you know, Rezart. This land,"—he swept a hand north, east, south and west—"is ours. And this,"—he pointed to the floor under our feet—"this is yours, Mira."

"No one will believe me."

He raised his eyebrows at me for daring to contradict him. Our blood runs in these hills, for better or worse. He raised me like a son, to own life like a man. But it was one of his dreams. Our property belonged to my brothers, even their future children, before I could claim it, according to tribal laws. There would be talk if Bac left the land to me, if neither he nor my brothers returned. "Bac, do you know what you're saying?"

"I do. I don't expect anyone to befriend or defend you when I'm gone, but my greatest hope is the village will honor me by leaving you alone."

"I'll go instead of you."

My brothers looked at me, eyes round in disbelief.

"Your mother would rise from the grave." He crossed himself. We all did.

"Bac, let me go. If anything were to happen, the land would be taken from me by harvest time, and you know it. You're better at words, at diplomacy. I can feed myself; teach me to shoot. I can't stand against the *Kanun*."

He grabbed a fish by the tail, skin crispy and ready to eat. "What, and leave Nikoll and Veli out to fight for me? And Luan? God rest his soul." He crossed himself again, opened his fish and pulled out the skeleton in one swift motion. "I told Rezart I'm leaving in two days. That is what I will do."

"Teach me for next time, then. Show me how to fight. I may need the skills here as much as on the road."

My three men and their knives stopped moving. Genti and Deda looked at me, then at Bac.

"I need to know how to kill with a knife," I said. I shaped my mouth into a chimney to let the heat escape from the food.

Deda spoke up. "I'll teach you. We'll start in the morning."

I didn't want to go to bed when everyone else retired. Tiredness wore at my feet and shoulders, but sleep was the furthest thing from my mind. Seeing my pillow reminded me of the other reason I couldn't lie down yet: I feared another nightmare of ghosts.

I sat on my bed until I heard three variations of snoring. I unhooked the window latch and climbed out to the staircase and descended. I crossed the main road quickly and walked past old Fejzi's backyard garden. Old Fejzi was long gone, but the name remained—a living example of the power of tradition. Along this walkway stood a mix of poplars and aspens, and beyond those was the riverbank.

I hurried to St. Mark's, our village chapel. I opened the door wide enough for my body to slip through—too much and the hinges would creak. Three candles were already lit. I plucked one from its hold and lit one, then three more.

I ducked my head and gently pulled my rosary over my head. I began at the Crucifix, syllables reverberating through my blood, sounds and rhythms I had come to know before I learned to speak:

"I believe in God, the Father Almighty, Creator of heaven and earth ..."

I missed my mother so much. I missed what life was like then. When she would sing while we fed the animals. When she would embroider our coats and shirts, how she rocked ever so slightly with the needle, back and forth.

I began again. "Forgive us our sins, save us from the fires of hell, lead all souls to Heaven, especially those most in need of thy mercy." Luan came to mind. Behind the memory of my brother was the question climbing up a cliff in the recesses of my mind: how many more would I lose? Who else? We hadn't heard from Nikoll or Veli in months. I shook my head as if I could kick the question back down into the canyon, to the abyss below.

"Hail Holy Queen," I whispered. "Mother of Mercy, our life, our sweetness, and our hope! To thee do we cry ..."

I stared into the flame to see my request. In the orange and yellow, I saw a smile; a new smile, not my brothers' or parents' but someone else's.

I took a deep breath and came back to the holy cadence, skipping more than I ought. "Saint Michael the Archangel, defend us in battle. Be our defense against wickedness and snares of the Devil. May God rebuke him, we humbly pray ..." And I saw myself from a bird's-eye view, screaming a battle charge.

Genti is there, and Deda, and men I don't recognize. I can hardly see through the gunsmoke; I can't hear through the yelling. I stop running only long enough to stab, kick, and hit with a rifle's gunstock.

I squeezed my eyes shut. I heard Rezart's voice saying, "This land is *ours.*"

I didn't stand up until I was thinking about the present, about tomorrow, getting my father ready, and a summer of endless work in the sun, instead of visions and memories.

In the piercingly clean air, I breathed in as much as I could, to clear my head. *I should be the one getting ready to leave.*

The next day was Genti's day to be with the herds. After breakfast, I met Deda outside. He insisted that learning to fight within the goats' pen would teach me awareness of my surroundings. Within the first hour, our vests were off and our shirts sweaty.

"You catch on quickly; that's good. But there will be no women to fight. None. Most men will be heavier and stronger than you." He circled around me and reconsidered. "No, they will *all* be heavier and stronger. You have agility on your side. And surprise."

He had my neck in the crook of his elbow in the blink of an eye.

I stepped on his foot and poked the butt of my knife into his side.

"Good. But, the other end, right? If the time comes."

"Deda."

"Fine. But then what?"

"Stab in the side and run."

"If you have to, but running away *with* the knife would be better. Angle it toward the ribs. Meanwhile, I still have my knife in hand. I could stab you in the back. Or another soldier might aim at you, straight-on."

"They wouldn't with their man behind me, surely."

"The bullet won't go through you to him."

It was beginning to overwhelm me—to be so close to another and take their life, their breath. It was sickening.

"Mira? Are you okay? Chances are, you won't need to learn all this."

Had the sun already set? I couldn't feel its warmth. "I do. I do need it. You heard Rezart Agim. They'll stop at nothing."

"Well, let's take a break, anyway."

Later, I found my father cleaning his gun. Sitting by the door was his bedroll, tied with a leather strap. A sleeve from an extra shirt stuck out from the side. I wrapped a few pieces of dried meat and a loaf of bread into a towel. I set coffee to boil, silently insisting we have a cup before he left. The sweetness of the coffee almost swallowed the acrid smell of the gun.

"Me next," I declared, trying to push away scenarios of my father needing to use his weapons. He grunted and chewed on his mustache, usually a sign his mind was on something. The coffee cup looked out of place in his thick hands.

The next morning, Bac, three of his friends and the other groups walked out of town with considerable fanfare. If I'd had a say, I would have preferred a quiet send-off. Tears stung, threatening to find the familiar courses down my cheeks to the corners of my lips. It would be a week, at most, until they returned.

I saw them first. I was with our herd above and south of our village. The sun was high. Four men with their heads lowered held one arm out to steady the weight they carried between them. Two of them had rifles slung over a shoulder. All four of them were missing their *plis*. Not a word from them. I called out to the sheep to start our descent home. I walked in parallel with the men, hastening more with each step.

The babbling flurry of commotion began before they entered the village.

"Mira! Mira!" one of the men barked. I abandoned the herd and broke into a sprint.

"Bac! Bac!" I cried. My headscarf fell off and I didn't care.

Like fruit flies overwhelming an exposed peach in summer, our neighbors bottlenecked at our front door.

"Let me through!"

"What do you need? Where are the others? What happened?" Everyone asked at once. A few women came forward and set to work with boiling water and a flurry of other things I didn't notice.

I could scarcely breathe.

The exhausted quartet laid my father on his sturdy bed and stepped back.

"Bac! Bac! No, please, no!" I cried. I held his hand in mine. *Bac.*

The crowd parted again to allow for Genti and Deda.

"Mira! What happened?" Deda said. Logic often leaves the room in moments of panic.

"Hush. Grab my blanket, and yours too. Don't bother him," I said.

"The bullet's in his shoulder," Blerti, one of the men in Bac's group, said.

"Oh, God!" I yelled.

My father shivered and sweated and swallowed all at once. I couldn't bring the blanket close enough to his chin. Although it was early afternoon, Deda added more logs to the fire to break Bac's fever. Consumed as I was, all the shoes scraping and scratching back and forth, more questions, orders and suggestions for tried-and-true remedies, clawed at me.

A cup of tea intended for Bac was placed in my hands. I clenched my teeth and began to beg without my voice, only moving my lips in a soliloquy: *Holy Mary, Mother of God, pray for us sinners, now and at the hour of our death ...*

Arta, Rinaj's wife, brought fresh bandages to Genti, tending to Bac's leg, and to Deda, who had opened his shirt. There was little to be done except to wipe it clean.

The men had set his leg with branches and their guns' leather straps. I stepped behind Genti and lightly touched my father's shoeless foot. His toes were cold through his crusty wool stockings. Finally, Blerti spoke up with the story.

"Two days ago, the barbarian Ottomans were shooting all around us. The traps they laid, holes in the ground, were hidden well, even in daylight, with branches and all. We were watching every other direction except in front of our feet. The hillside was so steep, his leg fell right into a hole and got twisted in roots and rocks. Then, they shot him in the shoulder. We pulled him out and got under cover as soon as we could. I don't know how they didn't kill all of us ... lucky they had bad aim." His attempt at a little humor failed, so he cleared his throat and continued. "We set the leg as best we could. The fever started last night, on our way home."

My father's eyes fluttered open to me for a moment, then closed again. He swallowed again and rubbed his dry, cracked lips together. Arta brought me a bowl of steaming broth. Deda put his arm under Bac's head. I moved back up to his side and slipped half-spoonfuls to his mouth.

"Just a little," I implored. *Bac, please. Not you, Bac. Please.* It should have been me. *I will be in the next raid,* I vowed to the Accursed Mountains.

Bac didn't make it through the night. His spirit was free to roam the mountaintops without his tiresome body. I knew his ghost would not linger; it would look for my mother's.

Within an hour, his body was cleaned and wrapped and placed in a damn box. The town crier came, holding his *plis* over his chest. He asked if there was anything specific he should include.

"Nothing more than you already know," Genti replied and patted the man on the shoulder.

He began to announce the news as he descended our stairs. His voice crumbled my heart into a thousand pieces, like dry leaves underfoot.

Every home had a chest of clothing reserved for funerals and weddings. I pulled it out from under my parents' bed and began to shake out and match the neckties and embroidered coats we would wear. Every piece was a work of art—my mother's skillful creations of the craft. For myself, I chose a black suit intended for Luan. The dizzying network of dark blue flowers and leaves roamed from wrist to shoulder and across the back. To feel my mother's presence, to wear my dead brother's clothing in order to bury my father—to continue at all—came from a peculiar strength that can rise at a time of misery.

The communal dirge led the way to St. Mark's. It reverberated between the mountains. I could not participate because of the weight I felt lodged in my throat. The cry cut through the heavy air, making space for Genti, Deda, Rinaj, and Blerti, carrying my father. I followed them and the village followed me.

In the cemetery, next to my mother's plot, I faded in and out of the priest's readings and recitations, "… the righteous perish, and no one takes it to heart; the devout are taken away, and no one understands that the righteous are taken away to be spared from evil. Those who walk uprightly enter into peace; they find rest as they lie in death …"

But not you, Bac. We needed you alive.

Afterward, the entire village came to our house to pay their respects. They shook my brothers' hands, then mine. They took my brothers by the shoulders and tried to find words between the crying and crying out. We borrowed as many cushions for seating as were offered. Most men stood. As the woman of the house, it was my duty to host, but it was all I could do to remain upright. I was grateful to Arta for carrying around our black tray painted with white and pink flowers. The tray was last used for my mother's funeral. *I am an orphan now.* On it were small glasses of *raki* catching the dwindling sun through the window. Everyone avoided eye contact but muttered their thanks to Arta.

Deda put a plate of cheese and bread in my hands. My mouth was too stale and dry to know what to do. Soft mumblings of conversation began to spread out underneath the condolences and kisses.

The sunlight coming through the front door suddenly dimmed. Rezart Agim stood in the doorway. His eyes acknowledged everyone with a single sweep of the house, and in four intentional steps, he stood before me. Instead of bending forward to console me as I sat, he knelt and took my hand. His eyes, dark as midnight, held mine. Light engulfed me. I felt detached, soaring from my layers of wool, guilt, and sorrow.

I pulled my hand away and covered my face with my handkerchief.

Later, I surrendered to the fact that I wouldn't sleep. I was too exhausted to slip outside, too tired to even consider unlocking the window. I simply lay on my side, twisting a lock of hair in my fingers. I could not feel my heart beating; I could not hear my breathing. The remnant of me lay wide awake, both stinging from a pain in my heart and blanketed in numbness.

When at last my eyelids began to feel heavy, our house was overcome with a fog, the fog from my nightmare the week before. A crack of light surged through me. My heart found its beat again, pounding out of my chest. My hands began to shake in their clamminess. I tilted my head away from my pillow.

"Good evening," said the form in a female voice.

"Mother?" Though the deepest part of me knew it was not. "Do … do I know you?"

"You don't. I need only to tell you something. Then you may sleep in peace."

"Sleep in peace?" Fear raked my back and anger charged my cheeks. "How dare you."

"You will see blood and salt. My son will show you both."

Then, the house was night again. I sat up against the stone wall and whimpered and shook and knew it was real.

Valentina Muskaj

"The *Ballisti!*" Spit flew through Baba Halil's teeth at the very word. He turned from a compact window framed by stone. His gray beard quivered. Baba Halil, our village's Sufi priest, was an obscenely patient man, but I had struck a deep and tender nerve. "Valentina, are you telling me ... you're joining them?" He gripped me by the shoulders. "They're finished, don't you know? They misplaced their hope. The Germans will let them rot without a second thought!" His translucent green eyes pierced me.

I bit my lip. "I'm not joining them. I'm going to infiltrate. They think we're dead. The Ballisti who were with the Italians when they torched your house and burned our fields don't know we're alive."

Sweat ran down his forehead.

"If I get in, I'll know their plans. I'll know if they're coming back this way. 'There is no luck, only hard work.' Isn't that what you always say, Baba? You'll remember I wasn't here when they set Tragjas on fire." I swallowed to push down the lump in my throat. "How do you think I feel? Next time, my father and his bum leg won't get away. And I won't forgive myself if there was more I could have done. "

To let the Ballisti win would be to give Albania to Hitler, tied up with a pretty bow.

Baba Halil fanned himself with his black robe, one of too many layers in this stifling heat. A turban was part of his everyday wear, but the war, and the heat, changed that. It was one of many things to be cast off. Baba Halil was of the Bektashi order of Sufism, teaching tolerance and compassion. It arrived generations ago, and it was Muslim enough to avoid military conscription and higher taxes imposed upon non-Muslims by the Ottoman Empire.

Our world flipped four years ago, when the Italians invaded and the king abdicated. In this upside-down world, everyone picked a side and was compelled to fight in some way. The Babas had chosen the side of intellectual subversion and diplomacy, mostly. They were willing to use violence as a means to regain our freedom.

I brushed past him and sat on a stool under the window. I rested my head against the wall and searched the rafters for an easier way back to our right-side-up world.

It was no mistake that our simple *teqe* rose into a dome. A higher ceiling illustrated the higher, soulful knowledge to be gained here, in the house of prayer. Lofty hypotheticals had been replaced with political scheming and useful skills, such as loading a gun.

My sister, Floriana, spoke up from her seat on the splintered floor. "I don't understand them. I, I, don't understand *why*."

"Ana, Val, people believe what they want to believe," Baba Halil said, simplifying the existence and purpose of the Ballisti. His tone softened, now that he understood I was not betraying everything I knew and everyone I cared for. "They've exchanged their brains for rifles and empty allegiances. There's no time to wonder why anymore."

I couldn't sit. I jumped up and paced. "Every night we're out there, before engaging in a shoot-out," I said, pushing my hair off my sweating neck and turning to face him, "if there's time, I double-check that they're not one of our neighbors."

"Neighbors? Neighbors! The day they chose Germany over their homeland is the day they became our enemies! They are—" Baba Halil turned away. "I can't ask you to go," he said.

"I'm not asking for your permission," I said. "I don't want to do any of this. I want to go back and teach, like before. But"—I took a deep breath and let it out—"here we are."

The air in the *teqe* smelled like cool, wet sand, no matter the season. "It's too dangerous," Baba Halil pleaded. "They might have left us alone, had we not provoked them. I don't want that to happen again."

"The burning, or the provocation?" I stood again to face him, eye to eye. "If we hadn't gone and blown their stores, the Germans would've gunned us down from the air. They may still! You, you were the first one to say we had to resist, remember? Tragjas needs you. Are you done, Baba?"

"No, no. I'm more scared now than when I gave that little speech. That's what it is." He wiped his forehead again. "It's worn me down, I suppose."

"Your fear may get you killed, if any of the parties interpret it as collaboration," I said. "If you act scared, they may think you're hiding someone."

His eyes slanted into resignation, then brightened with resolve. "I'll write up another article and see how I can help your father. Also"—a smile crossed his face—"what you said about hiding reminded me, what can be kept forever, but never once shared?"

Baba Halil and his riddles. It was a common bond between us. Riddles had taught me that there's always something to learn, even if it's right in front of you. I smiled. "You're going to have to find something harder than that," I said. "Secrets. Once you share them, you can't hide them anymore."

Baba Halil smiled.

I held my hand out to Ana to help her up. She looked at me with her ewe eyes and put her hand in mine, taking more of my strength than she needed.

Baba Halil put his arms over my shoulders and Ana's, and we walked slowly toward the front door. Baba Halil opened a storage bench built into the wall by the door. He pulled out a pair of pistols and set them on top of the lid. "There. There's your Ballisti uniform," he said.

"Should I ask where you got these?"

"No."

I looked at him solemnly. "Thank you, Baba."

Baba Halil glanced at Ana, then tucked his thumbs into his waistband—an endearing habit. "Ana, are you going on this little mission of Val's?"

She shook her head. "No. Val won't let me."

I caught the bitter quiver in her voice.

"Ana," I began. She waved away the rest of my sentence. Five years between us, she was my sister. My baby sister. Our friends sometimes called her 'Doctor,' the way she raced to care for others' cuts and rashes and bullet wounds.

"She didn't want to fight at all, and now she wants to be a spy." Ana looked at Baba Halil but she threw the words at me, stinging like nettle.

All at once, and all over again, I was filled with both resolve and anger at the world. "I'll do whatever I can."

"Yeah, now."

I grabbed the guns. "Let's go," I said.

"What is tonight?" Baba Halil asked.

"Night before the half moon," Ana replied.

When the moon was half-full each month, Ana, our friend Xhevi, and I had taken to digging potholes on the main road east of Tragjas, as indirect sabotage. At best, an Axis, or Ballisti, truck tire would catch it and it would flip the truck downhill. At the least, they would be stuck and behind their own schedule.

"Ah. So, less traffic, then?" Baba Halil said quietly. He had returned to his composed self.

"That's the idea," I said.

"Do not"—he raised a finger inches from my face—"give up. Ana, you can't give up, either." When Ana assured him she wouldn't, he took a step back. "But come home soon."

"As soon as I can," I said. A vague and vain promise.

"See you soon, Baba," Ana said.

"Until then, go with God."

I took in the view outside the *teqe's* humble door. Winter on this hill in southern Albania was grainy and dull. Spring rains transformed brown fields to fertile soil. And every summer of my life, wheat, corn, barley, and sugar beets grew full to bursting, covering the lazy slope from Tragjas to the flat land that stopped at the Ionian Sea. Every summer but this one.

The air here was generally breezy and humid, yet sometimes stagnant when the wind was too weak to push itself over the mountains.

Our livelihood lay between the mountains to our north and east, the sea to our west and the spring river south, in a valley. Every need was met in our cozy corner of the world. Tragjas was made up of almost one hundred houses grouped together by family name. The village well was built in the center of town, as it should be. The first generations built their houses in a large ring, wide enough for the donkeys and carts to circle, wide enough for a wedding and its dancing. A new house was built as each generation grew into adulthood and began a family of their own, next to or behind their parents.

Our house walls were cut roughly from the mountains around us. Tradition kept the homes whitewashed, and whitewashed again, every year. The slate roofs were cut from a quarry near Orikum, a nearby seaside village.

Ana and I walked back to our house, quiet, annoyed with each other, and hot. Ana and I were together day in and day out. We knew each other's thoughts and how stubborn we were. She was more stubborn, of course.

I couldn't read her mind, but seeing her with her hands in her pockets, high-kicking the weeds along the way, I had a pretty good guess. She resented me for not recruiting her to join my infiltration scheme.

"We'll carry on as planned tonight," I said. "Come on, Ana. It would be too obvious if we show up together at a Ballisti camp. Someone may recognize one of us."

"And someone may recognize you if you show up alone! It's a foolish, selfish idea, Val."

I plucked a few wild blackberries. My fingers turned blue-purple. I threw them in my mouth and clamped down hard. To have Ana upset at me cost me more than she knew.

"Mami!" Ana called out. Out of habit, we took the path along the house and through the ghost of the gate to the back yard. The gate and fence had been part of the fire's fuel.

All the women worked the land, same as the men. But the charred ground meant less fieldwork. And so, Mami was not harvesting but on her hands and knees, foraging for wild plums. She wore a coat to protect her sleeves and skin from the bushes' small thorns.

"Almost finished," she called out.

Ana and I waited for her at the patio table under the bougainvillea. The speed with which the vine filled in surprised me every year. It announced its tenacity and defiance with bright pink, paper-thin petals. I deemed it a living miracle for escaping the Italians' attack.

Our perpetually sun-kissed mother set down the half-full basket of plums and sighed. She sat with her legs straight out and pushed loose strands of dark hair from her temples. She held her right arm close to her body, a means of protecting her aching shoulder. Life was a labor of love.

"Mami, we may be gone longer than usual this time," I said. "Ana and I will go … east of here tonight."

I met Ana's eyes saying: *We?*

Mami nodded and kept her gaze out to the fields between the singed persimmon trees, then shifted her eyes more closely to our lone goat, Lucky. The rest of the herd had been snatched by starving enemies. "Don't tell me any more, my dear," Mami said.

She was right. Information was dangerous. Besides, my plan was more of an idea, with plenty of room for flexibility and mistakes.

"I'll pack you a bag. Maybe you'll be back for winter," she said. It was a wish, not even a subtle demand. A woman of the fields and mountains didn't lay out hope lightly.

Earlier in the year, when Ana and I told my parents we would be more actively involved in the Partizans' objectives, my father had approved. My mother? She glanced at each of us and she knew. She knew not to weep. She knew not to throw her strong, short arms in the air and shout curses at Il Duce or the Führer. No curses to the Ballisti, the Partizans, or the smaller party who wanted the king to return, all vying to fill the void of national power. She knew not to curse even my father. She would need to save her breath to pray over the candles she hoarded.

Floriana and I were finishing up an early supper of cornbread and yogurt when my father came in the front door.

I watched him as he entered. His first glance was to my mother, to the back of her head as she prepared a small ball of cheese from Lucky's milk. Was it too much to call her an alchemist?

Babi's cheeks sagged. He was a man of this unforgiving land, whose skin had nearly turned to leather after almost fifty years in the sun. His bushy eyebrows lay relaxed, tired on their edges. His frame was angular and deceptively strong. Even still, I worried about his weight loss. 'He's getting old,' my mother said with a shrug when I asked.

"Hi, Babi," I said.

"*Shpirtrat e Babit*," he whispered. Babi's life-breath.

He shuffled to the bucket of cool water next to Mami. I knew his bad knee gave him more trouble than he let on. He should have let other people harvest and plow, and plow and harvest, for him. But he didn't know how to work any other way.

"Lani and I finished the beet field. There's not much, but I expected worse," he said. Any other year, August was a month of unceasing work. "There's no hope for any wheat or barley, of course, but there are still some root vegetables."

Babi washed midway up his arms, the hair flat and thick. Many priorities and daily routines had been traded for survival alone. My mother insisted that cleanliness is what kept us healthy. Death may come in a blink, but it would not be from any disease.

With a deep exhale, he sat on a cushion next to the empty fireplace and closed his eyes. Throughout my childhood, there had been many nights I woke and saw my father staring into the fire in the main room. The first time I heard a mortar fall and crack the earth, he came to mind. I realized then that his drive was due to his time fighting for independence from the Ottoman Empire. He was a teenager then, and everyone around him was fighting against the Sultan, fighting for the right to live their existence their own way. His honor and loyalty preceded him. Even the nomadic Vlahs who lived on the outskirts of town each spring respected him.

On the nights a breeze came down from the mountains instead of the muggy sea, and fresh yogurt cooled his sweat, he recited old poetry. When he delivered these monologues, pride shone through my mother, in the crow's feet around her eyes and under her blushed cheeks.

*

I glanced at Ana. We slipped away to our bedroom to change clothes.

When we were little kids, we shared the room with our older brothers, Sokol and Arberi. They grew their mustaches as soon as they could, as much out of tradition as an excuse not to shave every day. They were dutiful, too, as they were part of the provocation Baba Halil referred to.

Arberi was engaged to one of our neighbors when he and Koli joined the National Liberation Movement. They were so excited, chattering on and on while they packed their bags full of dry foods and other odds and ends. They wore as many layers of shirts as possible.

Even still, Ana and I altered the clothing they left behind to fit us. We traded our billowing pants, loose around the legs and gathered at the ankles, for their wool ones. Stifling was a fair trade for practicality and resilience.

"Are you going to tell Babi?" Ana asked me as she buttoned a brown shirt.

"What is there to say?" I tucked Baba Halil's gifts into the back of my pants and covered them with one of Sokol's outgrown vests. Under Ana's bed, I saw the box holding Arberi's wedding shoes.

Last January, Koli and Arberi came home for a one-week holiday. The *nonas* brought three cakes in a seven-day span to support my mother's efforts to plump them up before they returned to the frontlines. The boys were almost jovial, engaged and interested in strategy and politics more than ever, unfazed by their slimmer bodies.

"What about you, Val? Don't you care?" Koli had asked me one day that week as my mother and I cut up a kid goat, sizzling from the spit.

I paused for a moment to create a serious tone severely lacking in the room. "No. I want everybody to be done with it and stay home. We're pawns, don't you see? What are we to them, to the Allies?" I didn't expect him to answer, but I waited a moment anyway. "Useful. We are a useful land between the Soviet Union and Turkey. Just as our land was a useful bridge five hundred years ago for the Turks to get to Italy.

Everything repeats." I waved my hand at him in a hopeless way.

Koli held up a finger. "Don't you mean, it *would have been* a useful bridge?"

"Of course." Ballisti, Partizans, the goats in the field—no one would deny the impact of Skenderbeu's quarter-century of bravery, keeping the Ottomans from invading the Continent.

"We're fighting for Albania, Val," Arberi said. "Don't you understand?"

"Sure." I left it at that. That was our last good conversation before they said goodbye.

We would give all of our heart, because that is what we do, in exchange for our land to be chopped up and given away by the Allies to our neighbors. It happened after the Great War, I had thought; why would this be any different?

But, I had changed since that argument. Now, I had to try.

When Ana and I emerged from the bedroom, sweat was already beading on my spine, sending a ripple of goosebumps over my arms. My father watched as I pulled back the large rug and removed three thick floorboards. I retrieved our rifles and gave one to Ana. The last round of bullets I put into the bottom of my shoulder bag.

My mother stood watching us, too, waiting with two bundles of food. She chewed her lips, a habit I had inherited.

"It's like all the other times we've left," I said. An empty confidence to a woman who hadn't seen her sons in over a year.

Mami kissed us once, twice, three times. She had said her piece already.

"Bye, Ba." I bent over and kissed him on the head. I saw the muscles twitching in his jaw. He grabbed my hand, squeezed it and pressed it to his lips, hidden by his stout mustache.

Ana and I headed for the forest east of town. Behind us, the sun began to transform the sea to shadows and dark glass. Helios, god of the sun, delighted in the mountains and cast them in oranges and yellows.

"Miss Val!" called two children. It was Lule and Mateo. I wanted to hide my gun from them, hide the world from them, but they knew. There was no hiding.

"When will we have school again?" Another thing lost to war.

Unique to Tragjas, an education tax was collected to send the best students to college abroad. My father and Baba Halil went. My marks were the top in my class and I was sent to France. By the end of my first year, I could switch between English and French without much difficulty. Upon my return, I assumed the role of schoolteacher, as Mr. Dugas was more than ready to retire.

"I don't know. I don't know," I said to my former students and their big, brown eyes.

Their faces fell. I was forced to close the school two years ago, and still they asked about its reopening whenever they saw me.

"But I have a riddle for you. I expect an answer the next time I see you." I tapped Lule on the nose. "Ready?"

Lule and Mateo jumped with joy and tried to contain their giggles. *Oh, God. Giggling.*

"The more of these you take, the more you leave behind. What are they?"

[Footprints.]

Tragjas was small enough that all of the kids were friends, practically family. Without fail, the start of each school day was marked by rambunctious cheers, yells and teasing. When he was the teacher, Mr. Dugas kept instruction serious and orderly. Maybe it was the commanding tone in his voice or that he was a father figure. My attempt to keep order with sharpness was ineffective.

One morning, I decided to not speak. I walked to the board and began to write. Chairs scraped to face forward, someone stifled a sorry cough, and jokes among cousins quieted. When I finished, I turned and asked one of the older students to read for the younger ones.

[I have no legs. I can't walk, but I run everywhere I go. What am I?]

[A river.]

That was the necessary magic: a riddle to grab their attention. And so it went, passing on riddles from Baba Halil, and ones I invented, every day until the summer solstice. Then, the children were excused to work the land with their parents under the baking sun.

I ruffled Mateo's hair. "Now, off you go! I'm certain your mothers are looking for you."

I took a long breath and pushed my fears, fears I dared not form into words, down deep, deeper, never deep enough.

Our rendezvous point was a cave on the other side of the first mountain.

We arrived by following carefully laid markers in the rich woodland. Xhevi was waiting for us. Already widowed last year at age twenty, she lived in Gjorm, a village north of the cave. She sheltered Allies and Ballisti alike as they passed through town. She played the part well, seemingly neutral in her black mourning dress and headscarf.

"Hello, ladies! What do you hear?" she said, before we even got a drink of water. She had one of those oval faces that couldn't smile as widely as her eager voice implied. Xhevi was direct, smarter than me, and obsessed with tucking her short hair behind her ears. A better friend I would never find.

I offered Xhevi our mother's dried fruit. "Where are the nearest Ballisti?"

Xhevi tossed a cherry into her mouth.

"Other than in Vlora, I mean." I'd debated the advantages of walking into the city they controlled or finding a cell in the field.

Xhevi stopped herself from tossing another cherry in her mouth. She looked at each of us. "What did I miss?"

Ana spoke up. "Listen to this: Val's joining them. Baba Halil gave her another gun, even. No, two. Isn't that right?"

I pulled one of them out from my waist and slapped it on the ground next to her.

Xhevi chewed with deliberation, wide-eyed.

"I'm not joining them," I said. "I am, but I'm not. Let me ask the questions. The less you two know about me, the better. Can you tell me where the nearest ones are camped?"

"Ballisti, the bastards," Xhevi said. "They're everywhere, Val, you know that. And just as many Italians, it seems. But yes, there are some on the other side of Gjorm. Pushing up to Tirana. They have a long way to go, and they're running out of food." She took another handful of fruit. I realized then how completely alone she must be, even as to finding food for herself, let alone defending herself, back home.

"You have to come and live with us. You're not to go home alone after tonight, do you understand?" I said.

Again, Xhevi stopped moving mid-bite. The slightest twitch in the corner of her mouth told me everything I suspected. "Okay," she said softly.

"Okay," I said firmly. "Now, who from Gjorm is Ballist?"

"Val. Gjorm is dead. If any men are still alive, they're scattered, joined up along the road to somewhere else. A courier may have come last year, every so often, saying one of our own has been killed, but that hasn't happened in a long time."

Xhevi licked her fingers. "Anyway, not only is your idea crazy, we can't do this without you."

I had no answer. My idea was decent, but the execution was as solid as the wind. I tied up the food and untied my boots to cool off. I inhaled and prayed my parents would be able to hide away enough food for winter before another raid. On the exhale, I prayed I would find the nearest group of Ballisti, to sow some hell.

"I wish we knew when it would rain," I said, moving on to the more immediate problem. "Then these potholes would turn to mud pits."

"That would be great. But how many holes can we keep digging? What else can we do?" Ana asked, looking at both of us.

"Xhevi?" I deflected.

All three of us looked out the cave's entrance, as if the view would inspire us.

"Transport," Xhevi decided. "It's all about transport."

The impatience almost ate us alive, but at last, the sun was low enough to give us adequate coverage in the flickering shadows of the forest.

I stood and wiped my hands on my pants and walked a few steps deeper into the cave. Above our heads, a deep, horizontal crevice held our store of shovels and a pick. A divine hiding place. We strapped the tools onto our backpacks, sealed our lips and set our jaws. Time to work.

Of course, the Ballisti were as capable as we were in traversing these mountains. We only had to be one step ahead, every time.

After a couple of hours of hiking on the slopes of pines and ash and granite, we were covered by night, dark as an eggplant. We stopped next to the road. Following it south led to Brataj, then Borsh, a coastal town full of fig trees and olive groves. From there, a two-day hike led to the Greek border.

"Ana, it's your turn to look out," I said.

Ana gave a single nod, crossed the road and scaled the rocky incline like a mountain goat. We waited for her 'all-clear' triple whistle, like a mourning dove. As soon as we heard it, Xhevi crossed the road and swung the pick.

Because our plan was based on the moon cycle, not the weather, some nights were harder than others. It was one of those nights where the packed dirt resisted our insistence. I found a clump of stones and worked around them. To break it up, I jumped onto the shoulders of the shovel head, over and over again, and wiggled the handle back and forth. Dust tickled my nose. I looked in Ana's direction every so often, by instinct.

Another hour and our first holes were complete. My legs and arms quivered from exertion. We sank back off the road and into the forest to rest a bit. To watch for any activity. The moon shone on select rock faces, and the orchestra of nocturnal animals reminded us we were not completely alone.

We made our way north to Gjorm, but not more than a mile, rotating jobs through the night. The sky was shifting to purple-gray when we heard last year's leaves crunching behind us.

"We could make that job much easier."

I turned and saw two men. Their thumbs were hooked around rifle straps slung over their shoulders.

"Who are you?" I said. Baba Halil's pistol was on the ground, so very far away.

"Defenders of Albania, like you," the other, taller one said. "Are you Muskaj's daughter?"

"Who's asking?"

He shrugged. "We're on an island surrounded by a sea of Ballisti. You hear who's in your camp. And who's not."

"We're fine, thank you, move along," I said.

"Are you sure? We got a shipment yesterday." He looked over at his comrade and spoke with an air of playfulness. "Endri, what did the nice British officer call that stuff?"

"Explosives, Kosta, explosives," Endri said. "Hell better than shovels."

"You're with the British?" I said.

"We're with the Movement. Free the People!" At this Kosta raised his right fist to his head, the Partizans' signature salute.

I lifted my fist in response.

"Step onto the road," I said to them. Keeping my eyes on them, I picked up my gun. Xhevi crossed from her side of the road and stood next to me.

The men stepped forward. They were dressed in dark green pants and shirts, well-made boots and tight-fitting caps shaped like fishing boats. In the still-sleepy morning light, Endri could not have been more than seventeen years old, at least ten years my junior. Kosta looked older, but not weary or jaded. He had a wide forehead, and his nose took a sharp turn downward at its tip. I surmised he had been fighting since the invasion.

"How many of you are there?" Kosta said.

"Why?"

"Curious." He looked up and down the road, a habit for all of us in these parts. "Now, how about Endri and I finish digging these?" They put down their backpacks. "We'll need them deeper to fit our explosives. You can light the fuse, as a sign of good faith that we're on the same side."

"I'm not an idiot," I said. If they were not fellow Partizans, we would already be dead.

"I know. You even speak French," he said casually.

Kosta and Endri lost no time getting to work; skinny as they were, they made digging look easy. I looked again in Ana's direction. I couldn't help it. I remembered what I said to Baba Halil and his weakening, dangerous fear. I would need to be more careful that my worry didn't put her in more danger.

The sun rose, revealing the forest by thousands of fragments of light, like peach and pale yellow roses. My shoulders hunched over and I bowed my head with the vulnerable feeling that came with the day.

"Three? That's all you have?" I said after Kosta and Endri installed the plastic explosives.

"We're lucky to have any," Kosta said. He pointed to a round piece. "This is the satchel charge. Connect the wire," he said, "and go." He unrolled the coil and walked to us.

"Will it reach up there?" Xhevi pointed to Ana's lookout point.

"It should."

The cord tangled in the bushes several times, but we made it up the hill. We sat down between prickly brush and boulders still cold from the night. The guys glanced from me to Ana.

"Right, sorry," I said and rushed a round of introductions.

My eyes burned to sleep.

"So, how long are we waiting?" Xhevi said around a yawn.

"Until we see an enemy truck. Or two. It's more efficient taking out a truck when you blow a crater, right?" Endri said. "We were on our way to stir up some trouble in Gjorm. Germans are on their way there. That's the rumor, anyway."

I felt as if a rock had fallen and landed at the bottom of my stomach. I glanced at Xhevi. Her face had turned an iridescent pearl-pale, stricken.

She cleared her throat. "Already?"

The calmness in her voice chilled me to the core. I coughed and tried to turn away any more attention from her. "Feeling pretty confident with these matches?" I asked the men.

Kosta shrugged. "I've learned quite a bit. And the Brits are as generous as can be, thank God. They wish we would fight the Germans only." He shook his head. "They don't get it."

"The Ballisti—" Kosta started.

"Bastards," Xhevi said.

Kosta and Endri looked at Xhevi, surprised.

"What? It's true," she said.

Kosta continued. "I think we all have our own stories. I am fine without ever seeing any of them again, so my explosives are impartial. The Italians are already running. Running home, if they can get past the Germans. Or us. They are prisoners on both sides. And converts. Scared, lost, and sorry, I think. But not me." He sniffed and snapped a small branch from the nearest bush. He broke it into smaller pieces until only shreds remained.

"I'll go up a bit further," Endri said. Before anyone could respond, he scampered up among the boulders to see more of the road.

I hoped a convoy would come soon. Sitting still was counterproductive to staying awake.

In a flash, Endri was beside us. "Light it up!"

I fumbled with the ignitor. Kosta ripped it from my hands. He sank lower behind the rock he sat against. The girls and I took his cue and slouched further into the bushes.

"Cover your ears. Three, two, one," he said, quite audibly, unafraid.

We waited a moment without any explosion. Then, the blast lifted me an inch from the ground and threw me against Kosta. I covered my head and bit my lip to keep any scream from escaping.

With that, the five of us would become the road bomb squad, attached to Captain Harris, SOE agent of British Military Intelligence.

Dita Arbani

"Dita! Come here!" Agon coughed and sputtered as dust fell on his head.

Dita jumped up from her digging on the other side of the compact cave. She shone her flashlight in Agon's direction. "What is it?"

He stepped down from a smooth stone that had put him at the right height under a cleft in the rock wall, as if the step was there by invitation. Or, to aid in hiding a treasure. In hands scratched and bleeding from his efforts in the narrow, rough crevice, he held a package. It was made of a crude, dark leather, folded upon itself several times over.

"Let's go outside to see it better," he said. Mottled mid-afternoon sun came through the proud sycamores and oaks. They were less than a dozen miles east of Tirana, Dita's hometown and the country's capital. To Dita, they might as well have been on a different planet. The constant honking of car horns and hissing buses had been replaced with leaves shaking in the breeze and chatty squirrels.

Agon and Dita stood next to each other. What he lacked in weight, Dita made up for. What she lacked in height, he made up for, but only by a few inches.

Agon looked at her and pushed his glasses further up his nose. "Ready?"

"Of course."

Slowly, they took turns opening the pleats. Dita held her breath. In the center lay a hammered cobalt ring. It was not striking but plain and simple, the stone oval and set in gold.

"Hey, hey! Not bad," he said.

"Not bad? It's an incredible find!"

Dita envisioned a party of bedraggled men and women, battle-tired Illyrians, ancestors to the modern-day Albanians. She pictured a woman leading them but leaning heavily on two men. Dita heard the panting of the entire tribe, focused solely on reaching the refuge of the cave.

"What do you think, first century?" she asked, spell broken.

"Yeah, maybe." Agon turned it like an expensive necklace on a rotating display in a shop window. A few pockmarks dotted the inside.

Dita stepped back. "Good job, Agon. What made you look up there?"

"A hunch," he said with a one-shoulder shrug.

"All those books you read, maybe?"

"Maybe." A shy smile crept over his face. They returned to their gear inside. He put the artifact in a toolbox labeled Treasure Chest. Agon was a few years younger than Dita, a decade if timidity were the measure of maturity. His shirt hung over his wide, bony shoulders, and his feet seemed too long for his legs; sports didn't suit him. He was a wallflower in meetings and general conversation. Researching, out in the field, was where he belonged.

Dita packed up her trowel, brush, and measuring tape in her tool bag. "I didn't find anything over here."

"We could come back," Agon offered.

"We don't have to tear down every cave."

Dita began walking down the path to Agon's car, but after a moment she stopped and turned around. She imagined the female leader tucking away this pouch in its hiding place; better to bury it than have it fall into the hands of an enemy. She hoped the tribe had found peace. "Some places ought to remain a mystery, I suppose."

"Blasphemy," Agon said. "And you call yourself a historian."

"I don't. I never have," she said in mock self-defense.

"What do you think he'll say?" Agon asked when they settled in his car. He began cruising downhill faster than Dita was comfortable with.

She held onto the arm rest. "Not much. History's not his thing."

"Kupi?" Agon's voice jumped half an octave. He twisted his neck from Dita to the road and back again.

"Oh! Kupi!" Too late. Dita's cheeks flushed. It did make more sense to ask about their boss, the Director of Cave Artifacts. "You meant *Kupi*. Kupi will be pleased. He won't *say* anything, of course. Have you noticed how he nods his head, clears his throat, and smoothes his hair, all at the same time, when he's satisfied with the progress of a project?"

"No, I hadn't noticed all that. I had noticed he's not much of a talker."

"Takes one to know one, right?" She wiggled her elbow into his arm.

"Wait, now, who did you think I was talking about?" Agon said.

Her cheeks burned, again. "Oh. No one, no one." Dita pointed to his bloody knuckles wrapped around the steering wheel. "You should bandage those."

He didn't fall for the diversion. "You're seeing someone?"

Dita propped her elbow on the car door and bit a fingernail, forgetting that her hands were still covered in cave dirt.

"Come on, you can tell me. I probably went to school with him."

That, she didn't doubt. Tirana was significantly more populated than it was five years ago, but within the twenty-something demographic, everyone knew someone through a friend or two.

Dita and Ilir had met six months earlier, among mutual friends, when the air was drunk on cherry blossoms and promises. She fell hard and fast for his deep look: short, charcoal-black hair and dark cocoa eyes. The first time his slim hand held hers through a rush-hour crowd, a thrill swept through her. A thrill she didn't want to let go of.

"Okay. Fine. Ilir Agolli."

"Agolli, Agolli. Nope, don't know him," Agon said.

They returned to the museum as their colleagues were leaving for the day. From the main floor, a flight of stairs took them down to the artifacts lab in the basement. Two of the walls there held high windows that let in sunlight at the sidewalk level. Under one of these windows, glass cabinets lined the wall. These contained ongoing projects not yet ready for display.

Dita and Agon cleaned and put away the tools without conversation. Agon wrote the date and the location on a label atop a transparent box. He placed the ring and its pouch inside. He entered the same information into a stately green record book listing all cave artifacts, from a dull knife to a royal-looking necklace.

With the ring stored safely, Agon turned to Dita.

"Shall we call it a day?"

"Let's."

Together, they pushed open the front doors into a crisp evening.

"Well?" Agon said.

"Well," her voice wavered. "Okay. Good work. And thanks for the ride today."

"Any time, Dita. See you tomorrow." He smiled his little smile.

Dita turned west for home, excited to draw the ring from memory into her sketchbook. That explained the little flutter she felt inside, she was certain.

Dita had started as a university intern at the national history museum and stayed after graduation, without a clear direction of what to do with her sociology degree. She quickly found out. She became unreasonably enamored with her countrymen as she organized files and assisted in creating displays of iconography and World War II memorabilia. Occasionally, she substituted as a docent if there was a group of English-speaking tourists. Now, she was part of the small Cave Artifacts team as an assistant curator. She hoped, one day, to be a department head.

Dita enjoyed the quiet, the calm, the order. Her co-workers were motivated and inspiring, too. She was proud of the stories on display at the museum. Most of all, she treasured decoding the past's mysteries.

Five years earlier, a beachgoer had found a trove of artifacts buried in a cave along the southern Ionian coast. Two years later, three more sites, all along the beach, were found containing ancient Illyrian coins and jewelry, the very last and most valued items of the dead. Since then, treasures in caves had been reported every few months. There were enough relics to clean, decipher, categorize, and display to keep them busy for the next ten years, if not longer.

Dita waited for the pedestrian light to turn green before crossing the street.

Her ancestors' practices shaped the code Dita saw in the life around her every day: strong family ties, keeping one's word, and unfailing hospitality. On the sidewalk, people made way for each other. She took for granted their innate, simple kindness, like helping a mother get a stroller onto a city bus. Their driving, on the other hand, was newfangled and slightly erratic.

Dita said "Good evening" to a *nona* in mourning black, a white handkerchief tied over her combed hair. The city's grandparents wore immaculately ironed tops and polyester skirts or slacks. Their raincoats were thirty years old and flawless. All the grandpas wore a hat or eyeglasses, or both. Young adults Dita's age had discarded the older style for faster fashion. Her parents' generation was stuck somewhere between: holding dearly and rightfully to what they had always known, and wondering which parts of globalization could simplify their lives.

Dita walked west, to a roundabout and through her neighborhood, past vegetable stands, two mini-marts, a handful of coffee bars and a bakery. She ducked into Auntie's. The warm aroma of baked goods relaxed her.

"Dita! How are you?" greeted Auntie as she scooted around to the front of the counter. Her eyes disappeared into her cheery cheeks. Her doughy hands, literally and figuratively, held Dita's. "How are your parents? You want the usual two loaves for your family? How's Nana?"

"Good, all good. The bread, yes, thank you. And, I'll have a half kilo of those, the orange-filling ones—" She pointed to a plate of mini-pastries covered in powdered sugar.

"Sofia's favorite, right?" Auntie knew everyone's favorite treat, including those of Dita's grandmother.

"They are," Dita said and dug a two-hundred *leke* coin out of her pocket. "Thanks, Auntie. See you soon!"

As she turned the corner from the bakery, Dita's one and only sister, Nora, called. Two years older, Nora had left home as soon as she could, quickly finding a life in Rome. Despite the distance and the pay-by-the-minute phone plans, the two of them were as tight as their matching curly hair. Nora was the cuddler, the doting one, the one more comfortable when she was touching someone else—twirling Dita's hair or linking her arm in their mother's.

She was the first person Dita had told about her fellowship application to the Etruscan Museum in Rome. It would be a boost to her career in the museum world, full of valuable experiences, large and small. Somehow, Nora had interpreted the possibility of the fellowship to mean she needed to convince Dita to move permanently to the Eternal City.

After the quick, initial pleasantries, Nora began another round of her Italy-will-be-the-best-thing-ever campaign.

"Did I already mention we'd be roommates?"

"Yes, of course. I don't know why you think you need to persuade me. I'll let you know as soon as I find out." She expected a response letter any day now.

Nora continued. "You could apply for a student visa and get into a history graduate program! Or I can start asking my friends and co-workers about a job once you finish the fellowship. Did you know I'm a twenty-minute bus ride from the Colosseum?"

And so on, as Dita climbed the stairs of her building, an exterior staircase open to the elements. She doubted Nora's banking friends ran in the same circles as Dita's prospective colleagues. It would be fun to be there among the ancient ruins, endless pizza and gelato. No, she didn't need any cajoling, though Nora made it sound more exotic than she felt it would be. But the unknowns, and the size, of Rome held little allure for her. There were as many things to be nervous about as there were exciting opportunities.

Dita hung up, smelling dinner before she arrived at her family's apartment on the fifth floor. Her stomach rumbled. Dita's keys jangled once, twice to the left to unlock the front door.

She slid out of her ballet flats and into her *shapka*. It was the only home she'd ever known, smelling slightly of mothballs, minty toothpaste, and plenty of spring-fresh floor cleaner. The air was somewhat humid despite, or because of, the cross-breeze flowing through the open windows. The cuckoo clock they'd bought on a family vacation in Switzerland one Christmas ticked steadily in the entryway. Her parents' television droned on in their room all day, every day.

Straight ahead, Nana sat in her preferred corner spot on their sofa. She had the best seat in the house, which looked out to the balcony. If she were to turn her head to the right, she could see Dita or anyone else coming through the front door.

"Hi, Nana!" Dita called. "Mami!"

"Finally!" Nana teased.

"In here!" Dita's mother said.

Dita passed the three bedrooms and bathroom to the open, combined living room and kitchen. A large, handwoven rug of brown, black, and red was held in place by the sofa and the loveseat, covered in matching stiff green leather. Decorating the sea-green walls were her parents' lone wedding photo, a cheap painting of a bowl of fruit, and touristy souvenir plates from Bari and Venice. That her travels had been limited, due to the complications of getting a tourist visa, had never bothered Dita. The itch to travel around her own country, though—that began with the job at the museum.

Between the furniture sat a small cabinet used as a side table. On its top, next to a red candy dish, lay a corkscrew-shaped piece of driftwood carved by her grandfather, Gjyshi. She had never known him, and Nana rarely spoke of him. Lena, Dita's mother, had been raised near the coast in the north, near Nana's brother, Gjoni, and sister, Tringa. Gjyshi was skilled with a carver's knife, beyond simple fisherman's skills. The piece Dita held had been deliberately carved as a visual maze— following one line was infinite. This had entranced Dita as a child. Nobody would miss it if she took it to Rome.

She kissed Nana on the forehead and finger-combed her gray hair, cropped short against her prominent jawbone.

"I've been waiting all day for you, sweetie," Nana said as she squeezed Dita's hand in hers.

"For these?" Dita dangled the bag of treats in front of Nana.

"Thank you," she said. She wasted no time indulging in a pastry. "But no, that's not why."

"This is the time I normally get home. What's on your mind?"

Nana's skin was weathered from a lifetime of work and play in the Mediterranean sun without a drop of sunscreen. An aura of Nivea face cream floated around her; Dita could recognize that "fragrance-free" scent anywhere. It might be sacrilegious to say it aloud, but Nana was as committed to that cream as she was to dyeing eggs deep red every Easter.

"Watch your mother," Nana said and winked. "That's why." Her tone sounded playful, but there was a serious undercurrent, and a ripple of doubt in her eyes.

"Mami?" Dita said, playing up the teasing manner. "What did you do now? Whatever you did, it can't be too bad—it smells delicious, as usual," Dita said. She crossed the room to Lena, and they greeted each other: right cheek, left cheek, right again.

"She forgot the bay leaves, Dita dear. I can't smell them," Nana said.

Lena rolled her eyes and grinned. "They're in, Mami." Inspecting for doneness, Lena poked with the spoon at the *gjell*, a casserole of potatoes, eggplant, carrots, peppers, garlic—always and forever garlic—and tomatoes. And bay leaves. "I promise. Wouldn't be *gjell* without them." A wide, happy smile passed among the three of them.

The kitchen took up one wall and no more. Cool gray cabinetry complemented the smooth floor tile throughout the entire apartment. To the left of the kitchen was a wall of windows, facing northeast. A sliding door opened to the tight balcony, just wide enough for four people to sit side by side, and a bistro table.

"Nora called me with more reasons to move there." Dita leaned her weight onto one leg and peeled a tangerine. The citrus cleansed her nose of the richness of the *gjell*.

"She's excited to have you there, that's all," her mother said. "How was work?"

"Great. This morning, Meta came by—"

"Big Boss Meta, right?"

"Right. He told me to prepare a few words for the opening ceremony of the Independence Retrospective exhibit, on behalf of my team. Kupi's been out for two weeks now. I guess he's really sick."

Lena *hmph*ed.

"Even still, I don't know why he would ask me to speak." She shook her head. "Then, Agon and I went digging for most of the day. We found a ring."

"Wow!" Lena said. She was Dita's biggest fan.

"Yeah."

Dita sat next to Nana on the sofa. "The exhibit is ready, Nana. I gave a couple pictures of you and Gjyshi, and your friends, to the railroad building display."

The railroad was far away from their livelihood but closely aligned to national industry. They had done their required stint working there, then went home to the rivers and lakes of the north as soon as they could. Lena once told Dita she could still see her father sitting on his anchored boat with a knife in one hand, its handle carved with outlines of mountains and flowers. If Dita could wish on a star, she would wish to feel the rough boat planks and the wind on her face at sunset with her grandfather beside her.

Dita held Nana's hand. Crocheting had taken a back seat to her advancing arthritis, but her previous pieces were tight, sturdy, and all over the house. A coverlet on each bed, a blue and green lap blanket spread over the top of the sofa, a white table runner—everywhere Nana.

"Remember one time, when I was maybe nine or ten, you told me the legend of Aeneas?" Dita asked.

"Go on," Nana said.

"Well, we found more proof of the story. An archeological crew found more coins from Caesar's time. They're cleaning them this week."

"Oh, that's nice," Nana replied.

*

Nana had moved in with the family when Dita was one year old, as soon as her grandfather passed away. When they were little girls, Nana took Dita and Nora by local train to the nearest beach in Durrës most summer days. More often than not, other kids arrived with their grandmothers. These were the girls' summer friends, because they did not attend the same school.

Dita loved to run along the edge of the waves as they taunted her little feet. When the sun got too strong, Nana and the girls hid from the blistering heat under beach towels and umbrellas. On those sweltering afternoons, Nana would begin to tell them a myth about the three dervishes or the Kulshedra, the legendary female dragon, and her tricks. Most days, the three of them made it halfway through the story before falling asleep, inebriated with sunshine.

At home, over the summer months and the winters, too, Nana taught Dita and Nora to play chess while she fixed dinner or crocheted. She could be found cleaning around the house, running errands, meeting friends for coffee, constantly on the move.

Women—don't let the plates fall, keep them spinning, don't stop.

Nana often had little surprises, like sweet pastries from Auntie's Bakery, on the table when Dita came home from school. She gobbled them up while Nana carried on rhetorical arguments with politicians in the newspaper.

Nana was prone to repeating conventional phrases such as, "Stop playing if you start to sweat; you'll catch a cold." Or, "Don't go to the kitchen empty-handed, carry some dishes." Or, of utmost importance at home, "Where are your *shapka*? Don't walk around barefoot!"

Dita took her grandfather's driftwood and spun it in her fingers. Spinning, twirling, dancing. "Nana, did you wear a *xhubleta* for your wedding?"

"Ha! No, definitely not. As the sister of a fisherman, marrying another fisherman, there was no money. Nowhere to keep it, anyway!"

"Right."

"I'm telling you, your *gjyshi* needed someone to help with all the fish, the gutting, the selling, and my face was nicer to look at, believe it or not. That's what he said once, anyway; it was his way of being sweet."

"Oh, I believe it, Nana. Do you want to go back, go and visit?"

"Visit what? There's nothing there for me."

"You know, what it was like, how's it changed, how's it the same."

Nana's shoulders rounded in a sigh. "Dita, it may sound romantic to you, but it wasn't easy. Nothing was easy."

"I'm sorry, Nana." Dita felt ashamed for imagining an easy life of selling fish or simple days as a shepherd in the mountains.

"I want you to understand this: I lost everything. But"—she curved her knotted, thick fingers around Dita's chin—"look at what I have now."

Dita nodded, scrunching her face. She needed to change the conversation; Nana had lived in the past long enough.

"You think the acceptance letter got lost in the mail?" Dita smiled. "It slipped behind someone's desk, maybe?" She breathed into the driftwood. What were her troubles compared to what her grandparents might have experienced? Yes, she would take this familial artifact with her to Rome. She would get the letter. Mail was slow, that's all.

On cue for a company man at a predictable job, the front door opened and Dita's father, Murat, entered.

"Hello, hello!" he shouted cheerfully to the entire apartment. Dita heard him toss his keys onto the entry table. She knew he would first find Lena, setting the table at the moment, and kiss her hello, then find the other ladies of the house.

"*Shpirti*," he said and kissed Dita on the cheek.

He bent over Nana and sandwiched her hands in his. "Sofia, how are you today?"

"I'm well, and you?" Sofia smiled.

"Let's eat," Lena said.

Murat gently pulled Nana to standing and held out his elbow to walk her to the table.

The day of the exhibit's opening arrived.

Dita dressed up: she wore the black wrap dress that hit her curves, red hoop earrings, and a single mist of Fiorucci. She dug into the depths of her sister's wardrobe to find those black heels Nora bought last Christmas. She put them by the front door.

In the bathroom, she performed a quick self-assessment. There was nothing to be done about the acne in the center of her cheeks. She had washed and set her hair the night before. She gave it a good shake and she was ready.

Nana sat at the table eating her toast. Dita mused that she could eat from the floor if she ever had to, Lena kept it that pristine. Two generations of impeccable cleaning. But Dita doubted she would be able to meet their standard, in Rome or elsewhere.

"Good morning, Nana," Dita said.

Lena walked into the kitchen, putting on her earrings, followed by Murat and his cloud of soap and shaving cream scents. He'd gone bald the popular way—a salt-and-pepper ring wrapped from ear to ear. He finished buttoning his collar and sat down.

"Good morning, all," Murat said.

Dita reciprocated and finished her hard-boiled egg with olive oil and salt in record time. Next, she scooped four heaping teaspoons of finely ground coffee into the *xhezve*. She filled it with water and set it to boil. She kept watch. At-home espresso machines were gaining in popularity, but not here, not yet. They stood by the Turkish way of having coffee.

Otherwise, Dita thought of her parents as open to new ideas. Dita put so much sugar in it, the process didn't matter to her.

When the coffee boiled, Dita poured it into their everyday cups. She was too nervous to sit and drink it slowly. She shot it back in one swallow, washed the cup and placed it on the drying rack.

"You'll do great," Lena said, reading Dita like an open book.

Dita shook out the jitters from her hands. She planted extra kisses on the matriarch and hurried out the door, into the commotion of the city astir.

Dita hustled up the museum's two dozen marble steps and passed under the sprawling mosaic of gallant freedom fighters, partisans, and Independence intellectuals spread across the front of the building. She lowered her head in gratitude. A hefty tug on the front door and ascending another flight of stairs put Dita on the main floor, with offices and bathrooms to the right and left. She could hear staff members' voices down the hall. Exhibition rooms on the second floor opened to a mezzanine above her. Morning sun peered through windows near the roofline.

Dita left her bag and coat in the staff room. Agon met her in the hallway. When he saw her, and only for a second, he stood motionless.

He rubbed his head. "Two of the placards are on the wrong stands."

"What? You reviewed them all," she said. Her stomach tightened. The dignitaries, including the prime minister himself, were expected at eleven.

"I missed these. We'll need a wrench to switch them. I was on my way to find the janitor."

"Let's find him, then." She set out at a clip, as quickly as she could, considering heels were not her expert mode of transportation. Agon kept up.

No expectations, her father often said. No expectations meant no surprises. No surprises meant a challenge like this could be met object-ively, without being upset it didn't go the way one expected. Kupi should have been here. But in his absence, and with the anticipated talk, she felt the responsibility on her shoulders.

They passed heavy trophy cases neatly, if not unnecessarily, display-ing photos of various foreign government officials standing in front of the museum, and a few certificates of recognition from crooked minis-ters. Why they had to be on display was a mystery. But that was not her department, Dita reminded herself.

They walked the entire main floor looking for the janitor or a clean-ing lady. The air tasted thick and sweet from yesterday's floor wax treatment. At the east end, Agon and Dita took the stairs down to the maintenance and storage rooms, heels and boots creating an overlap-ping rhythm of click and thud, click and thud.

A janitor rescued them with a wrench for the placard stands minutes before the front doors opened at ten o'clock. Dita hoped Ilir would be one of the first to arrive. She caught her reflection in a window and ruf-fled her hair.

The officials arrived, with a cluster of journalists and photographers following close behind. The museum director, Mr. Meta, greeted them and led the way. Dita and Agon brought up the rear.

"Do you think they really care?" Dita asked, with a flick of her head to the ministers and their protégés.

"If it gets their face in the newspapers, yes," he replied.

When the cameras were ready, Meta opened with dull statements lined with platitudes.

"We should've set up chairs," Dita whispered to Agon, irritated with herself. She scratched at the scar on her foot, a relic of playing games in the street as a kid. It rubbed against the rim of her shoes. This is why she didn't have heels of her own.

Mr. Meta called upon Dita. She walked to the front, widened her stance a bit and let out a quick exhale. She refused to be nervous in front of these people. Some men shifted on their feet.

"Ladies and — " She looked up and saw that she was the sole woman in the room. "Excuse me. Gentlemen, welcome." She flashed a genuine smile. "We are honored to host you on the opening day of our exhibit, 'Independence: A Retrospective.' My name is Dita Arbani, an assistant curator of the Cave Artifacts team. Our department's contribution is a collection of pieces found in caves from Butrinti to Lezhe. Some artifacts may seem insignificant to us today, but if they were buried to be safe from thieves and the salty sea, then they must have been worth the effort. We hope you enjoy a look at the past. May it spark curiosity and renew your appreciation for those who came before us. Thank you."

She sidled to the back of the crowd.

"That's all?" Agon teased.

"I'm not the director. You do it next time," Dita said. She was certain he would rather give up reading for a year than give a speech.

He shook his head and Dita pressed her lips together to keep her laugh inside.

Throughout the day, visitors came and went with polite nods and thank-yous. Sunlight accentuated every part of the hall in turn as it waltzed across the tall windows. Dita walked slowly through the exhibit. She was familiar with most of it but wanted to peruse the first years of the previous century.

"Learning anything new?" Agon sauntered to Dita's side.

"Hey. Yes, always."

They walked on. Standing at the beginning of the post-World War II section, an older woman dressed in a brown skirt and matching jacket wiped her eyes over and over again.

"Madam? Are you okay?" By far the dumbest thing Dita could have said.

The lady, with her tawny and gray fixed curls, did not attempt to hide her dejection. "I lost my brothers and my sister to the trials, to the internment camps." The woman's hands trembled as she rubbed her nose with a handkerchief. She looked at Dita with pleading, red-rimmed eyes. "They were good. They were good people." She squeezed her knobbed fingers tightly, one hand over the other. "I haven't forgotten them, not for a day. Not a single day."

"Of course you haven't. I'm so sorry," was all Dita could eke out. Her throat tightened. She wanted to discover cobalt rings and ancient coins, but she also had to acknowledge the injustices. Dita bit her lip and waited.

The woman took a shuddering breath. "Ah well, what can you do?" She squared her shoulders and wished them a good day.

Dita glanced at Agon and found him concentrating, eyes fixed on one spot.

"You okay?" Dita watched him. His jaw muscles protruded, clenched.

"Yeah, yeah. My grandparents were thrown in prison, too. But they made it out. Trying to imagine what it was like." He shook his head to chase away the imagery and gave her a 'forgive me' look.

Dita led Agon out of the exhibit, away from the past.

"It would be nice to grab a drink with the whole team to celebrate," she suggested.

"Yeah?"

"But these heels!" One reason, one very good reason, to go straight home.

"I don't get it." Agon raised his hands innocently. "They look painful, so why wear them? I wouldn't last a minute."

Another reason to go home right away? Ilir hadn't come. And he had said he would.

Dita was one of the few staff members to stay until closing time. As she made her way to her coat and bag, she saw Ilir taking the main terrazzo stairs two at a time. His starched shirt was opened to the first button. His straight dark jeans stayed up with the help of a thick belt. He had confessed once that his older sister was his personal shopper and kept him looking dapper.

Dita's disappointment and annoyance dissolved. After a few sweet apologies and out-of-breath excuses of meetings and talkative co-workers from Ilir, Dita offered to be his personal tour guide.

"Please," Ilir said. His smile lit his face and lit her world.

The private walk-through began with sketches and primitive photographs of war-burnt villages in the early twentieth century. Men of the northern mountains stood in an awkward, defiant row. Their white shirts billowed in the sleeves and cuffed at the wrists. Their dark vests gave them a surprising formality for a bunch of shepherds. Strips of black zigzagged down their white woolen pants as lightning or, perhaps finally, a visual for what thunder must look like.

The women stood in the background. Not a single smile. Strong in every way, the warp and weft of each family.

The mountains and their seclusion. Dita didn't know, really, if that's how they still dressed, but the detail of their clothing was remarkable. She had never been high and deep into the Accursed Mountains, called the Albanian Alps by foreigners. By the time the roads were passable and clear of snow, school was out and she and Nora had always had the beach on their mind. Now, as an adult, she hadn't found the time to go.

She had never taken a ferry across the dammed-up Drin River in the north or Lake Ohrid on the Macedonian border. She had never been to the natural spring called the Blue Eye in the south. These far-off places were not more than a day's drive away. After Rome, she swore to herself, she would travel more.

Dita and Ilir moved on, through daily life for townsfolk in the 1930s; pictures and a few small paintings depicted mules and carts heavy-laden with the harvest bound for market.

"Durrës looks so different now, right?" Dita said.

"Yeah, I guess."

Beyond the pictorial timeline, descriptions of accomplishments, infrastructure, and economy were printed on large signs, invoking very little imagination. That's why she loved the artifacts, the discoveries. They were windows. Unbreakable windows to a world she could play out in her dreams yet never truly enter. Would she want to live in a time when disease was more rampant? In a time, less than one hundred years ago, when other countries dictated the rules? Or, when, as in the 1970s, one had to choose their words and actions carefully so as to not be misinterpreted and purged? No. But, there was a spirit she was desperate to be a part of, an inextricable *belonging* that she wanted, that she could see in the dark eyes in every photograph.

A significant portion of the cave objects had been dated to the mid-twentieth century. Dita lingered here, keen to tell Ilir the stories behind some of the artifacts. She attempted to temper her excitement.

"… And this is a chain bracelet we found near Butrinti."

"Hm." Ilir nodded and smiled.

She knew that nod and smile. It was what she did when her father explained the ins and outs of business taxes.

"Come on, I'm starving." Dita grabbed his arm. "Agriano's pasta is calling my name."

"Now you're talking," Ilir said.

The next morning, Agon sat at his desk, facing Dita at her desk, the staircase behind her. Dita had the cobalt ring under her microscope for cleaning, hoping this would reveal its details.

The door at the top of the stairs opened. Dita put down her brush. Meta was accompanied by a man she had never seen before. His black suit sleeves ran long to his palms, and his pants gathered at his polished shoes. Either the newcomer had forgotten to shave or his five o'clock shadow was already showing mid-morning. His jutting torso and straight posture suggested an extraordinary effort to not look nervous. But his darting eyes betrayed him.

"If I may have your attention, please," Meta boomed, louder than was necessary. He cleared his throat and stood with his hands behind his back. "After much deliberation, I'm pleased to introduce the new Director of Cave Artifacts, Mr. Gazmir Raco."

Dita's jaw dropped.

"I am confident you all will make him feel welcome in our museum family." With that, he turned back up the stairs, his pot belly in front and a trailing scent of stale cigarettes, and Raco, behind.

Dita called after him. "Sir? What about Kupi?"

"What about him?" Then, the door closed.

Mira

The night after my father's burial, I sat on the back side of our house under the full moon and gave her my opinions and fears. Owls in the distance had their opinions, too. All was black and purple shadows. The moon chose what it highlighted—curves of trees, faces of stones lying half-buried in the earth. The scents in the air could not have been more perfect: a braid of new grass, snowmelt river water, and new pine needles.

It was another night when sleep evaded me. With Bac gone, nights like these came more often.

"Can't sleep?" said a voice in the dark. I jumped in surprise and clapped my hands over my mouth. I turned my head to the east side of the house. A man, composed of moonlight and dark folds of clothing, walked toward me.

"I apologize. I did not intend to scare you." It was Rezart Agim. His voice was quiet and soft, not like it was in his passionate speech at Rinaj's house. "May I?" He pointed to the ground next to me.

"Yes, of course," I said. "I could find a bench."

"No need." He straightened one leg and relaxed against the wall.

We were still and silent for several moments. I could count on one hand how many conversations I had had with older men, and alone. My eyes raced from side to side, as if I could search the *Kanun* and its prohibition of the current situation. I was not allowed to sit next to a man, without a chaperone, in the middle of the night. Certainly, it was forbidden.

Of course, I was not supposed to go to that meeting, either.

"What do you think of those up there?" he asked.

"The stars?" I kept my voice at a whisper.

"Yes."

I sighed, and a shudder ran through me. "They remind me of the patterns my mother would embroider. What are they to you?"

Rezart looked at me. The moon illuminated his forehead, broad and pondering. His eyes were set too deep in the shadows of his brow to see any detail. His mustache twitched, with the touch of a smile, as if he would let me in on a secret.

He seemed to study me, though my back faced the moon. I felt rooted to the earth. I willed him to find me trustworthy and sincere. I looked down at my hands before he could see anything different. Sadness or naïveté, for example.

He looked up and sent his answer to the stars. "They're my guide. I was taught several constellations, and they help to orient me. If only to remind me of where I am."

"You forget?"

His shoulders rolled in a chuckle. "Sometimes, yes."

I didn't know what to say next. Instead of boiling over, the fear of being caught with Rezart returned to a simmer. The pinpoints of light high in the sky flickered like small flames in an open fire. I squeezed my eyes shut, then opened them again. More flickering pinpoints.

I wanted him to tell me about the constellations, about anything. But first, the task at hand looming over my village's life.

"I want to be—"

"I walk when I—" Rezart looked at me, surprised. That enigmatic smile again. "Please, go ahead."

"I was there at your meeting, if you remember."

"I remember."

I thought I must sound like a shrill blue jay next to his warm voice.

"You will think I'm a fool, but I did not know the situation was so bad—the Ottomans' cruelty. I want to be trained to be in the next raid. My brother, Deda, has taught me everything he knows. I haven't used a gun, but I can fight. I can't sit here."

He rubbed his arm, then sat without a sound, without shuffling or turning his head, for what seemed like a long time.

A slight breeze rippled through my sleeves. It stirred the revenge inside me. In fact, it fanned the flames. I still smelled the tangy blood and the foul sweat on my father's body. My head tied Vengeance to early summer, despite its buds, blooms, and longer days full of light. Hand-in-hand.

Rezart cleared his throat and spoke at a normal, conversational volume. "Your father was a good man. It was an honor to know him. I didn't think it possible, but I respect him more for—"

Tears sprang from my eyes, entirely unwelcome, but Love loves with abandon.

"—for bringing you." He wiped one hand over his mustache. "That is, I would be honored to fight alongside another Zeka."

I bowed my head, and gratitude and disbelief caught in my ribs, my throat, my shaking fingers. When I recovered enough to speak, I realized he had changed his plans. "You came back for my father's funeral?"

"I've met more bad men than good, and he deserved more than my early return. I'll leave tomorrow to recruit among the other tribes further north, as planned. Those who can fight will come with me. We will come through here again next week on our way to Scutari. To whatever is left of it." He stilled his hands and looked at me straight. "You may join us. Unless you change your mind."

I wiped my eyes and inhaled all the mountain air I could. "I will be ready and waiting." I exhaled something of a laugh at the relief washing over me. "You were saying something about walking?"

"Oh yes," Rezart said, "I walk when I can't sleep, sometimes. That is all. That's how I came upon you here."

"Yes. I do too. Sometimes. Other times, I sit and let the night pass."

"I see," he said. He stood and set his weight on his left foot.

I rose and wiped the dust and dirt from the seat of my pants.

"Good night, Mira." Rezart put his hand to his chest and bowed.

I heard the owls again, airing their questions.

"See you next week," I said.

"Next week." And the night swallowed him.

Genti and Deda understood I would join them. Our conversations revolved around my training, their experiences, and the farm.

"The fancier their coats, the higher ranking they are. You know it's a general when their gold ribbons reach their elbows."

"If nothing else, just run and take cover."

"You'll never appreciate a fire like you do when you're sleeping out in the open."

I wrapped all the dry food and divided it evenly into our packs. I washed all our clothing. I cleaned out the goats' pen and their shelter under the house, too. I swept out the fireplace. I dusted the mantel and hoped my mother would be proud. I wanted to be ready when Rezart returned.

I asked Gjergji to tend our goats and sheep.

"I'd rather come with you all," he said. "I'm old enough."

"I know. But how many men are left?" We looked around Bujan and were hard-pressed to find a house not missing its head and at least one of its sons. "And you have your lady in waiting."

"You're right. I'll take care of everybody."

"Good. That's what we need."

The next morning, on our way to the well, I stopped mid-step. I slapped Deda on the arm. Coming up the hill to the entrance of town was a quiet sight of destitution. Two women with two children walked in our direction, their eyes downcast. The women carried smoke-stained bundles on their backs, and one had a bundle wrapped around her front.

I dropped the pail and jogged to the survivors, for that is what they must have been.

"Where are you from?" I said. There was no need for other questions. All the answers were written on their faces.

"From Gralishte. We had everything. Now, nothing."

"Are they coming this way?" Stupid words, as soon as they left my mouth.

"No, they're scared of the mountains' curse."

"That's right. That's right. Let them think that," I said. I shook my head to push away the emotion and bring logic front and center. "You're here now."

A quick, refreshing wind blew between us. I wanted to believe it was a sign of hope. "Come to our house. We have food."

I squatted down and spoke to the children. "Hello, my name is Mira. What's your name?"

One buried his face in his mother's skirt. He looked to be no more than three, with his hair cropped within a quarter-inch of his scalp. This makes for thicker, fuller hair, according to the *nonas* of every village since time immemorial.

"You can talk to her," one of the women encouraged. "He's Beni. I'm Mindi," Deep creases pinched near her eyebrows. Her light brown hair peeked from underneath her gray-white headscarf.

"And this is Elise," Mindi said, pulling back the layers of fabric that kept the baby strapped to her.

The other boy, not much older than Beni, took a half step away from Mindi and, with all of his bravery, said, "Rudi." He stepped back and looked at my shoes. His head was covered in whorls of brown-black curls.

"I'm Musine," said the other woman, who shook my hand, then Deda's. She could not have been much older than me, in her early twenties.

"Welcome," Deda said quietly.

"Please, come with us. Our house is right here." I gestured.

"I'll get the water," Deda said.

There was a collective sigh of relief when I opened the door.

"Sit," I urged them, motioning to the cushions on the floor around the fireplace. "You are welcome here. I'll make coffee."

"Thank you," said Mindi. Both of the boys gathered around her, mumbling and whining.

"Oh! Breakfast! Have you eaten?" I asked. I didn't wait for them to reply but went straight for the leftovers.

The boys reached for the bread as soon as I set it on the low table. I put the cheese out, too.

Mindi held them back. "Wait. We'll wash first."

The boys complied, with a huff.

I measured three spoonfuls of coffee beans and removed the lid of the cylindrical grinder. It was bronze, engraved with rings of waves and curlicues every few inches. I closed the lid and turned the handle on top. The familiar sound of crunching and cracking beans followed, like dropping a handful of wet river stones and hearing them fall, one on top of the other.

"Here we are," Deda said when he opened the door.

Beni and Rudi rushed to help Deda carry the water. I smiled at their little hands, wrapping around the rope of the bucket. The boys rinsed their hands and hurried back to Mindi with expectant eyes. Mindi smiled at them and gave them permission to eat.

"Thank you," she said to me.

"Of course."

I turned my attention back to the coffee. I held onto the long handle of the *xhezve* and poured in the powdery grounds. The base of the small pot was wide and narrowed at the top. I filled it with water and set it to boil.

Between sips of coffee, we learned that Mindi and Musine were sisters. Mindi lived under her husband's protection and Musine under their father's. Until the men were taken as prisoners.

"They bound all the men still alive from Gralishte. And as they left, the Ottoman soldiers threw a torch into each house." Mindi wiped her face with her strong hand. "I assume my husband is dead. I can only hope he assumes the same for me. There is no pain in death; it is peaceful. But the pain of not knowing ..." Mindi's voice trailed off, and she stared into the bottom of her cup.

Deda and I told them of Bac's death and that we were to leave soon to join the fight, like our brothers.

"Would you,"—I glanced at Deda, then looked back at the women—"would you stay here and care for our land and animals while we are gone?"

I stopped short of guaranteeing their safety here in Bujan. "There's food," I added. "And our neighbors will ..." I considered my words. How would our neighbors treat women from Gralishte? We were holding onto all the food we could to make it through winter. Would our people be willing to take in five more? "... our neighbors will be here if you need."

"Mindi is a great cook," Musine said.

Elise squirmed and squealed. Mindi loosened her from the swaddle. A pudgy face and pudgy hands poked out from her head covering and sweater dress. She was well fed, I thought, as I imagined corn mush dripping down her chin, in better days.

"And Musine is good with animals. She was caring for ours before, before they were stolen," Mindi said. She *tsk*ed and shook her head.

"Good," Deda said. "I'll show you around when you're ready."

"Thank you." The women placed their hands across their chests. "Thank you."

We did what we could to get them comfortable. Mindi and the children slept on my father's pallet. Deda's bed was given to Musine; he would sleep in the stable— Genti, too. The women's gratitude and tears began again.

It was mid-morning when we went outside, the sun almost parallel with the mountain peaks. At this time of year, our mountains were on full display, a delight to the senses. The animals sounded their chorus of thanks to the sun, grateful for the new green shooting up from earth and trees. Bees buzzed en masse around new salvia, yellow hawkweed, Queen Anne's lace and early yarrow. It was a sight: pasture-covered hill after rolling hill, broken only by heavy clumps of oaks, chestnuts and linden. Plum trees and stunted rock walls divided fields. All of it laid over the ebbs and flows of the mountains themselves.

Deda led our guests to the pens and the animals. The boys seemed to relax a bit when they saw the goats and hens. The clucking gave Elise a start. She puckered her lower lip, ready to cry, and looked up at Mindi for reassurance. Mindi patted Elise's behind and swayed side to side.

"We will have chicks in a few months. And the mama goats will have babies, too, and soon," Deda said. I could hear in his voice that he was as keen as I was to see them smile.

"Soon?" Rudi said, in a way only a little kid can.

Word traveled like lightning. All the women of the village came to meet Mindi and Musine, shaking their hands and squeezing the children's cheeks.

As we walked to our family's field to introduce them to Genti, we ran into Gjergji.

"Gjergji," I said. "These women, Mindi and Musine, and Mindi's children, have just escaped Gralishte. Can I count on you to help them, should they need it?"

I turned to Beni and Rudi. "Gjergji is the best fisherman in town. He will teach you, won't you, Gjergji?"

Gjergji, arguably the kindest soul on earth, simply placed his hand over his heart and bowed. A promise, a greeting, honor above all.

Over the next few days, our new friends learned our routines and met other neighbors. The daily chores varied little from their own back home; it was more a matter of learning where tools were stored and where our land boundaries lay.

As part of my final preparations, I altered two pairs of Luan's pants to fit me. Gjergji's mother made a jacket for me. It was not my mother's embroidery, but she had sewn a ribbon, loop after loop, onto the arms and around the cuffs. It was no accident that my entire wardrobe was black on black on black.

Then at last, the seven days were up. And Rezart had promised. My first, my only, intention was to watch the road for him.

Mindi, Musine and I sat on the front steps of our house facing the rest of town and the road from the north. The children had gained back most of their energy from their journey and found their voices to speak again.

"Let's go feed the goats, Beni," said Rudi. They looked at me for approval.

"Of course, yes," I replied.

On any other day, even the previous day, I would have walked over to the pen with them. But even that was too much for me. My mind was not here anymore, here at home in Bujan. The tension of idleness and need for action had put me on edge. I kept my arms wrapped around my chest and bounced my foot. Even my brothers had found time to spare, anticipating. They leaned against the wall and sharpened their knives.

"Don't worry, Mira. He's the best," Genti said, without looking up. The best at recruiting and the best at avoiding bullets. What other skills did one need when face to face with demons in the flesh? I remembered what Rezart said at the meeting about burned and pillaged houses, and the sorry state of Musine, Mindi and her children was enough to make me want to march ahead alone. I wanted to do my part. I wanted the barbarians to pay. Only the good sense my mother passed on to me, according to my father, held me until more men could support me.

Finally. The ground began to grumble from horse hooves. The goats came to attention and bleated. Rudi and Beni ran to their mother. Genti and Deda put away their knives and stepped forward.

Battle-ready men and their horses circled the village well. They were mimics of each other, from their wool pants and black boots to their sun-wrinkled, freckled faces. Rezart was not among them.

I stepped in front of my brothers.

"Where is Rezart Agim?"

The shock of me speaking to them read plainly on their faces. The one in front coughed and shifted on his horse.

"Good morning, Miss." Then he looked at Genti and Deda, ignoring my question. "We are twenty-four of Rezart's men." His voice was formal, as if reciting a decree. "And we have come on his behalf to ask for your sister's hand in marriage."

My eyebrows shot toward heaven. I turned my head and saw Genti and Deda wore the same expression.

Genti recovered more quickly, properly concerned about the immediate need to offer hospitality. "Please, water your horses and rest. We will bring some food." Genti looked around at the village women with pleading eyes.

Gjergji needed no instruction. He began hauling water at a clip.

I calculated and planned, in my head. There was the practical—I would have a place in the world. And there was the personal—I would be near the battle. Our house could become a headquarters, if need be. A refuge to others. Our property would be secure if, God forbid, there was ever any question of ownership. My intentions to fight were clear when Rezart and I talked under the moon last week. I did not see his advantage in marrying me.

"Why didn't he come himself?" I said.

"You know the *Kanun's* tradition," the same man replied. A mole on the side of his nose distinguished him. His vest told me his village embroiderer was equal to my mother's skill.

The *Kanun* said that the man's representatives, not the man himself, must ask for the girl's hand.

"Yes," I replied, sensing the pressure of the situation. I commanded my heart to stay in my chest. I rested my hands on my hips. "I also know that of the twenty-four, twelve must be blood relations. Did you stay true to this?" I said, grateful for my listening ears and my father's insistence on my education as to tribal inner workings rather than mysterious things like constellations.

The men looked from one to another, then back at me, and nodded.

"Oh." How could so many of his blood relations defy death?

The women returned with provisions. Some men had dismounted, ready to rest and devour the food and drink. I suppose this conversation was already taking longer than they had expected.

"Men of the house of Zeka, what will your answer be?" said the man with the mole.

I took another step forward. I lifted my hand to allow the lead horse to smell me. I rubbed the side of his chestnut nose, shining like copper in the sun. A confidence grew in my voice, a voice I didn't know I had, from my heart. "Sir, you may tell Rezart Agim I have no dowry to offer."

I heard more than one gasp in the crowd of neighbors and warriors.

"If he accepts this, he can meet me at the chapel at seven o'clock. I'll be there, and ready." I turned back to the house. Over my shoulder I shouted, "Seven o'clock!"

No one mentioned the law in the *Kanun* that said we must wait four weeks between the engagement and the wedding.

I took one glance at my brothers. Their mouths still gaped open. I swear at that moment, I felt my mother wrap her arm around my shoulders and lean her head against mine, and smile.

Even so. "Why me?" I said.

Deda's face shaped-shifted from stunned to stern to wily. "Do you see any other young woman who speaks the way you do?"

A buzzing began in my head. It was as if a swarm of bees had found a way into my mind. I walked back to the house, blinded by the overwhelming feeling of what I had agreed to. Mindi and Musine held their hands in knots, faces as surprised as I felt.

To marry Rezart was, in part, for them. For them, for my family, for my land. But I cannot deny the glowing smile inside when I thought of the conversation we had shared last week.

I am sure Rudi and Beni didn't understand what had transpired, but they jumped around, sensing the energy in the house. They ceased only when Mindi held them by their shoulders.

"Well, ladies, how do we prepare for a wedding?" I asked. "I will not wear a *xhubleta*, if that's what you're thinking. It weighs a thousand pounds. I'll bathe, and if you'll braid my hair, please. I'll need clean shoes and," I looked around the house for other chores before a wedding. "And, if you could brush this coat out, that would be nice."

Blerti's wife, Mada, rapped on the doorframe excitedly despite the front door being open, to visitors and to hungry flies. Arta and her daughter arrived behind her. They waited their turn to kiss and squeeze me. "We'll take care of the dinner. It will be lovely. Oh, Mira!"

Eagerness and yes, happiness, shone on their faces as well. With Mada, they set out to find food fit for a respectable wedding feast.

I grabbed two buckets to fill for a bath.

"No, no! We'll go!" Musine took them from me. Mindi shooed the little boys out of the house.

In an instant, I was alone. I sank to a cushion.

If my mother were alive, she would have accepted their congratulations with her radiant smile. Then she would have made sure my waistband, shawl, and blouse were free of any tears. If she were alive.

I lifted my hand and watched it tremble.

Val

Kosta put his hands on his hips. "He'll need to meet you, of course, our guy Harris. And get some sort of agreement from Major Prifti that you're assigned to him now."

"We're not assigned to anyone," I said. "Who's Prifti?"

"The commander down in Saranda," Endri said.

"Running your own show, are you?" Kosta struck his thumb against his nose. "Right."

"Are you surprised? Show me some weapons and better training than I can get from my father and I will get in formation, but until then …"

"No, no, we understand," Endri said. "We're surrounded by the enemy, right? Harris is on his way to Tragjas. He hopes to set up a contact there. May we join you?"

"You said you were on your way to Gjorm."

"We were, but we accomplished our mission with you."

"Fine. Keep your eyes out." As if I needed to remind them. We walked back to Tragjas with little conversation.

We stopped in front of our house.

"Follow the road," I told the guys. "Before you leave town, turn right. The *teqe* is tucked around the curve in the road. Baba Halil will welcome you. I'm sure it can be Harris's HQ. Please tell Baba Halil we'll be there after we sleep a bit," I said.

"See you then," Kosta said.

Xhevi, Ana and I slipped inside before our neighbors, or more schoolchildren, could see us. Our parents were surprised to see us again so soon, and close to happy when I told them exactly how much my plans had changed.

"We'll go and meet this Brit at the *teqe* tonight. Then, who knows where?" I said. I hoped I sounded adventurous.

"I don't expect you slept," my mother sympathized.

"Not a wink," Ana said, her arm hung over Mami's shoulders. "Did you?"

"Babi and his snoring slept for me. That counts, right?"

We crawled into our beds. Xhevi squeezed in next to me. My mind attempted to work, spinning the 'whos' and 'what nows' and a thousand other questions. My body, as strong as I needed it to be, gave way, and for the first time in a long time, sleep buried my worries.

I woke to our bedroom door creaking open. I sat upright and looked out the window. Dusk.

"Checking on you," Mami whispered.

"Thanks." I shook Xhevi's shoulder. "Come on, wake up, girls." I swung my legs to the floor. I scanned the simple and sturdy wardrobe in the corner. "Think we'll be gone through the winter with this Harris?"

Ana moaned to be left alone. I threw a blue knit scarf at her. Mami made it several years ago. It was one big loop, long enough to cover my neck and my head. I rarely used it. "Come on, sleepyhead." I grabbed the scarf and rolled it into my bag.

"Be right there," she grumbled.

In the main room, Mami had another handkerchief full of dried food ready. Babi gave me the flint from the mantel.

"I can't take this," I said.

"I have another," he insisted. I cast a doubtful eye at him but put it in my pocket. We said goodbye speedily and took the shortcut between neighbors' houses to the *teqe*. With a hop over the retaining wall, we righted our clothes and packs and hurried across the small courtyard. Ana opened the door.

"You're here!" Baba Halil walked toward us with his arms outstretched. "Come in! Yesterday feels like a lifetime ago, doesn't it?"

"You're telling me," I said.

Behind Baba Halil stood Kosta, Endri and, presumably, Harris, their commander. Our commander.

"Ladies, may I introduce Captain Harris." Baba Halil turned and opened his palm to Harris, glaringly foreign with his blond hair and pencil-thin mustache.

"These young men told me about your work," he said as a greeting, an introduction, and the start of a meeting, all in one.

"We're doing what we can with what we have. It's not much." I pointed to his boxes. "Moving in?"

"Sort of, yes."

I saw a few cargo boxes, stencil-painted in letters and numbers. Dented corners indicated a hard landing. One piece, presumably a crate like the others, sat on Baba Halil's storage bench.

Harris cleared his throat. "My orders are to keep giving them hell on the roads. This disrupts, or delays, the arrival of incoming troops and supplies. As of right now, they're mostly coming up from Greece."

"Yes." I waited. But that was all.

He raised his eyebrows, and wrinkles formed in his forehead. "It won't be easy."

"We know hard," I said.

So, to the south we went. We relied heavily on supply drops from the British. Weeks went by, back-and-forth between the main drop zone and our next piece of road. As soon as we had explosives and matches and cover of night, we had work to do. Without the support to engage with the enemy, only to sabotage their path, we didn't usually stick around. Revenge was sweeter, though, the times we were able to salvage boots or food from the trucks we disposed of.

We stayed above the road, hiking, scrambling on our toes and holding onto broken trees when there wasn't a safe path to follow. For us, an achievement was marked by the number of days it took for the Nazis to repair the road to continue north. "We need to move inland," was a phrase we heard from Harris often to avoid skirmishes with the Ballisti and the converted Italian prisoners. And, to find shelter. This pushed us further into the coastal mountains.

We found as many caves as we could, because any family who harbored us might have been killed for aiding the enemy. My heart broke for the families in villages more remote than Tragjas. They were the true victims of war—their few sheep and goats were stolen by every warring party. A growing voice inside me questioned the value of our explosions at their expense. Did they need the roads as much as the Germans? Did other Partizans ruin farmland the way the Italians had ruined ours? I dropped the answer into a deep well until the reverberations of 'no' relieved me of culpability.

Autumn shriveled into winter. I remembered my mother's subtle hope. Guilt wrapped like cold arms around me on the days we could do nothing but wait for a supply drop from the British, squatting in the mud or sleeping in frosty pine forests.

A north wind brought cold rain, pelting and fast. Desperate for a refuge as much from the storm as the barren hills, we knocked on the door of a shepherd's house near Sasaj. A mother and her two daughters graciously took us in. A small box of Harris's food ration he presented as payment may have swayed her decision. Even with the four walls, I felt exposed. I didn't like it; I wanted a forest or at least a mountainside.

"If we had more men," Harris fumed, once we were as comfortable as we could be among the household's fleas and two goats, "we could target anyone able to escape the traps we've set!"

I exchanged glances with the others. Harris was blue eyes on the job, straightforward, even. Supply drops were unreliable, given the weather and the German air force playing chase; one of the Brits' supply planes and its crew had crashed a month earlier. We heard stories of a few British agents coming in for a job and leaving soon thereafter. Harris never went home, but focused on the mission.

Like the rest of us, he was cold and wet and ready to eat. But, of all the times to unload, he chose a night when we were guests.

"We've got to get these Ballis—" I said.

"Bastards," Xhevi interjected.

"Off our backs first, Harris," I finished.

"If you get the Germans, the Ballisti will be forced to follow," he replied.

The daughters, in that bumbling age between childhood and womanhood, put a plate and a few forks in front of us. Boiled greens circled a healthy disc of cornbread and a generous spoonful of lentils. The girls sulked into a corner and stared at us with wide eyes.

"It's more than that," Endri said. His black cherry eyes flitted to Harris and back to the fire. His voice cracked a little. I could see in the way he held his shoulders that he wanted so badly to prove himself a good soldier.

"Bah," Harris said. He gave up.

I motioned for the girls to come closer to the fire. Reluctantly, they did. They sat on their knees, but not before I saw the holes along the seams of their shoes.

"Let me see," I told the older one.

"I'm fine, miss, thank you," she said.

I repeated myself.

All eyes were on us now. She swiveled her feet out in front of herself.

"Shit," I whispered. The side of one shoe was split open, and her toes were scrunched at the top. I waved my hand at her. "Give them to me."

"No, please," she said.

"Not another word." I removed my leather boots and set them next to her.

Her broken shoes pressed my feet on all sides—not ideal for walking miles every day. It was a non-issue.

The next day, we had a minute to rest in the forest behind and south of Sasaj. Harris offered an extra lace to keep my new shoes together.

I thanked him.

"Are you certain that was a good decision?"

I tied the lace around the middle of my foot. "A girl with shitty shoes in winter? Yeah, Harris, I'm certain."

"You're a soldier."

I stood. "It's done, Harris."

By early December, our outstanding missions and the German machine guns had pushed us beyond Mount Çika, all the way to Pilur. This was as far as the Ballisti could venture from their supply in Vlora.

It seemed we had caught Zeus's attention with our explosives: it stormed, showered or drizzled for a week, unceasingly. It's possible he was on our side, his bolts aimed at the Nazis, and we were merely tangled in his crosshairs. Lightning bolts aimed at the Nazis ... yes, that was a pleasant thought.

Pilur was a terrible place, like Sasaj. At one time, I imagined, Pilur was full of grazing sheep among the rocks and green grass and contented families. Gray day after gray day, it became hard to know what time it was. We hiked with heightened trepidation, wandering in a cold mist, two days straight without a fire to dry our feet. I wrapped my head with my blue scarf.

"Today, our aim is a shelter—a roof and four walls," Harris said. We were too tired to talk, to think ahead, or even to be cautious. We moved forward, by collective will, up and around the foothills of Pilur, keeping the road and the sea at our right hand. I looked to the granite and shale mountains trying to shine beyond the hill. They begged the sun to cast one more ray of light. If mountains could beg.

The sun heard their request, because a sliver of winter's evening sun came through the clouds and landed on a shepherd's shelter. Such huts were built throughout the lands, for a shepherd who was too far from home with his herd.

Kosta sprinted ahead to the feeble door and knocked. "Hello?"

I began to shiver from a weakness I had never known. I fell to my knees among the slippery crags and glistening mica.

"Val!" Ana yelled.

I'm okay. I'll get there.

Pistol in one hand, Kosta rotated the latch and pushed his way in. He waved an 'all clear' to us.

Endri, with his cherub cheeks and the wisdom of an elder, had collected bits of brush and half-burned sticks along the way. He dumped these onto the stony fire pit in the middle of the dirt floor.

From his precious pack of matches, Harris lit a precious cigarette. Instead of shaking it out, he tossed it into Endri's pitiful pile of twigs.

I collapsed to the ground and closed my eyes.

In the morning, I woke to the feeling of icicles jabbing outward from the insides of my feet. This collided with a sensation of hot coals on the skin of my toes. From under a thick coating of sleepiness, I built up my tough, outer shell to fend off the agony. Like an actor wearing a mask, I protected myself with mental theatrics, telling myself it wasn't all that bad, that others had endured much worse than me.

I sat up, with the intention of pacing to bring blood to my feet while the others slept. I pressed down my heels to stand.

A wave of nausea knocked me flat. The pain traveled to my head, squeezing my bones on its way. My body rattled with chills.

"Val? What is it?"

"Ana, my feet."

She lay behind me, where she received none of the fire's benefits.

"We took off your shoes last night. You were out cold. We need to get your socks off."

The others began to stir from their light sleep and offered a groggy "morning" to everyone. We had dropped the "good" months ago.

"*Immersion foot*, if you want the English name for it," Harris said and offered me his flask. "Here."

I stared at him for a moment. "Thank you." I took a long swallow, and my whole chest burned. My feet, though, felt like they had been stuck in a mean ice bath.

In fact, it was Ana and Xhevi peeling away bits of socks from my exposed toes. The girls alternated between sucking in air and pressing the tip of their tongue to their upper lip in effort and in disgust. It was a grisly sight.

Endri removed his coat. Without a word, he gave Ana his shirt to wrap my feet. He put his coat back on and buttoned it up to his neck.

"This isn't …" Xhevi mumbled.

"Hush," Ana replied, concentrating on my sock stuck to the layers of skin and burn.

My feet were spotted, itchy as hell, and swollen. I clamped my eyes shut.

In the quietest voice I had ever heard from him, Kosta said, "Scoot her to the fire. But, not too close, now."

I couldn't have them worrying over me so much. "How about this one?" I said aloud. "I have no feet, no hands, and no wings, but I always climb higher. What am I?"

"Val, come on," Endri said. His pursed lips and lowered eyelids told me he was pushed to the brink.

"Okay, okay. I'll let you off easy. Smoke, that's what."

It worked. He smiled, and the others did, too. But it wasn't enough. Endri and Kosta left to find anything they could add to the fire.

Each wall of the hut held one small window. The thatched roof was blackened from fire smoke, and the eaves were open to the elements. It made for minimal air circulation. Remnants of cigarette paper lay scattered about the ground. Pebbles in the dirt floor found every sore spot on my side.

The guys returned with an armful of branches each.

It took all my strength to be present and not slip into sleep or blackout or both. "So what now, Harris?" Like it was my first day on the job.

His eyebrows furrowed, and in the light he looked five years older. He coughed and waved the smoke away. "Start a chimney business," he joked.

We actually laughed.

"Set up the road, come back and light it up at sunrise."

"When there's a convoy," Kosta said.

"When there's a convoy," Harris promised.

"Well, I can't dig, but I can still shoot," I said. "We're not too far from the road, are we? I can use your rifle, Kosta."

"Like hell," Kosta said. He was pushed to the edge, too. He saw the hurt and surprise on my face before I could hide it.

Harris chimed in. "Take care of yourself." A friendly order. He pulled his coat more closely to his chest and sat against the wall facing the door. "We'll head out after we rest a bit."

With permission to sleep again, we rose in and out of naps for hours.

Later, Xhevi and the men tightened their belts and secured the explosives on their backs.

"Work as fast as you can." I wanted my words to carry more weight and wisdom because of my disabled state.

Endri took one last drag of his cigarette and handed it to me.

"Thanks," I said.

"We'll be back before you know it." Xhevi tucked her hair behind her ears and kissed the top of my head.

Ana stayed with me. On their way out, a gust of winter almost extinguished the fire. It smelled of old olives and rosemary. The flames were spindly, looking like I felt: not reaching my full potential.

After a while, Ana inhaled and I knew something was on her mind. "You think they're alive?" she said.

"Who?"

"Sokol. Arberi."

My vision blurred with tears. "I don't know."

"You don't think it's fate? That Kosta and Endri ... that they've taken our brothers' place?"

"Ana."

Sizzle-pop went the fire. It seduced me, weak as it was, with its constancy and comfort. My heavy eyelids fell without my consent.

Before the war, I had the sweetest dreams, full of plump quince and ripe cherries. Now, when my fitful sleep wasn't drowning in the regular nightmare of the sea and its monsters, it was full of empty, stomping shoes, wandering in a space with no ground and no sky.

It was still dark when our crew returned.

Endri squatted in front of the dwindling fire and rubbed his shins. "Harris, you have any more in that flask?"

Harris chuckled and passed it around. "The lines are at that boulder there in front of the hut. Now, keep your eyes and ears open."

At last, we heard the winter birds' first tweets and chirps. Then, a grumble like distant thunder.

I sat up on an elbow. "They're coming."

Kosta, Harris and Endri holstered their pistols and hoisted the rifles. I caught Endri's gaze as he fitted his cap. There was a drive, a spark, written in his eyes. He was gone before I could form a question.

The rumble of diesel grew. Each minute was a lifetime.

"They should be lit by now, if they're the five-minute ones," I whispered.

"Does Harris have any other kind?" Ana replied.

Then why aren't they back yet, I wondered.

A shot rang out, close, and I yelped. Another and another, before any explosive.

Xhevi looked out the south window with a pair of binoculars. Her face scrunched and her lips curled. "The boys are—" She paused. "The boys have cover, but closer to the road. The first two trucks are—"

Boom! A fantastic explosion and the searing sound of gas finished Xhevi's sentence.

A barrage of machine-gun fire. Heavy and shiny-sounding, like coins falling into a pitcher.

"Germans," I said.

"Definitely. Our boys are behind the rock, guns down."

"How many are in the convoy?"

"Four, to be sure. Well, now two. Maybe more around the curve in the road."

"How many did you lay?" I asked, butterfly wings tingling in my fingertips.

"Five."

"Five? Harris has been carrying five?"

"I was carrying one," Xhevi said.

More distinct rifle shots from our boys. I heard yelling; a harsh, barking voice. *"Feuer!"* I heard desperation in its tone. More shots fired.

The other road bombs went off, one after the other.

Stillness.

An engine blew up, and the light from it brightened our faces for a moment. Stillness again.

Another span of lifetimes passed until the boys came back. They smiled, victorious, and shivering.

"You got them all?" I asked, incredulous.

"One truck fell off the cliff," Endri said.

"Endri here started on the middle drivers before they could meet all our hard work," Harris reported.

"Are there any trucks left? Working, I mean," Ana said.

"Yes. One's a pile of metal, one's upside down, and the other's upright, with the dead Germans sitting inside," Kosta said.

Ana nodded. "Good. We can use the truck to get Val home. I'll be right back. Going to get some of their boots, or tires, if that's what it takes, to make some decent"—she raised her eyebrows at me—"shoes for you."

Xhevi remained by the window and kept watch. Kosta and Endri joined her.

Harris stood over me. "How are your feet?"

I shrugged. "I'll make it." I looked toward the window. "How is she?"

"Almost. There. She's there, at the upside-down one," Xhevi said. She tucked a curl behind her ear.

My bare hands felt a vibration in the dirt.

"What's that?" I asked. "Kosta! It's them! Go! More are coming! Ana!"

I bit my lip until I tasted blood. I'll recognize that unmistakable tremble until the day I die.

"Go! Ana!" I screamed. I scrambled to my knees. Endri put his arm under mine to lift me up. From the window facing the sea and the road, we saw Kosta take cover behind a boulder jutting from the hillside like a middle finger. "A—"

Xhevi clamped her hand over my mouth. "Don't tell them her name," she whispered.

A truck stopped. The Nazi in the passenger seat exited with a gun pointed at my only sister.

Kosta aimed.

Ana raised her hands slowly. All my blood drained to my feet. They throbbed with the pulse of my heartbeat. Xhevi and Endri held me up, keeping me from falling into an ocean of loss and disgrace. She went to the trucks because of my obstinacy. I groaned, deep and weak.

We watched Ana shuffle to the back of the truck. The Nazi closed the door and they drove away. She never lifted her head. She didn't give us away. Our Doctor and a better soldier than I.

Kosta returned and stood still in the doorway. The sunrise behind him cast his face in awful shadows. We waited. Then, he took a step and turned and kicked and pounded the door. He screamed the voice of rage, pure and simple, aching and overbearing. He kicked and he punched over and over, so hard, so fast the door had no chance to respond.

I swung my tender feet out of the commandeered German truck in front of my house. I put my heels to the ground and stood with the strength of a dormouse carrying Atlas's burden. A humid chill riding on the gray clouds swooped in from the sea. My mother ran to me, held me close, then turned away when I told her about Ana. My father rubbed his hand over his face. How could their baby be gone, too?

Xhevi stayed with me while the guys went to see Baba Halil. I couldn't blame them for escaping the painful silence under our roof. I stayed close to the fire to thaw my feet but didn't bring attention to them. I couldn't feel them. I couldn't feel much of anything other than thick, thick shame.

The men, and Baba Halil, came for dinner. I looked right away at a canvas-draped case that Baba Halil carried in his arms.

"What's that?" I asked, before saying hello.

"Ah, this. Another gift from the Brits. Well, they left it. Didn't give it to me, per se." Under the canvas was a metallic box, but the top half of each end was dotted with holes. Inside was a pigeon. There was just enough light in the room to see it tilt its head in static degrees and survey the room.

I swore we locked eyes.

"Baba Halil, Harris, please, sit down," my father gestured. We sat in front of our low, round table on the sheep rugs of my youth. My mother filled the table with lentils, grilled onions, pickled cabbage, salted fish, beets with olive oil, cornbread and goat cheese.

"A Major Thomas came two days after you left," Baba Halil said. "He stayed in the *teqe* for some time, off and on. He didn't tell me much but that he sent messages, attached to the bird's leg, to his contact in Elbasan. The only other thing I know is that it needs to be let out of the cage every few days if it's not needed for a mission. Into a larger, but enclosed space."

"The pigeon takes messages to Elbasan? And returns?" I said.

Baba Halil caught a crumb of cornbread and wiped his beard. "Indeed." He coughed and looked into his glass of *raki*. He lifted it in the air and, when he had everyone's attention, he spoke reverently, "The Major was killed last week. He was a good man."

The cornbread and lentils stuck like mud in my mouth. All of our "I'm sorrys" jumbled over each other, fighting through the smoke and despondency on their way to Harris. We listened and watched the fire, and made space for that weight to settle.

"When do we use it?" Endri said, in a hushed voice.

"Only if there's significant news. Right, Harris?" Baba Halil said.

Harris stared at his hands folded in his lap a moment longer, then looked at Baba Halil and only Baba Halil. "I wasn't trained with them. But yes, I wouldn't send it more than absolutely necessary."

"And the contact will do the same, or send instructions."

"Right," Endri said.

Baba Halil continued. "He said the birds are quite reliable, because they have one thing in mind: to get home. They don't need a road to drive on, you know?"

Mami burst out into a wail.

"I'm sorry," Baba Halil said. He chewed on his bottom lip.

He put the blanket back over the birdcage.

"Harris," I said. "Can we take the bird with us?"

He bowed his head. "She's all yours."

I blinked, surprised by his choice of words. I didn't press.

Kosta and my father began a conversation between themselves. Xhevi complimented my mother on the food. Mami hadn't eaten a bite. My father added three more logs to the fire.

Baba Halil leaned over to me and whispered, "One more thing about the bird. I named her 'Shpresa.'" He shrugged one shoulder, to shake off the embarrassment or lighten the mood, I wasn't sure.

I couldn't help but crack a smile, my cheek muscles rebelling against atrophy. Optimistic Baba Halil naming a bird 'Hope' in the middle of a war.

"I'm sorry about Ana," he said. "She'll find a way."

I contorted my lips and those damn tears threatened to resurface. I shook my head.

"There are a few other things," Baba Halil said gently, "that Major Thomas did for Shpresa. May I show you?"

We turned away from my parents, wanting to protect them from any reminder of the reason their children weren't home. Inside her cage was a food tin. It was half-full of dried berries and uncooked maize. In another tin, next to the food, was an inch-wide roll of paper. It was all but used up.

"What he did, he unrolled it, wrote his note and then tore it off. He rolled it as small as he possibly could, with the writing on the inside, of course."

"Okay. I don't think I can write that small."

Baba Halil continued. "When you're ready to put the paper in that canister, pull her leg straight behind, not out to the side."

"And she'll go to Elbasan?" It seemed impossible.

"Yes. Push her up into the air to give her a head start." He winked.

Harris stood to take his leave when my mother cleared the empty plates. I reached up to shake his hand. He squatted between Baba Halil and me. "My turn now," Harris said and coughed politely.

"Something easy, Harris," I said.

"Right." He shifted his weight. "So. With me gone—"

"Sorry?" I stammered. "Harris, you're leaving us?"

"My time is up, yes. You will report to Major Prifti as soon as your feet are well enough. He's rough around the edges, but keep your head down and you'll be fine. Take the bird with you. Like I said, she's all yours."

Baba Halil, and my house full of people, people I loved, fell away. I zeroed in on the captain. "But Ana, Harris. I need to get to Ana."

He sighed. "I understand. I'm afraid it'll put her in more danger to ask around. If I can ask the right people, in person, I'll find a way to let you know. My advice? Get home as soon as all this is over. This is where she'll come, too, no?"

I bobbed my head because I couldn't speak. My bottom lip betrayed me. I shook his hand with all the strength of a picked flower.

Harris left to catch his scheduled rescue boat.

My feet throbbed like glowing embers and stung like pokers stabbing a fire.

Dita

Dita wore black jeans and a thermal top under her denim jacket. Ilir was waiting for her outside her building, at the bottom of the stairs. Right cheek, left cheek, right again, and sweetly on the lips.

As they walked to dinner, Ilir and Dita passed by families pushing strollers, with their little ones bundled like penguins. Stray dogs were beginning their night of hunting for food in the trash bins. A man sold cigarettes from a box bungee-tied to the back of his bicycle. Giggling high school students walked as if they owned the night among the bass of cruising cars and the gritty air.

Dita and Ilir strolled along the Lana River. Businesses lined each side, interrupted only by veins of city streets leading to neighborhoods.

She knew where they were going without asking.

Ilir held the pizzeria's door open for Dita. An employee scraped a fresh pizza from the wood-burning oven and called out, "Hot!" He whipped back to the oven with his paddle to shift the pizzas around so they would receive equal heat. Passionate music popped from speakers placed throughout the restaurant, wires dangling from one to the other as though the job wasn't quite finished. The smell of salty cheese and sweet tomato made Dita's mouth water. A toddler squealed with excitement as his pizza was cut into smaller pieces.

Dita and Ilir found a table set at a diamond's angle and sat next to each other to have a view of the street, the life outside.

A waiter arrived in a hurry, all but running into them.

"Easy, man, we're in no rush," Ilir said. The waiter's shoulders dropped.

Ilir worked in imports-exports. His easy smile enchanted Dita and his customers alike. Everyone was a friend, all on the same level. He was the life of any party, charming, hands on his hips that said he was open and willing to talk to anyone, anytime. He usually told exaggerated stories too loudly, to gather everyone in, to have command of the room. Dita preferred to talk to two or three friends quietly. What is life without balance?

The waiter mumbled something about not having enough employees. He folded his hands and asked for their orders with concern and patience.

Dita decided on the plainest, most simple option. "The margherita, please. And a salad, too," she said, looking to balance the pizza and last night's pasta with a small plate of carrots and lettuce.

"A prosciutto and mushroom for me," Ilir said with a big smile. "And a Birra Tirana. You too, Dita?"

"No, the house white, thank you."

"Birra Tirana and a white wine, then," Ilir finished. The waiter swept away and past the oven to the kitchen. Chair legs screeched against the tile floor as a family got up to leave.

Dita turned to see what had caught Ilir's attention: a live soccer match being shown on one of the televisions, between Italy and Serbia. Dita people-watched.

"So, I got my dad's car washed this morning." Ilir slapped an unopened pack of cigarettes against his palm. "You'll never guess what I forgot."

"Your wallet?"

"Nope. See, I went to one of those automatic, drive-thru places. I forgot to roll up the back window." He lit the cigarette, grinning from ear to ear, proud of a good story.

"Oh no!" Dita cupped her cheeks.

The waiter reappeared with their drinks and a condiment caddy.

"Yeah, so, I bought some towels and spent the rest of the morning trying to dry the seats," Ilir said.

"What else can you do?" Dita lifted her glass to his. "*Gëzuar.*"

"*Gëzuar.*"

The game was now 1-0, Serbia. A table full of downhearted fans sat under the television. Their lack of cheering told a sports novice like Dita that the Italians needed a big play to keep hope in the air. Hell would freeze before anyone here would cheer for Serbia.

Dita took a sip of her Pinot. "So, get this. Kupi, my boss, is out, and a new guy who nobody's heard of, is in. As director of my team."

"What?"

"I know."

"But why?" Ilir sank his shoulders and pressed his forearms into the table.

"'But why?' You know how things work, Liri."

"Did you want the job?"

"I mean, I'm leaving, right? But, get someone who's at least *interested* in history. Not some 'businessman.'" She glanced at Ilir. "Sorry." She assumed Raco was one of those self-inflated modern merchants.

"What's his name?" Ilir said, keeping an eye on the game.

"Raco. Gazmir Raco."

Ilir's gaze came back to Dita, flickered, registered, and reset all in a blink.

"What?"

"Nothing." He took a swing of his beer. "Except, if it's the same Gazmir Raco, he just left the company."

"Yours? Why?"

"He wasn't pulling his weight, supposedly. Also, his position has been filled by the owner's nephew."

It was Dita's turn now to take a deep swallow. "See?"

Italy lost, 2-0.

Dita closed the front door softly and placed her purse next to a silver dish and two empty candlesticks on the entry table. She slipped into her *shapka* and glanced in the mirror above the table out of habit.

The kitchen light glowed and the rest of the house was dark. Her parents sat on the loveseat together watching an overseas sitcom.

"You didn't have to wait up," Dita said.

"We didn't," Murat replied. "This came." He picked up an envelope from the coffee table and handed it to her.

Dita puffed her cheeks and exhaled. She took it to the dull lamp over the stove and wiggled a finger under the envelope's flap. Her parents joined her. Lena switched on the brighter, overhead light.

Ms. Arbani,

We are pleased to inform you that you have been accepted into our one-year fellowship at the Etruscan Museum ...

"I've been accepted!"

"Congratulations!" Her parents radiated pride and hugged her.

"Thank you!" It felt like something that happened to other people, to her friend Luljana or Ilir, not her. "Nora will be so happy!"

"Let's celebrate, want to?" Lena said. "Grab the sherry," she motioned with her chin to the glass cabinet between the living room furniture.

Free of dust behind the door sat crystal glasses for *raki* and dessert dishes used on New Year's. In the center of the shelf was a handmade book, leather-bound and small enough to fit in Dita's palm. It was her only link to her maternal great-grandmother, the legendary fighter Mira Zeka. The pages were folded in such a way as to be pockets for pressed flowers. Dita hadn't touched it in years, afraid it would crumble in her hands. She remembered the song she and Nora had made up to memorize the flowers inside: "Snow drop, violet, yarrow, lace, rose, aster, each in its place." Also on the shelf was a notebook from her paternal great-aunt Val, a Partizan and badass guerilla fighter during World War II. Whenever Dita felt sad, she studied Val's notes. It put life in perspective quite quickly. Tonight, though, was not one of those times. Dita grazed her fingers over the books, these priceless artifacts in her family's home, took the glassware and sherry, and gently closed the cabinet door.

"To opportunity and ... adventure," Lena said.

"To history," Murat added and raised his sherry.

"To living history," Dita said, satisfied.

Dita called Nora, as promised, in the morning.

"I knew it!" her sister shouted, popping the receiver. "Smarty pants."

Dita laughed, dissolving pounds of tension. It would be good to be with Nora again.

A few weeks passed deeper into autumn. The trees lining the sidewalks around town looked pitiful and lonely as they shed their leaves. The days were darker earlier, of course. Every year, the change in light and temperature sparked a craving in Dita to eat warm, rich foods like beef stew and anything baked.

After work one day, Dita was in the kitchen with her hip pressed against the counter, picking at her mother's chicken and potatoes. Her fingers glistened from the oil and juices. Truly, love elevated food from good to irresistible. What else could make such a simple dish so delectable?

Nana sat in her spot on the sofa facing the balcony and the television. A sliver of bare legs peeked out between her black skirt and beige knee-highs. A red lap blanket, another one of her works of art and craft, lay draped over her legs. The crocheting hook and yarn looked awkward moving through her fingers. After a few turns of her wrists, she began the repetitive motion, tremulously. Dita could see this doily project wasn't up to par among Nana's better works. But it was something.

"Nana, where are your *shapka*?"

Nana Sofia looked at her feet. "Huh. I guess I just forgot them." Her grandmother shrugged and continued crocheting.

"You?" Dita almost laughed, but then a wave of concern rushed through her. Was this the beginning of her grandmother's decline? House shoes were practically another layer of skin, and Dita had never, ever seen her walk across the house without them.

Nana wiggled her toes absently.

The jingle of her father's key and the thump of the front door closing echoed in the apartment. "Is it my birthday?" Murat called out. "Smells so good!"

He greeted his ladies of the house, as always.

"Babi, I'm going out tonight, so you can have my serving of dinner," Dita said.

He adjusted his glasses and rubbed his hands together. "I won't let you down."

She looked down at the meal she would miss. The way the pieces of chicken lay looked like the Cape of Rodoni she'd seen on a map earlier in the day at work. Yesterday, a treasure-hunter had delivered a small pot and two knives. He had discovered them at a certain Rodoni Castle. The land on which it was built was narrow and curled in shape, like a pirate's hook. It jutted out to sea long enough to create a small bay.

Ambiguous memories of middle school geography class resurfaced. The hilltop above the bay offered a prime, unobstructed view for the state military. Recently, Dita had learned that Enver Hoxha, the country's dictator, had built deep tunnels into the cliffside and filled them with cannons. As a consequence, the entire cape had been inaccessible to the public for the better part of the twentieth century.

Dita eyed Nana. She wanted to ask Nana so many things, now that she wasn't working on that in-depth fellowship application. Now that she worked with their national history every day. Now, it seemed natural that she make a career of working with her country's story. She felt stupid for not realizing it earlier, surrounded as she was by her family's treasures in the glass cabinet, and Nana herself.

After the second war, the People's Party created a world of isolation under the guise of communism. Life was rife with espionage among neighbors and betrayal among friends. The Youth worked in the summers, pulling and pushing the entire country toward progress by building dams, roads, and factories. Family farms became collectives, and the yields became state property. Finally, ten years ago, a semblance of democracy had emerged, under which money translated to power and the country sought to Westernize itself.

In the name of national research and her own curiosity, Dita crossed the room and knelt in front of her grandmother. "Nana, have you ever been to Rodoni?"

"Rodoni. There's something there, isn't there?" Nana said, turning the question back to Dita. "What is it? My sister would talk about it."

Lena entered the room at that moment. "Really?" She cast a dubious glance at Dita. "It wasn't like you could go there, or anywhere, for a weekend getaway. Privately owned cars were forbidden. You remember when we got our car, Dita?"

"Of course." Despite the darkness of the past, she felt an urge to run to the beach caves, to the stories Nana told when she was younger, to sleep among the grapevines planted on sun-soaked terraces two generations ago, to eat from wild blackberries on the beaches. That was the life she wanted. There were two sides to the coin: fruitful and satisfying on one side, torturous and paranoid on the other, as the grieving woman at the exhibit could attest.

Dita's phone buzzed. She kissed her mother goodbye. She squeezed Nana in a hug.

"I'll see you tomorrow," Dita said.

"Gold," Nana whispered and put a finger to her lips.

Shivers ran over Dita's heart. She willed every muscle, every fiber in her being to be still, to not make a sound.

"Gold at Rodoni. That's it. You know, Miss History." She clutched her own wrist.

"No, Nana," she whispered back. "I don't know, tell me." Dita stole a glimpse at her mom. The Swiss clock cuckooed.

"Yes, yes. It's there, somewhere," Nana said.

Dita wiped away a surprising run of tears. She hugged her mother again and left, depending on the stair handrail for the first time in her life as her crying blurred her vision.

Dita greeted Ilir in a daze.

He held her at arm's length under the yellow-orange streetlight. She peeked at him long enough to see the question written on his face. "My grandmother," she whispered. More tears.

"What did she say?"

Dita clenched her teeth to get a grip. She hated how her nose turned cold when she cried.

"'Gold at Rodoni.'"

"Okay," he said in a confused tone. "Why does that make you cry?"

"I don't know. I don't know, it feels like … if I knew about that, then I would know everything I need to, like I would really understand her life. Maybe. I don't know."

"Do you still want to go out?"

Dita shook her head, as if waking from a dream, and wiped her face again. "Yes, yes, of course."

Mira

BUJAN, JUNE 1911

Enthusiastic chatter filled the air before the church yard came into view. When we turned the corner, I heard:

"There she is!"

Guns cocked and shots fired into the air.

"Save your bullets!" I yelled, to no avail.

The man who asked for me on behalf of Rezart stepped forward. "I am Qazim."

He bowed with his hand on his heart. Before any other words could be exchanged, the other four shots rang out.

When the ecstatic cheering calmed, Qazim continued, "I am pleased you accepted."

Right away, Qazim and I found ourselves in the middle of a swarm of people.

"Rezart and I have been friends since we were young. I have been trying to convince Rezart not to be scared of women." He smiled and winked.

It had been too long since I had seen so many smiles. Even the robins and the river seemed more excited than usual.

In my next breath, voices quieted and, in a communal agreement, my neighbors, friends, and Rezart's men parted. Rezart stood before me.

He was dressed in black from head to toe, save for a white shirt buttoned to the top. He had combed his hair. His face seemed younger and brighter, and even his cheeks seemed to shine.

He first gripped Genti's arm and shook his hand. They brought their heads to touch, as their ancestors had once greeted each other. He then repeated the gesture with Deda.

Rezart gave me a single nod with a pleased smile. The sunlight caught his left iris, exposing a treasure of dark amber. I was speechless. He held out his arm to me. I held onto his elbow. Again, the crowd parted and we entered the chapel together. It was a simple chapel with a steeple, built from local stone. A refuge built from nature's refuge.

Everyone rushed in behind us, eager to be witnesses within earshot. The less lucky ones, including most of Rezart's men, packed themselves into the open windows from the outside. The cross-breeze cooled our provincial sanctuary. A kaleidoscope of rainbows spilled onto the wooden planks through the stained glass near the bell tower.

The priest, who had come with Rezart, was about my father's age, and round and rolling in every direction.

"Brothers and sisters …" he began. I was still upside down and inside out. But, of all the things I felt, I did not feel fear. Rezart kept his eyes on the priest throughout the ceremony, only looking in my direction when the priest addressed me.

If there had been no *besa,* his word of loyalty and honor to me until his last breath, if there had been no oath to God Almighty, the kiss he gave me would have been enough. I had no expectations, no preconceived notions, but when his lips fit over my bottom lip and his fingers grazed my jawbone, I was bathed in gold. It was like coming out of a cold, rushing river: renewed, alive, and gasping for air. Yes, I could have defeated an army with a kiss like that.

The dinner afterwards was arranged in the flat land behind my family's home at the edge of town. Three fires shouted to the heavens, though the sun hadn't yet set. Rinaj and his *çifteli* and the drummer, one of Rezart's twenty-four, sat slightly up the eastern hill to let the sound carry over the gentle valley and onto the ripples of the river.

How Arta and the other women managed to find so much food on such short notice was nothing less than a miracle. The roasted goat intended for Rezart and his return had become the meat for our wedding. Musine and Mindi must have baked two dozen cornbreads, using everyone's fireplaces. I smiled at the idea of them running from house to house. Cheeses, bowls of yogurt, and abundant bottles of last year's *raki* were set on all the tables.

First things first: the toast. Rezart raised his glass. Qazim and Rinaj held a bottle each and filled any empty glasses.

"Welcome!" Rezart began. "It is an honor to count you all as witnesses, as brothers, as family. If you will join me,"—he raised his glass again, but now not alone—"to Mira, a woman of strength and generosity. *Gëzuar!*"

Despite our black attire and the dagger of pain nagging at my heart to no end, we were cocooned inside a globe of joy. The music weaved through the salty foods, the sweet, dried fruits, and the drink.

Rezart stood beside me. Our arms touched ever so lightly. Children approached me with big smiles, and their hands held gifts behind their backs: wildflowers gathered into bouquets, roots and all. When there was a break in receiving celebrants, Rezart's thumb brushed my back.

Time passed like a lazy, sunny day. A few widows presented bottles of homemade liqueur they had found in the backs of cupboards, waiting, aging. The women held my hands and kissed me over and over again, showering me in love. There was a certain current of code within each family, within each clan, to live together, to die together—but not an outpouring like this.

Perhaps it was the beat of the goatskin and the dizzying strumming of the *çifteli*, perhaps it was in the stability I was beginning to feel from Rezart, but I could no longer resist the desire to dance. *I will allow myself this.* My feet fluttered to join the women already dancing among the fires. I tried to squeeze in behind Arta, who was at the front of the line. She immediately traded places with me. Custom dictated that the leader hold a handkerchief in their lead hand, my right hand. Without a misstep, she gave it to me and took my left hand. I wound the handkerchief between my fingers. My heart thrummed in unison with the drum. With the next downbeat, my right foot stomped and my right wrist twirled. One foot forward, one back, one kick forward, grapevining into a trance, around and around until the sun rose.

Rezart and I were the last to leave, kissing and hugging everyone before they walked home, drunk on happiness.

He led me to old Nosi's house, its stones tinged pink with the sunrise. The scent of sweet hay on the roof tickled my nose. He opened the wooden door, but he held me back with his hand around my elbow. I smiled as I remembered the tradition: together, we stepped in with our right feet. Equal parts superstition and symbolism. We were inextricable now.

Rezart's bedroll and leather pack sat in a corner. The last embers of a fire remained in the pit in the center of the single-room house. The coolness of the air pinched my cheeks.

"I'll get it going again," Rezart said and got down on his hands and knees. He chose the smallest pieces of kindling and, with tight lips, blew into the coals. A pile of short logs waited within arm's reach of the fire.

He stood, satisfied with the new fire. "Are you hungry?"

"In fact, I am. I danced so much I forgot all about eating," I said.

"You were beautiful."

I bowed my head away from him.

Rezart opened his pack and brought out a white cloth tied in a bulky knot.

We sat in front of the fire, legs crossed. Our knees touched. I untied the bundle. Spread out, the fabric was an apron.

"Who gave this to you?" I asked, wiping a tear of laughter from my eye.

"Arta, I think. Arta?" From his coat pocket, he pulled out a pouch of tobacco. "Do you mind if I smoke?" He lifted the pipe in the air.

I looked at him. Never had I known a man to consider asking anyone, a woman, about their smoking preferences. "Who are you?"

Rezart shrugged like a shy little boy.

"Go ahead," I said. I reached for a handful of dried figs. "Maybe one day I'll learn how to smoke like a man. Anyway, yes, we have an Arta."

Like the rush that comes from removing a river stone from its place, I wanted him to know everyone in town, to know them like I knew them. I told him about Gjergji, how Rinaj the *çifteli* player and my father were best friends, about wine-making every September. He listened, looking away only to cut up two apples.

With food in me and warmth all around, I felt sleepy. My arms and legs were as strong as leaves caught in a drenching rain. The room had brightened with daylight during my short stories.

"I can't stay awake any longer, Rezart." I was too tired to figure out any sort of bed or blanket. The ground would work fine.

"Of course." He stood with ease and retrieved his bedroll. The fire crackled.

He opened his woolen blanket to its fullest size. The crease remained indented along the folds, when it was his alone. He took care to flatten the crease and the edges.

"And, if I may, before we lie down," he said.

I smiled.

He put his hand into his vest pocket. "I would like to give you this."

He offered a book. It fit in the palm of my hand. The edges curled, and most were ripped to some degree. Stiff papers had been folded into fourths and bound with thick, dark thread. The folds were on the bottom rather than the top, to create pockets. I turned one page at a time and pulled each pocket apart. Tucked inside each lay a pressed flower.

My lips parted at the beauty of the gift. I looked at him and saw vulnerability, plain as day.

"Thank you. This is …" I shook my head, at a loss for words.

"Let's sleep." He gestured for me to lie down between the fire and himself. I curled the book into my chest and closed my eyes.

Crickets' chirps woke me sometime later. I lay still and listened for other sounds. Above the insects were the birds' songs, flitting and sporadic. An octave below, the honeybees and bumblebees soothed, dull and constant. I imagined their legs full of pollen as they landed on open wildflowers.

The sound of puffs of air came to my attention. I turned with caution to look at Rezart, ignorant of how deep a sleeper he might or might not be. When he inhaled, his cheeks grew slightly, his mustache rose, yet his lips remained closed. Then came the puffing sound as his lips parted to allow the exhale to escape, like a fire's bellow. Soft, relaxed, and incongruous with the warrior's reputation.

I sat up on my elbow to take in the sun on his forehead, his high cheekbones. I couldn't help but smile at his ears, how they came to a point more than most.

A whiff of smoke caught in my throat and I stifled a cough. It was too much; it brought him out of his sleep. Rezart turned to his side and faced me, still asleep but without the puffy exhalations. His eyelashes were so, so dark and dense.

"Good morning," Rezart mumbled.

I started. "Go back to sleep," I whispered. Pulling someone from their slumber was an ill omen.

"I was walking." He opened his eyes and found my hand, like it was something he had done a thousand times. He brushed his thumb over my knuckles and closed his eyes again. "In a green field, with you, in my dream. But I think it's better to not leave you waiting for me, here and now."

I squeezed his hand, all of this new, every bit of it: lying inside on a sunny day, holding hands with a man, a man who was also my husband.

"I can hear the sea, the waves," he said.

"What do they sound like?"

Without letting go of my hand, Rezart sat up and looked at me.

"It sounds like the winter wind through the pine trees. You know what I mean?"

I smiled. "Yes. There's a pine forest above our northernmost plot. It's so quiet until the wind comes. And it's different from the summer wind."

He agreed and reached for his cup to drink some water. Before he drank, he offered it to me.

"I'll make some coffee," he said.

"You make coffee?"

"Out in the field, I'm famous for my coffee." The irony was not lost that our roots in coffee came from the empire we sought to banish.

On the low table behind us sat a loaf of cornbread and the necessary provisions for coffee. The house had been arranged with every accommodation.

"Did Arta set all this up, too?" I turned and set about reviving the fire.

"No." A smile flickered across his face. "Qazim hinted at it but, once my men were on their way here, I managed to acquire this"—he waved his hand over the food and coffee—"on my own, from fellow fighters up north. They were happy to oblige when I told them the news."

"But you didn't have an answer yet."

"True. I hoped."

We smiled enough that our teeth almost showed.

The bitter scent of the coffee beans bit my tongue. I salivated. We sipped our coffee and stared at the fire. I drained my cup until the last drop.

"Mira," Rezart began, eyes focused on my face.

"Yes?" I said too quickly, and high-pitched.

"I wondered …" He pressed his lips together and then let go, turning them white, then pink again. "I wondered if I could unbraid your hair."

He broke any defense still standing. I was river mud through his cool fingers, wax to his flame, dandelion seeds in his summer breeze.

"Yes. You may." I turned my back to him and faced the window.

He loosened my hair to my scalp. He rested his fingers on my shoulders, then moved to my collar. I held my breath and felt he was holding his, too. We removed my short, black jacket. A current ran under his hands, first only over my arms, then it ran to my ribs and my hips.

"Mira," he whispered.

I flushed and turned to face him.

"Yes." My reply to the question he sent over every inch of me without speaking another word.

Val

"Cheaters! All of you!" Kosta threw his cards down in mock frustration. I tilted my head back to be sure the stars saw our rare laughter. The Ionian air swept around us, heavy with humidity. Endri swept up the cards and handed them to me over the supply box we had drawn to the campfire.

"One more and I'm done," Endri said. He crossed his arms and tucked his hands into his coat. How we didn't taint him with our sarcasm and cursing was a wonder. "The last game is always my luckiest."

"Yeah, sure." Xhevi rolled her eyes.

It was hard to look at Xhevi. She kept Ana at the forefront of my mind relentlessly. Some days, I wished we had never met Kosta and Endri on the road that night. Most days. Because then my Ana would be home in Tragjas.

I glanced at Kosta to confirm another round. It was hard to look at him, too. If I looked too closely, I might have found a crack in his armor. It took him all spring to build it up around his grief, anger, and guilt after Ana was taken. None too soon, either, as his inner turmoil pushed the three of us to the brink of our patience.

"I'm watching you," Kosta said. He pointed at me with a cigarette between his fingers.

I plucked it from his hands and took a deep drag. "I'll meet you here tomorrow, too," I said to Kosta.

In the past nine months, the tide had turned against the Ballisti and their friends, the Germans. Our Partizans had suited up and organized. We wore matching uniforms and caps with red stars. I didn't care much for the fight songs or the dress, but it was better than the alternatives.

Our general objective now was to push any remaining Nazis north to the ports and prisons. If they weren't gunned down first. The successes shifted our orders from bomb squad to cleanup crew along the coast. We were sweepers, confirming every possible enemy outpost was indeed deserted. So far, no surprises, no stragglers.

The next morning, the sun peeked over the blood-stained mountains. I had come to appreciate the serenity that dawn commands, a stillness not to be broken until the sun has turned from its orange whisper to its inspired yellow glow.

I sat up and stretched. My peeling, blistering toes had healed to be mostly healthy again. Only on nights like last night, when it rained, did they tingle and ache, in memory of wet socks and pregnant clouds.

I began the day double-checking that I had packed everything in my rucksack: extra underclothes, a map, bag of seeds for Shpresa, first-aid kit. I began to survey and organize our dwindling inventory, hoping we would soon be notified (by pigeon) that our time was up. Time to move on, done even with the sweeping.

Shpresa was a dutiful compatriot. With that five-minute tutorial from Baba Halil, I had become her primary handler. She broke the anxiety that preyed on us. It showed up in our shaking hands, in our inability to answer a simple question, in our short tempers. One look at her and we all melted. As thanks, we doted on her with abandon. Every time I sent her off with news, I felt useful.

I had never met the comrade to whom Shpresa trekked, time and time again. They had a good hand, precise and patient, a testament to our generation's rigid primary education. I had no confirmation the comrade was a 'he,' but that's how I thought of them because their handwriting was straight and sharp. Mine was precise, too, but more round, more curvy. His small writing required my pocket magnifying glass.

Early on, we began to add personal notes following the official communication—riddles, in particular. I soon looked forward to the recipient's sense of humor through the word puzzles sent back with Shpresa. The riddles were fresh air.

[*What walks on four legs in the morning, two at midday, and three in the evening?*] Was the first riddle.

I replied as quickly as I could: [*Man. Oldest riddle in history. I'm almost insulted. Try again.*]

I meticulously tore off the riddles written on the bottom half of the paper and kept them in a pocket inside my rucksack. The top half I threw into the next campfire, so as to not compromise any whereabouts or orders.

[*I have rivers but no water, oceans but no fish, forests but no trees and cities but no people. What am I?*]

Two days later, I replied: [*a map*]

And so it had gone for eight months now: strategy, riddle, logistics, riddle.

[*You keep this only after giving it to someone.*

I'd very much like to meet you. Find you when this is over?]

I wished to write more often but felt I shouldn't until I had an official reason.

[*Your word. Yes.*]

From the corner of my eye, I saw Shpresa alight on top of her cage. I jogged over to her and tickled the black spot on the left side of her neck.

I read the riddle first: [*If six children and two dogs are under an*

umbrella that only covers two children and one dog, why is no one wet?]
It was hard to wipe the smile from my face. I bit my lip and looked at
the sky. The clean, cloudless sky. I knew: [*It's not raining.*]

At last, the three sleepyheads woke up. I never quizzed them with
the riddles.

"Shpresa came back."

Instantly, they looked at her in her cage. We would nuzzle our noses
to her beak if we could.

"We need to move up to Filikuri Beach," I said.

Within an hour we were hiking along the road. Traveling north, step-
by-step closer to home, we kept the sea and its wind to our left. Zeus
was kind and blew in some cloud cover as we hiked, blurring the hours.

*I do not have wings, but I move across the sky. I don't have eyes, but
I can cry. What am I?*

A cloud.

Near the crest of a hill, I raised my hand to stop and we dropped to
our knees. At the top, in the crook of a curve, sat a house on a cliff. We
were easy targets for anyone watching from the inside, as there was
nothing to hide behind. We readied our pistols.

The disheveled state of the house announced its abandonment by its
residents. Its bones were solid, strong enough for the sea winds. Fraz-
zled but still upright, like all of us. In good times, what a view the
residents must have had. It took even less imagination to see it the way
the Germans would have, as a checkpoint.

I steadied my hands with an exhale through narrow lips. I signaled
for Kosta and Xhevi to secure the back side, the side facing the sea.
Endri and I rushed to the front wall and crouched under a front window.
The sun parted the clouds to illuminate our arrival. *Aren't we all sacred?
Can't we all have sunny days again?*

I'm convinced Shpresa knew when to be quiet as a tomb. I kept my
body flat against the wall and bent my knees into a squat to see inside.

In the expanding sunlight sat a crooked table and a tired, crude bench. A fire pit held its last ashes. The sea breeze diminished any distinct sounds, but I heard a gruff, scratching noise.

Kosta and Xhevi came around and squatted underneath the window on the other side of the front door. Kosta only needed to stretch his neck to assess the other part of the interior, the part of the house behind me.

His eyes widened. He raised two fingers. He laid his hand flat against his cheek. Two people sleeping.

With hand motions, I told Kosta to open the door. I would cover him through the window.

I stood fully. Indeed, two bodies lay on the ground amidst a few empty bottles. I heard that noise again. It was coming from them; they were snoring.

Kosta opened the door.

Pow!

"Kosta!" Xhevi screamed.

"Ah!" The other German shouted and scrambled to get up. He scanned the room and saw he was severely outnumbered.

"Kosta! What did you do?" My voice cracked. I looked at him and the German he'd killed, shot straight through the middle of his chest, like a target.

Kosta lowered his arm, stepped into the house, and raised his gun again at the still-alive Nazi.

"Kosta!" I yelled at him through the window. "Kosta! Put your gun down. Put your gun down."

Kosta kept his back to me. The floor absorbed the *thunk* of the gun.

"Endri, Xhevi, tie up the other one," I said.

I left Shpresa and went inside. I put myself in front of Kosta. I raked my hands through my hair and looked at Kosta. There it was, the crack in his armor I didn't want to see. It oozed heart and care and concern and clarity and insanity.

"What was that?"

His gaze was glazed over, but his reply was crystal clear. "Ana. That was for Ana."

Ana and her wild hair in the sunshine. I could hear the goats braying behind her. Her laugh echoed in my head, and I twisted my lips, pushing my cry out to the sea.

The burn of homegrown 80-proof moonshine stung my eyes. Bastards, greedy and weak. It was a drink reserved for a host to serve their respected guests, and these guys weren't strong enough for it. We cleaned them of their pocket knives and identification papers.

The German groaned over and over and yelled angry words, presumably curses, between groaning. "*Mein kopf!*" He tilted forward. The muscles around his jaw bulged as he sucked air in through his teeth for relief. He was missing his jacket, and his sleeves were rolled up. He was well-built. His skin was so white, rings of purple wrapped around his arm hairs. His eyes sat close to his thin nose. He squeezed them shut, no doubt from a headache I did not envy.

Our French, Italian, and Greek—and English—were better than our conversational German. I stood in front of him and evaluated his, and his dead comrade's, situation.

"Tie his feet for good measure. Deserters, I bet. What do you guys think?" I said, glancing at my squad. My family.

"Likely, I suppose," Xhevi said, holding their identification. "That one," she said, nodding toward the blond one, the one Kosta didn't kill, "is a Hans Gunter." She tapped his papers in her palm.

Gunter looked up. His face hardened.

Another option was that they had failed to make it to their rendezvous point to be shipped home. Their blunder would cost them time in prison.

"*Disertores?*" I asked.

It was enough. *"Nein! Heil Hitler!"* Then he spat at my feet.

"Option two, then," I said.

No, I reconsidered. We're not all sacred. And not everyone deserves sunny days.

Dita

"A Gimlet, please," Dita ordered for herself when she and Ilir arrived at Bar Grand.

Ilir ordered a beer brewed and bottled a couple of hours south, in the city of Korca.

"Next time we come, we might be sitting inside," Dita said as they waited for their drinks. "I can feel the weather changing, a little."

"Yeah, maybe so," Ilir said.

Most of the seating at Bar Grand was al fresco. Dita's bones seemed to rattle with the techno music the DJ played from the back corner. She tucked her shoulder into the back of Ilir's arm a little deeper and smiled. They walked through happy, energized conversations laid out over cushy patio furniture and flickering tea lights.

Dita and Ilir were the last to arrive, rounding out their friend crew to a total of six. Everyone shifted to place them in the middle, dividing the sexes—all the women to Dita's left and all the men on Ilir's side. That's how it was done everywhere, whether it was at a special dinner or neighbors conversing in a courtyard.

Dita hugged her girlfriends. The guys stood and waited in turn to greet her: handshake and right cheek, left cheek, over the too-small, round table standing between them.

Ilir settled into a story about cars. Dita held one hand underneath her drink and wrapped the other around the stem.

Gold at Rodoni. Dita saw herself with white hair, half mad with sun exposure, chipping away at the decrepit castle with a dull pickaxe, to find Nana's truth. If that's how long it would take, then so be it.

Dita took a sip and used all her effort to concentrate on the conversation.

"… not only did he arrive two minutes before closing, but then he went on a rant as to why we should lower the interest rate even more, just for him!" recounted Zana, a loan officer at a foreign bank. Everyone *tsked*, took a sip of their drinks, and waited for another story. They didn't have to wait long.

"I started going to a gym," announced Luljana, an endless fountain of energy and news. "I love it. I've only been going for two days, but they have everything. TVs, music—you forget you're working out. If you guys want to come, I get guest passes each month."

"Thanks, Luljana, but that sounds terrible," Dita said and lovingly patted her knee. Luljana and Zana laughed. "Now, if I had to get sweaty to get a frappé, that would be worth it."

Luljana's glistening hair fell in front of her as she picked out the stale pistachios from the dish in the middle. It would take Dita her whole lunch break just to dry her tangly whirlpool of hair, not to mention the actual workout. Dita's showers—rather, her hair-washing days—were carefully planned around the weather, important events, and how much energy she had to deal with the curls.

"Dita, once you get to Rome, you'll walk everywhere, even more than here; you won't need a gym," replied Luljana, who was always sugar-sweetly amazed at anyone for any sort of accomplishment, past, present, or future. "But really, the gym. It's great."

Rome. Would she be able to find her own friends or only be the tag-along little sister? Dita felt sure she would learn a lot, not the least of which would be improving her high school Italian. And she did have a sweet spot for gelato. Who didn't?

Later, a scruffy-looking boy, no older than eight and skinny as a rail, solemnly meandered through the tables. In his half-raised right hand he held white cones made of printer paper. Inside were freshly roasted almonds. He didn't advertise or announce the snacks. His bored eyes scanned the customers without focusing on anyone at all, looking for a sale.

This was not his first night of selling almonds—he was at Ilir's side in a heartbeat when he waved him over. Ilir dropped more than enough leke into the boy's stubby hand.

"Keep it. Be a good boy," he said and clapped him on the shoulder. The boy skillfully tilted his arm up to keep all the almonds from falling in every direction. He bowed his head, cracked a smile, and walked away.

Ilir put his arms over the back of the couch, one around Dita, and reclined. She looked at him and his generosity and her heart melted a bit more. He threw a wink at her. He exaggerated his stories, sure, and told them too loudly, yes, but there was a layer of goodness that magnetized her.

Dita poured a handful of warm almonds into her hand. Everyone slipped into their second or third rounds except Dita. She should probably get home. She wanted to go home. The music's steady beats filled in the gaps as conversations lulled. Except Ilir's. He turned away from Dita to better tell the guys about his plans to get a BMW 3 series from his cousin's friend in Germany.

Ah, well. Home would have to wait.

Dita turned to Zana. "Are you going to Vienna again this New Year's?"

"Yes, I got the tickets last week. Super cheap."

"Great. Your uncle is there, right?" Luljana said. She shot back the last bit of her Cosmo.

"Both of them now," Zana said. "My dad's brothers and their families. My nephew turned four last month." She tilted her head and pouted her lip to tell them how cute he is.

"Aw, fun," Dita said. But, honestly, she had no clue if four years old was fun. The underlying pressure to have children lay as thick as mosquitoes over a swamp in August.

"When will you leave, Dita?" Luljana said.

"Well, Nora's coming for New Year's, then I'll go with her." There. Now that she had said it to other people, she had to follow through with it and keep her word. Still, she struggled to pull up the requisite anchor — her calling to stay home tugged at her.

At last, everyone parted ways. Ilir's etiquette on walking her home had yet to get old. The sidewalks were built to be wide enough for two and a half people. Heels clicked along in both directions. A gypsy, piled in her layers of clothing, held out a hand to passersby. Pharmacies' neon green crosses blinked and flashed. Fresh pizza tempted them at every other corner.

"That used to be me, you know," Ilir said.

He broke her out of her mental jumble of work, moving, Rome, Nana. "What? Who?" Dita said.

"My little brother sold almonds when I was a kid. My parents opened up a kiosk selling anything we could find: a pair of scissors, a bag of chips, pencils, whatever. But the cigarettes and newspapers—those always sold the best."

"Really?" Pity and pride swelled in her at once. There was still so much they didn't know about each other.

"We sold popcorn on the beaches in the summers, too." In the street lights, his eyes were at once matter-of-fact, embarrassed and searching for Dita's approval. "Maybe that's how I got into business."

"Maybe." She leaned her head against his arm and they walked on, stepping on squashed cigarette butts and empty wrappers from chocolate croissants. Cars paused at red lights, considered to be more of a suggestion at this time of night. A trio of young men and their laughs and smokes stepped onto the street to pass Dita and Ilir.

"Anyway. Won't go back to that, right?" he said and squeezed her hand tighter.

"Right."

Dita made a beeline for Agon in the lab the next morning. "What do you know about Rodoni?"

"Rodoni, Rodoni." He rubbed his thumb over a breakout of zits on his jaw and rotated his chair back and forth. "Rodoni Castle. A fortress built by Albanians six hundred years ago on the cape. One side of it is built into the hill; the other three sides are surrounded by water. Hard to reach and easy to get away. Most of it has been acquired by the Adriatic Sea. If I remember correctly."

"Secrets and all," Dita said.

"Secrets and all," he repeated, staring at her. He snapped his fingers, remembering another tidbit. "After Skenderbeu's time, it was part of the trade route, a landing point to and from Italy."

"Trade. Trade means money."

"Mostly true," he said. "Don't forget: there's trade on the books. And there's trade not on the books. We have a solid history of piracy."

"Right." Dita smiled widely. "Queen Teuta was badass."

"Also true." Second only to Skenderbeu as a national hero, Teuta took over Adriatic domination when her husband died, around the time the Roman Republic was rising. She was successful enough in riches and battle that, after a few years, the Romans felt the need to send tens of thousands of their army and navy to put an end to her reign.

"Okay. Thanks," Dita said, trying to sound professional.

"Oh, come on, it wasn't that much. Quiz me on Skenderbeu's battles and I'll be here all day."

"My grandmother said there's gold there, at Rodoni." It spilled out of her mouth in a hurry. It was her life's new aim, and she would stop at nothing.

Agon skidded his shoes along the floor and brought his chair to a stop. "Well. That would be something."

"Right?" Dita set down her purse. Before there are missions with detailed objectives, there are dreams. This was hers. "Where should we start?"

Agon spun around and pushed up his glasses. He faced the bookcase on the other side of the room.

She waited. She couldn't wait. "You can't see the titles from here. Can you?"

"Not a one." He walked across the room and tapped a shelf with his finger. He pulled a book with a blue spine and red type and returned to their desks. He gave her the book, titled *Ottoman Commerce 1466-1865.*

"It can't be any earlier than 1450 AD, when it was built," he said. "Your trade idea is a good one. Let's start there."

"*My* trade idea?"

"Yeah. It's your project, you get all the credit—"

"And all the responsibility. Thanks." She sat down with the book. "You may continue with your credit-less work," she joked.

"Why, thank you, I will," Agon said, a good sport.

The rest of the morning passed quietly. In the book, the photographs of merchants' entries in their record books varied. Some included the product, price, and quantity. Others skipped the quantity altogether, and on still others the ink had been smeared beyond recognition.

Dita rubbed her head. Far and away, Durrës was the most important port in Albania, seconded by Vlora in the south. The cape of Rodoni was large enough to harbor fishing boats, not warships or merchant fleets.

Dita stretched, stiff from reading. She put her pleather bag over her shoulder and stepped outside for lunch. It was one of those days where the blue in the sky was medium and the sun was in and out of the clouds. The breeze had people walking with sweaters tied around their waists or over their shoulders, just in case. It was a beautiful, late-fall mix of conviction and uncertainty that mirrored Dita's internal weather: Ilir, the lack of answers at work, how fun it would be with Nora. Equally, the anchor keeping her moored was quite heavy. She needed to find the strength to pull it up in order to cross the sea to a trove of opportunity in Rome. But, Nana. Nana, the queen.

The museum possessed the entire north end of the main square. The statue of Skenderbeu, the national hero against the Ottomans, on his muscular horse brought up the south. The spiritual presence of the men he led to battle, to freedom, to death, was alive and well. Dita walked in the direction of the monument, then turned right and along a large city park. There seemed to be fewer and fewer green spaces as each month passed. At the beginning of the block, government buildings loomed large and dampened the city's sounds.

Dita replayed Meta's words over in her head. "What about him?" he had said of Kupi. Kupi had made it clear he was passionate about the caves' treasures and wanted every lead followed. The mystery of his firing made Dita itchy. She felt like she was walking on a life-size board game without knowing the rules.

At the end of the administrative buildings, the city was again uninhibited. Music and noise oozed from every orifice of the city: car stereos, televisions from the long series of shops, and kids calling out to one another.

The *byrek* lady and her flaky, buttery hand pies had set up shop in a corner kiosk the same week Dita began her internship at the museum.

Nothing short of divine coincidence, really. Every culture has a version of warm, stuffed dough. *Byrek* was theirs, Dita's. She quickened her step. If this was street food, who would want a fancy dinner?

"Four, please," she told the lady, "two cheese and two with tomato."

Dita called Agon as she waited. "Meet me at Skenderbeu in five?" she said as soon as he answered.

She heard his grin through the phone. "Make it ten. I'm almost finished cataloging some Scutari coins."

They hung up and Dita's order was ready. The heat of them surprised her. "Ow!" She dropped them without thinking and waved her hand in the air. Dirt from the sidewalk quickly stuck to the pastry and the tomato filling.

"I'm sorry," she said to the lady, who only laughed and told Dita to wait.

While she waited, she adjusted her bag and plotted her next steps for Nana and her gold. Exploring Rodoni would be a great excuse to get away with Ilir for a day.

With the fresh byrek in her hands, she tapped through her phone to call Ilir. At the thought of him, butterflies in her stomach lit and scattered in every direction.

"Hey, what's up?" he answered. The rush in his voice rippled through her.

"Hi! How are you?" Dita said.

"Fine, you know, meetings all day and all day meetings." A sniff of a laugh came through the phone. "You?"

"Good, good, I'm getting lunch," she said, waiting for a string of cars to pass before she crossed the street. The butterflies had found a place to rest but still fluttered their wings, nervous about her proposal. "Listen, do you want to go to Rodoni Castle this weekend?"

"What's there?" More skeptical than enthusiastic, but okay.

"Rodoni Castle," she emphasized. "We, I mean the museum, have some new pieces from there. It's the place my grandma mentioned. I've never been, and it's right on the water. Maybe there's a restaurant nearby? Then we could come back after lunch."

"My dad's birthday is tomorrow, sorry," he said. "But next weekend?"

"Sure," Dita said. "Do you think we could use his car?"

"Yeah, should be fine. It'll be cold, you know."

"Right. It's the off-season. We'll have it all to ourselves."

He cleared his throat, like rocks tumbling over one another.

Dita found some deeply buried confidence and poked at him, "Are you brave enough for the cold?"

"All right, all right. Bring a jacket," he said. "I'm free tonight. Dinner?"

"Sure. Seven?"

"Seven," he said.

Agon walked up as Dita put away her phone. "Byrek. Mmm," Agon said, lifting his portion in the air as a way to say 'cheers.' "Thank you, but I'm the one who should be buying," he said.

She waved away his chivalry.

"It should be you moving upstairs," Agon said after a minute. "Director of Cave Artifacts," he mused with his nose in the air.

"A title only, and you know it. Why don't you throw your name in the hat? I imagine Raco won't be here long."

He shook his head heartily. "No, no, no. I don't want an office."

"I didn't think so." She waved her hand in the air to prove her point. The city pigeons interpreted this as a 'come here' and crowded around her feet, begging, pecking, and cooing. Dita enjoyed her *byrek* and the sun warming her back rather than the phantom of doubt hiding in the corners of her heart. What if there was no gold? And, what if Rome was awful? Like moonlight on water, her hesitation flickered with the unknown.

"Rome will be good," Agon said through a mouthful. *Can he read minds?* she wondered.

He shooed the pigeons away with his feet. "You'll have a great time."

Dita glanced at him, measuring his tone. "Anyway. Ilir and I are going to Rodoni next weekend." She caught stray flakes of dough with her tongue before they ran away in the wind.

"Can you even get to the castle?"

"I don't know," Dita replied with a bite in her mouth. "We'll find out."

Agon shifted his weight to his other foot and peeled down the wrapper for more.

"Great. Call me if you find the gold?" he said.

"Of course."

"Are you going scuba diving?"

"In October? Are you mad?" Dita said. "*Should* I go scuba diving?" She threw her wrapper in the trash. "Do you think that's where the gold is?"

"Not necessarily, but three-quarters of the castle is underwater, right? According to the books." He licked his lips with his last bite. "It's like our own *Titanic*, you know? There's good stuff down there. There must be. Buried in sand and seaweed." He crumpled his wrappers into a ball. "Skenderbeu was the only thing keeping the Sultan from the rest of Europe. So, the Venetians actually found their pockets quite deep when ol' Gjergji said he needed to build another fortress."

Dita chuckled at Agon's nickname for the mighty commander. She imagined boatloads of money coming from the Italians, and the Pope, to pay the laborers and the quarry for the stone. No, the men were too good for that. They worked without pay, she mused, and instead Skenderbeu used the money to pay the quarry, to buy food and weapons.

"You think there's lunch near the castle?"

"Of course," Agon said. "I'm sure some fisherman and his wife set up a great little spot. No *byrek*, though, probably."

They walked slowly back to work. Dita felt cheated she couldn't take a nap—a nap with a belly full of byrek.

When they got to the museum's front steps, Dita shook off her drowsiness, thinking of Nana and how she might feel cheated, too. Cheated, that she, Sofia, would never find a way to tell her adopted mother Mira, "You did it. You and Rezart did it. We're free." Not even to her headstone.

"I'm going to talk to Raco," Dita said in the museum foyer, where they traded the commotion for an academic hush.

"About Rodoni?"

"Yes. Let's make it official. Why not?"

"Want me to come with you?"

Dita shook her head and kept walking. "Thanks, though. I'll be down soon."

She knocked on Raco's office door. Spreadsheets and statements and invoices and stationery with official letterhead were strewn across his desk. He seemed exasperated by her already. But Dita took a step inside. She clasped her hands in front of her. "Mr. Raco, I have a request. I would like to lead a small team to explore Rodoni Castle."

"Explore?"

"To, um, uncover anything left behind."

"By whom?"

Dita explained its place in a trade route to Italy. "A couple of utensils were recently found there. And, as you are well aware, our Skenderbeu built it. Surely, there's more, don't you think?"

"I don't see the significance or what value would be added."

"What value?" She opened her arms for emphasis. "Sir, this is what we do."

"It's not a cave." Raco tapped a pen against his chin, daring her to counter that.

"Sir, I have personal experience, some family, actually, who says there's …" She didn't want to tell him exactly how valuable the potential findings were. "Jewelry there."

Raco leaned back in his chair. He glanced down at the papers in front of him, then squinted his eyes at Dita.

"Ms. Arbani, you must be new. We cannot open projects on hearsay, on family stories. I believe it is still government property, is it not?" He paused. "In fact, it is still government property."

"But, couldn't you—" She wanted so much to have the iron will of her Aunt Valentina, that iron will that drew the circles around 'Home' over and over again in her notebook.

"Furthermore, it is difficult to reach, it is not a cave, and no one is interested in visiting. Except you, it seems."

"But—"

"No, Ms. Arbani. That's a no."

She didn't need to say anything when she returned to the lab in the basement. Agon didn't need to ask.

"I'm still going," she whispered across their desks. "Nana's not crazy."

Agon nodded in agreement.

The next Saturday, Dita and Ilir breezed out of town and into the flat countryside that stretched out before them. Half-built villas painted salmon pink and canary yellow popped up among the latent fields. Ilir tapped out, on the steering wheel, the rhythm of the American pop music on the radio. His dad's car smelled of cologne.

Dita was eager to arrive, to be that much closer to Nana's mystery at Rodoni. She leaned her head against the window and watched a few birds. Not a single flap of wings, only soaring.

Dita sat up and turned down the volume. "Would you rather swim like fish or fly like birds, all the time, one or the other?"

"Swim."

"Wow, that was quick. You don't want to think about it?"

"I already have." He continued drumming and added in the head bobbing. "The water has lots of food, you can go anywhere, and you're protected from the sun. And," he pointed with his index finger, "you can catch a current and float, not even swim."

"You could catch a current in the air, too. Coast, like those guys up there." It was easy to play the devil's advocate with Ilir, because he was so certain of everything. All the time. "You can get food by land or sea if you're a bird. You can go anywhere when you fly, too."

Ilir *tsk-tsked*, disagreeing. "No, you have to land at some point. And birds over land, like eagles, need land food, like rabbits or mice. Sea birds need small fish and *still* need land, for their nests and all."

"Okay, fine, but you can be protected from the sun in the top of a tree."

"Boring," Ilir said.

Dita put her hands up in surrender. "Fish it is."

Other than the two streetlights and the shambled mosque in the last quarter-mile, there was nothing else to suggest civilization. Dita was relieved to see a hotel-restaurant at the very end of the rough gravel road.

"More than a fisherman's shack," Dita mumbled. Floor-to-ceiling windows with thick wooden frames lined the front wall. Sheer curtains had been drawn, and the heavier layers stood at attention, waiting for their turn to help warm the room when the Adriatic's true winter set in.

Ilir put the car in park, but neither of them opened a door. "Looks good," Ilir said.

"Inviting, yes. But first, the castle. Remember, we're not really supposed to be here, wandering around, so …" She put her fingers to her lips.

"Mira, I don't see a soul. But that"—he looked up at the darkening clouds—"on the other hand …"

"Adventure! Come on. You won't get a cold, I promise. This would have been an easy day for Skenderbeu. Can you imagine camping out here, year round?"

Ilir shook his head and grabbed an umbrella from the backseat. Dita smelled rain on its way. The wind picked up its intensity: the prelude. Rain and lightning: the epic verse. Dita adjusted her tool bag across her body. She felt cold with anticipation and slipped her hand into Ilir's.

The surrounding fields varied, with thin and dormant grass, proud weeds and mouse holes. The sheep grazing nearby must have had a part to play in keeping it shorn and matted. Within a few minutes of walking, the open space became dense forest filled with stiff shrubs, scratchy groundcover, and feeble trees fighting for space and sun. The grooved and permanent path sank a hand's width deeper than the ground to each side of it. The downslope to the sea was full of boulders and briars. Dita and Ilir concentrated on the trail, riddled with roots ripe for tripping visitors. This was an invitation exclusively for the intrepid and inquisitive. Halfway down, donkeys' hoof prints created natural stairs. Their permanence supported the idea of this route once being important to merchants. Dita stopped to put her fist inside the prints.

"Centuries of storms didn't wash them away," she said to herself. "There was that much travel."

Ilir stopped to wait for her, farther down the trail. Dita stood and braced herself against the rock face beside her. Ahead and below, she saw the only stout tower left standing of Rodoni Castle. The water surrounded it, cool azure blue, thanks to the clouds, and nothing short of dreamy.

Thunder rumbled overhead.

Before removing her hand from the rock face, Dita noticed that initials and names had been etched into it, inside roughly drawn hearts. She fought a tight feeling in her throat. This was special, a special place. Some people had ventured here, past the outlandish cannon-stuffed tunnels, to proclaim their heart's desire, albeit quietly and in an abandoned corner of the world.

Dita sighed and returned to the present moment. She looked over her shoulder, then carefully hurried to catch up with Ilir. They ran across the small stretch of sand and under what was once one of the castle's main arches. They stopped in the first of several alcoves built into the outer wall. The width was sufficient for both of them, but the height was lacking. Ilir bent over to step inside. They sat on the ground—a mix of sand, gravel, dirt and weeds.

Then, as if to welcome them to the castle, the dark, mad sky opened.

The temperature dropped quickly, and Dita shuddered. Ilir curled his arm around her. The rain was loud; the air smelled sweet and only slightly salty. The atmosphere, and their successful adventure, inspired a kiss. That kiss led to another and another. Determined raindrops, blown in sideways, found their cheeks and their noses.

"We made it," Dita spoke into his lips, barely audible over the downpour. Maybe he didn't care the way she did. But, finally, she had arrived somewhere important in her story.

Opposite from where they stood, the tower rose at least thirty feet in the air. Behind them, on the other side of the fortress wall, the sea slammed and receded under the strict orders of the moon's pull.

The alcove stretched long and deep, sort of an exposed tunnel open to the rest of the property. It was separated into seven areas, and in the center of each, in the outer wall, was a small hole looking out to the cyan and navy blue sea. The rectangular beige stones, cut in various sizes, were unremarkable in themselves but assembled with a care that comes with experience and dedication. There were a few layers of thin, red bricks in corners, apparently more modern efforts to keep the salt water from claiming more than it already had.

Ilir checked his phone signal, and a 'pfft' fluttered through his lips in disappointment.

"I wonder what this part of the castle used to be," Dita said. "Look-out spaces, I suppose, except … except when it was new, there would've been something, a room of sorts, on the other side of this wall. Not water."

"'Castle' is a little generous, don't you think?" Ilir asked, raising his voice over the thunder.

Dita tilted her head. "Maybe. Fortress, I guess. A solid fortress."

"Solid? Except for the part that has been washed out, you mean?"

"Right. Except that part." Dita mirrored his wink and smile.

For all the drama the rain created, it barreled past faster than Dita expected. Within twenty minutes, they could see the back side of the storm. In its wake, it left mud, mud, and more mud between the tower and their alcove.

Ilir braved the mud to stretch his long legs and smoke a cigarette. Dita breathed and exhaled. Her heart began to settle, with Ilir, the storm, and the past surrounding them.

She pulled out her sketchbook from her toolbag. She drew broadly, quickly, the basic shapes of this outer wall and the tower. Then, slowly, she detailed the varying bricks and stones.

It was easy to imagine it as a landing point for merchants from Venice, or as an ideal hideout from the Ottomans; choose a century between the fifteenth and twentieth.

Dita stood up and brushed her right hand along the stone wall. She half-closed her eyes and wondered. *Who were you? What did you do here? Did you stay and fight, or escape? Can you hear me?* The wall scratched her fingertips. She was taking another step when her index finger caught on a loose stone.

Her feet stopped, her finger curled, and her heart beat faster. She stepped back and bent down to be in front of it. She wiggled the yellow-gray brick. It shifted less than an inch. Dita continued to move it side to side, like a loose tooth.

"Ilir?" she called.

Her hand quivered over the stone. *Nana,* she whispered in her head.

Ilir returned and bowed his tall frame over her. "What is it?"

Her palms turned sticky. Her fingers felt stiff from the cold and the constricted effort. She jiggled the brick. Scrape, scrape. It resisted the change Dita forced upon it; its jagged edges dug into her fingertips.

"A loose brick?" Ilir said.

At last, it came out.

"There is a reason it's loose. Do you have a lighter?" she said. "No, wait, I have a flashlight." Her fingers were familiar with the shapes of tools in her work bag. She pulled it out of its designated pocket without looking.

Dita looked inside the stone's cavity with the dim light. The sound of her heartbeat in her ears drowned out the waves. She peered inside.

Dita let out a yelp. "Nana!" she shrieked again.

As if reaching for an injured bird, she slid her hand into the empty space. She pulled out a dark, leather cord, long enough to fit around a wrist. A gold nugget lay in the middle, secured by rounds and round of thin wire. A beautiful bracelet. Dita stared at it, breathless. The coldness in her joints, her knees cramped on the ground, Ilir breathing above her—all of it fell away as if she were holding the last remaining flower of an exotic species.

"This is what she meant!"

"Do you want to take it?" Ilir said.

"Do I want to take it?" she repeated, giddy. Her head spun. "Of course! It's what Nana was talking about! This is it! I have to show her!"

"All right, then, let's go." He sounded upbeat, either for Dita's happiness or to return to the cityscape, she wasn't sure.

Dita looked up and around nervously, again aware of the present moment. "Yeah, let's get out of here."

"Lunch? You still want lunch?"

Dita smiled. She dropped the flashlight in its place. "Of course." She rolled the bracelet in a piece of fabric and placed it in an empty pocket.

The hike back to the car and restaurant was tricky with the fresh mud. Dita held tightly to her bag because of the steep slope down to the sea on one side of the path. They came to the sheep field, where the rain had pitted the ground with potholes.

"Careful," Ilir said. He held out his hand.

"Whoa, this is slippery." Dita looked for the highest ground before taking each step. "You think they'll let us in the restaurant with our muddy shoes?"

"I think they'll be grateful for any business."

Dita closed the trunk of Ilir's car with her bag and the bracelet inside. Then she called her mother. There was no ring. No connection. Dead zone.

Her stomach growled.

Two sets of double doors opened to a large, open dining area. The stuccoed walls glimmered with a shimmer of silver. A disco ball sat on a corner shelf, a standard novelty for restaurants she frequented. Modern-day dinner music added a beat to the otherwise soft ambience.

Instead of menus, a waiter ran through the fresh offerings: green salad, homemade fried cheese, bread, and olives. "And, we have today's catch, of course."

Dita's mouth watered. "All of it, please. And an order of fries, if you have some."

"And a bottle of merlot," Ilir added.

"Of course," the young waiter replied.

Dita put her elbows on the table and looked out at the sea view. She pressed her lips between her fingers, imagining how Nana would react when she got home.

The waiter set a wire vase stuffed with thin, packaged breadsticks from Italy, called *grissini,* in the middle of the table and left.

"I can hear the gears in your head. Did your grandma say if it was hers?" Ilir said.

"Actually, no." She tore open a packet of the crunchy *grissini* and began to chomp away like a rabbit.

"Where do you think it's from?"

"I have no idea."

"How did she know about it?"

"She mentioned her sister, but other than that ..." Chomp, chomp. "She acts like she's open and will talk, but then she goes back, you can see it on her face, and it's dark."

Eventually, the sumptuous meal, and the red wine, weighed down the somersaults of adrenaline in Dita's belly. She leaned back and wiggled her fingers around her waistband to allow room for the satisfying food and drink. Ilir made a cross with his silverware in the center of his polished-off plate.

After coffee, Dita and Ilir sauntered out of the restaurant. The questions about the gold began to bubble again.

"I've got to call my mom," she said. Her phone had found a spot of service.

"Mami? Are you there? We found it!" The connection seemed hollow and far away. "Mami, can you hear me?"

"Dita? I can't, I can't hear you." Even with the patchy reception, Dita heard a shaking in her mother's voice.

"Mami?"

"Dita?"

Dita relied more on the air between to carry her words rather than the phone signal. "Mami, what's wrong?" She raised her voice to a shout, as if that would help. "I'm coming home. Bye."

"Everything okay?" Ilir turned the ignition on.

"I don't know."

Mira

A few days after the wedding, five men from our village, Rezart and his twenty-four, Genti, Deda and I gathered in the center of town. The gray sky, unusual for this time of year, was tense and ready to cry. It stirred an unease in me.

Prepare, the clouds whispered. *More burned houses, more death. You do not yet know the sweet, stinging smell of gunpowder. But you will.*

All the body heat sat thick and immobile among the pack horses, laden mules, and men ready for a fight. The men looked to Rezart for direction. I saw a touch of softness around their eyes; they had good hearts. They were as true to solemnity and determination as the mountains that raised them.

There are no quick goodbyes here in the mountains. Arta and others blubbered over us again and again. Genti gave Mindi and Musine full charge of our property. I kept tight-lipped lest any empty promises of return might tumble out. Mindi's children wrapped their small arms around my neck and squeezed.

Fear ought to have been nearby, telling me it was too dangerous and futile. But with each passing minute, my toes wiggled in my boots, desperate for action, ready to meet the army that had taken my father and

Luan. One could assume they had killed my older brothers, too.

The plan was to make our way south, executing ambushes as needed until, together with the tribes from the east and northwest, we would attack at Scutari, an all-important city where trade and culture were equally successful and valued. It sat at the crossroads of Montenegro and the rest of Albania. When Rezart explained this, a current sparked through the men. Chins lifted a bit higher. Strength in numbers.

Rezart said goodbye to Gjergji, Arta, and the others who had aided him with the wedding plans. His gaze settled on me. Time to go. Rezart mounted his beautiful gray horse, Plak, first. He held his hand out for me. I took it, wedged my foot in the stirrup and clambered up.

"Haj!" he called out, and we set off.

I held onto the back of the saddle to turn around. Bujan dropped out of sight quickly. We followed a narrow path that led us up and down along the southern wall of the valley. Plak found his reliable cadence, leading our ensemble. I relaxed around Rezart's hips and legs.

"How old is Plak?" I said, wondering if he was true to his name, 'Old Man.'

"Not old at all. But he's gray, so ..." he shrugged.

I smiled at his sense of humor.

"How are you?" he said.

I set my chin on his shoulder. "Fine, thank you." I searched the sky and found an eagle: our symbol of freedom and the symbol of our land.

At each crest, the wind rejuvenated us. The shade of the valleys was as cool as our storehouse back home. The hills and crevices, covered in summer green, pleased the eye, but the mules were neither fooled nor deterred. Green meant rain, yet they plodded through supple soil and lots of mud with ease.

We stayed slow and steady because we did not have any spare horses. As it was, the men of Bujan were already doubled up with some of Rezart's men.

We followed the river, and on the third day, we arrived at Berishe, my father's last assignment. I crossed myself as soon as I dismounted. We wandered through the abandonment, the skeleton of it. Respect for the dead and abject disbelief rendered me silent. Blackened, crumbling stones. No roofs. Rugs and clothes that should have been vivid with color. Within a few minutes, I came back to Plak and cradled my forehead against his saddle. I couldn't look anymore. I removed my coat and unbuttoned my shirt at the collar. Anything to breathe.

Two feet scuffed the dirt next to me and stopped. Rezart wrapped a hand around my side.

"*Zemra,*" he whispered.

I drew in a sharp breath and found sanctuary in his open arm. If only my tears could retreat, too. I brought my head to his, and he touched my chin with all the weight of a feather.

In his other hand, he held curtains, defiantly intact. He put them up in a saddlebag. "Bandages," he said in a cautious voice, focused on the task at hand.

I nodded. He stroked my nose with his finger. I turned away. I did not come along for him to carry me. "I won't be a distraction for you." I wiped my face clean.

"That never crossed my mind." Rezart turned and whistled to the men, our warriors. "*Hajde!* Let's go!"

Despair, in her gray and faint-indigo rags, stood next to me. When I sat in the saddle behind Rezart, she raised her hand for me to help her up. I hesitated and looked ahead at the road. I sought out Revenge instead. I wanted blood for blood. Revenge would cut through this suffocation.

There she was. She appeared in a rush, in a rage. She shoved aside Despair and hopped up behind me unaided.

I scooted a finger's width closer to Rezart to accommodate her substantial size.

"There's room for me until your dying day." She put her hands around my waist. "Isn't that right?"

I tilted my head in agreement, oh so slightly. My voice, my measly courage was down the road, running away with a holy fear of her. I breathed deeply and held on to Rezart's hips. I kissed his shoulder to apologize for my new friend, my new secret.

My imagination played out a scene. I don't know where or when, but I saw knives and fire.

Each day on the road my body ached and protested the saddle. But each day, the knives multiplied, twisted, flying in the air. They caught light. They almost sang. At first, the fire was an ordinary campfire in the distance, uninteresting and uninterested in me. By the end of the third day, I was close enough to feel its heat all around.

Every evening, we set up camp near a mountainside or in the thick of a forest, so long as it was near a waterfall or the river. The men caught game or fish. The time between dinner and sleep was spent telling stories and making portable traps. We only had three tents among us. The men slept close together and near a boulder to provide as much warmth as possible.

Despite the weariness of the road, I found it difficult to sleep. One night, Rezart curled around me. He rested his hand on my shoulder to test my wakefulness. I responded with a shift in my hips. He put his lips on my earlobe.

"*Zemra*, let's walk. Come with me."

I twisted my head back to him. "But." I was quickly finding my courage in bed with him. I stayed my hand on his leg. "Maybe more of that would put me to sleep?"

"Of course. Later, I promise."

We tied on our waistbands, pistols and knives, and vests and walked northeast from the camp. Rezart held my hand in his and we hiked uphill through aspens, pines, and elms. I worried about Musine, Mindi and the kids, that somehow the Ottomans had slipped past us. I envisioned every village we were to pass would know Berishe's fate, that we were too late for anyone, everyone. Images of orphans and shadows and their shouting stumbled over themselves in my mind.

When we neared the ridgeline, Rezart pulled my hand down, motioning me to crawl on my belly.

The trees spilled over the other side, but about one hundred yards down, we saw a clearing lit by a fading fire. Ottoman fighters sat near it; I saw five clearly. Their voices were loud and obnoxious and foreign. My skin crawled.

"You, Azmir, Rinaj, your brothers and I will attack tomorrow night, almost dawn, when they"—he tilted his head toward the soldiers—"will most likely be asleep. What do you think?"

I could only see Luan's bright, open face smiling at me.

An owl hooted. My knuckles ached from clenching the earth.

We slipped back the way we came.

As the ground leveled, the trees thinned to a field full of tall grass, alive with singing, nocturnal insects. I stood against a tree and waited for Rezart. The staggering display of stars and the crescent moon all but blinded me. I seared the light into my memory, a piece of peace despite the despair, fear, and Revenge's looming presence.

Rezart reached for my hand.

I let out the breath I had been holding since the ridge top. "Why didn't we take them earlier?"

"They arrived today too, like us. How fortunate we did not have a campfire." He kept his gaze on the stars for a moment, then looked at me. He looped an arm through mine and pulled me in front of him. My legs straddled his.

"Tell me something," Rezart said.

His hands slid down my arms until he held my hands. The skin of his fingers was thick, the muscles underneath were strong. I laid my forehead against his. A memory, full of night light, came to mind.

"Your mother came to me," I said. His bright eyes shone. "I didn't know who she was, then. There wasn't any detail, really, only a silhouette in a fog." The dewy air stuck to my cheeks, and I recounted the entirety of the vision.

"I wish you would have known her," he said.

"And you mine. I was only ten." A smile came to my lips. "She might've chosen someone else. Did I tell you she was one of the village matchmakers?"

He broke into a deep smile. Rezart whispered, "Do not speak ill of the dead, hmm?"

"Of course not," I replied, my lips finding his.

We stepped back into the forest, dark as a deep well, and found the rest of each other with all our senses but sight. Rezart kept his promises.

The next night, the attack went according to Rezart's plan, until we arrived at their campsite. We had spread around their tight circle, knives in hand. Moisture sizzled out of the green branches, making the air smoky. With one particular pop from the fire, an Ottoman across the ring woke with a start. His eyes, big and round, lighted on me first.

My muscles betrayed me—useless, helpless. His face tightened, and he reached for his sword. In the next moment, his eyes bulged and a knife emerged between his front ribs. A thick line of blood ran down his shirt, running to the ground.

I looked up and saw Azmir, one of Rezart's twenty-four, holding the handle. I didn't hear the fire hissing, no cries or grunts. My heart's pulse beat with such strength, I could feel it in my forearms, my thighs, my fingers. I had never felt such a thing. Even my scalp tingled.

Then, everything was loud, so loud, filling and bursting in my ears. Short cries of surprise and agony. Deep groans of effort, blocking punches, and of thrusting knives into bodies.

"Mira!" Rinaj called. There was only time to give me the slightest tilt of his chin.

In one move, a move Deda taught me, I swiveled around and down on a knee, knife raised. Behind me, an Ottoman readied his sword to slice me. I raised up into a lunge and thrust my weapon into his stomach, into that white shirt peeking from below his waistband. I pressed all my weight into my shoulders until he doubled over.

My dreams of knives and fire had come true.

Half of the premonition from the ghost of Rezart's mother, of seeing blood, ran down my knife.

I made it to the bottom of the hill before I threw up. When I finished, Rinaj scooped me up and carried me to the edge of camp.

"Thank you. You can put me down now. I'll be fine." But I wasn't fine. I sank to my knees. My throat burned. My bones felt as fluid as the blood throbbing through me. My breathing was tired, aching to get enough air to all of me.

"Next time, I will look them in the eye," I whispered.

Rezart heard me. "You didn't look at them?"

"At him. I only fought one."

None of the men sat to recover, like I did. Instead, they stood around me. The Ottomans' guns weighed heavily on their shoulders. We took no prisoners.

"I know what you're thinking," I said to all of them. "The *Kanun*, the damn *Kanun* and the rules of engagement. Where is their code?" I motioned to the hilltop where the bodies of the entire Ottoman squad lay waiting for birds of prey. "Ripping women from their homes, stealing their food, and burning everything on their way out? Are you defending them?"

"Of course not. If they have a code, they don't honor it. But we do," Rezart said.

"Honor! Ha! Do not speak of them and of honor in the same sentence. I'll look them in their eyes, but it will be to confirm they're dead. Not for honor, not for the *Kanun*!"

I stood and walked ahead, shaking and alone, to camp. I stormed into our tent, as much as one can while crawling on weak hands and knees. I sat on our bedroll and drank from the water canteen until my insides felt full and cool.

Rezart came in and sat beside me, quietly. "*Zemra.*"

I bobbed my head, permission that he might continue.

"I didn't yet ask: were you hurt at all? Are you okay?"

"No."

He stayed and waited. A few early birds began to sing their wake-up call in the trees surrounding us.

I reached for his hand, then both sides of his jaw and led his body over mine. He covered my anger, my nerves, and the satisfaction of the mission. There was no time to remove our stockings. I ripped his sleeve with my trembling fingers. Then, I knew only oblivion, a complete detachment from this world to one of bliss.

Days later, we made camp near the former village of Koman. We situated ourselves such that a mountain, patchy with scrub brush and birds' nests, was at our back and the forest protected us in front. On the second day, when the sunlight was midway to the horizon, a trilogy of mourning dove-like trills rippled through the trees. It was our signal that an outsider was within sight. An enemy would have been shot outright.

Rezart flattened me against a rock. I crouched to my knees and I put my hand on my knife and glared up to our lookout post.

Ymer, a burly man with shoulders as wide as a door, was the one on guard. "You'll stop there." Our men and their loaded guns were well-hidden by bushes and boulders.

The visitor raised his hands and stopped in my line of sight. Rezart was between us. "I have a message for Rezart Agim." His voice was high, as much from nervousness as youth.

Ymer, still hidden in the trees, replied, "From whom?"

"From Pejani."

I could feel dozens of eyes on Rezart, waiting to mimic his response. The crease over his left eyebrow relaxed. He smiled and lowered his knife. I stood and walked one step behind my husband.

"I am Rezart Agim," he said, even-toned, which was friendly for the public Rezart, the one everyone rightfully admired.

The young man dismounted. "It's an honor to meet you." He laid his hand against his chest and bowed.

"And you honor us. Come, rest, and we'll hear this message from Pejani." Rezart reached for me. The boy's eyes flicked to Rezart's hand holding mine, then boldly looked at me. I caught his stare and he turned his attention straight ahead.

We led him back to the firepit, tucked into our part of the mountain.

"First," Rezart said, "tell us your name."

"Pejani, sir. I am one of Pejani's sons, his middle one. I am Hasan." His eagerness to say the right thing to the legendary Rezart was sweet.

Rezart insisted Pejani sit in the shade. Rezart sat across from him, squinting from the sun, and introduced me, Azmir and the others not on guard or hunting for rabbits or an unlucky deer. Azmir brought a bladder of *raki*. Hasan's shoulders eased with the welcome reception. There was space now for exhaustion, and it revealed itself, dark around his eyes.

Rezart lifted the bladder and wished health and victory to the house of Pejani. He offered it first to Hasan. The hearty round of *"gëzuar"* was swallowed up by the ancient stone and wilderness.

"Tell us, how is your father? Your family?" Azmir said.

"My father is well and comes with the Kiri and Drishti tribes. We have camped at Boks. He says we must meet together at Rragam." He paused and became nervous again. "After we rout the Ottomans presently camped there."

Rezart pursed his lips and concurred. "Rragam. The west side, or the end rather, of the River Drin, and the east side of Scutari. Yes, that will be good. How soon can he get there?"

"Our tribe could be there in a day. But it is three from here. Can you leave tomorrow?"

"Of course, of course. You will stay with us. How many Ottomans did you avoid on your way?"

A wonder that he reached us at all.

"None, sir."

I jerked my head up, searching for the jest, the tease in his eyes. I glanced at Rezart. His eyes were thoughtful and focused.

"None?"

"No, sir."

I offered, "They're all in Scutari, then?"

Rezart lifted his *plis* and scratched his head. "Must be. They can't leave it. If you hold Scutari, you hold this entire region up to, and up against, the Serbs. And if that's not enough, it's an easy ride to the coast, to Italy and the rest of Europe."

We made quick work of packing in the morning. Three days away from more cold-hearted bastards. Rezart sent two of his men ahead as scouts. Hasan was now under Rezart's protection and as such rode directly behind us. The bees of anticipation buzzed excitedly in my mind.

By the end of the day, my eyelids and forehead ached from watching for an ambush. My legs were raw and stiff from riding with every muscle wound tight like the strings of a *çifteli*.

I spent the second day behind Rezart reliving the midnight prophecy of blood and salt. The blood I knew—it was behind us, drying on the bodies of the Ottoman soldiers. But the salt?

Val

I stepped outside the house overlooking the sea. Every part of me rattled and rocked from this encounter with the German soldiers. One of them killed point-blank by Kosta. I would need to send Shpresa.

The sky had closed up. A gust of wind ran a chill through me. Around the back side of the house, I set Shpresa down. I laid my head against the wall and closed my eyes.

"Need some paper?" Xhevi came around the corner with a few sticks in her arms.

"Yes, actually, but it has to be this special kind. I'm abbreviating as much as I can."

[Capturd Gmn at Filik. 1 dead. Send transp.]

I tapped the pen against my lips.

[*How can a man go 8 days with no slp?*]

I rolled the paper tightly, pushed it into the holder and screwed the lid. I whispered into Shpresa's head. "Safe travels. If he needs a hint, tell him to get some sleep *tonight*." I let her go. She faltered a bit from the wind, steadied, then soared.

The salty air seeped through my chapped lips and tingled my tongue.

142

My fingers bumped over the pebbles, cool dirt and pathetic grass. I began to smooth the ground to be my impromptu canvas.

I looked out to the horizon. It reminded me of an old mirror, spotted and murky. The sea lay dark and upset, churning toward high tide. I made a few wiggles in the dirt as clouds.

"I'm hungry," Xhevi said, interrupting my thoughts. I was glad for the interruption—I would not have been satisfied with a monotone scene because, right then, my heart bled every color.

I echoed aloud what I had to believe: "She'll be back soon."

"Of course," Xhevi said.

In the meantime, we would need a cooking fire and food to cook, and Xhevi was hungry. My stomach grumbled. I latched Shpresa's cage and stood. "I'll help you gather more sticks."

I glanced back once more at the moody, liquid landscape.

Kosta, the only one not gathering sticks and kindling, stood on the north edge of the cliff. The sea wind fought his hair, but it was too thick to dance in the breeze.

"Maybe we can all meet here next summer. Do you guys swim?" Kosta said. His defense was up again.

"Me?" I said. "I can see the bay from my bedroom window." If he noticed that wasn't an answer, he didn't press me. I could swim well enough, but I would bet a new pair of boots I was the weakest of us four.

"Anyway, I'll go down and catch some fish," Kosta said.

I raised an eyebrow.

"I'm fine."

I looked in through the side window.

"That German's not going anywhere. Did you see how mortified he was?" Kosta said.

Despite the angry spit, yes, I had.

"You coming, Endri?" Kosta walked to the west side and looked for a path down to the water.

Endri stopped mid-step, arms full of firewood. He slowly turned his head in our direction as if he had been caught red-handed. In another life, he was a clown.

"All right, all right. Grab the nets, let's go," Kosta ordered lightly. We had found a few essential fishing supplies in the house.

Xhevi got a fire started, ready for fresh fish. I swung the front door open to check on the prisoner.

Ana, a few years ago, the river water splashing over her faint freckles, sun glinting through each droplet.

With a sure hand, I grabbed the Germans' canteens. I left them outside on the ground, by the closed door.

"All right, who's ready to be beat again?" I asked. No one responded. With bellies full of fish and the crackling fire, we were almost asleep sitting up. I shuffled the cards slowly. "Fine. That's okay, I'll remain the champion, I don't mind." No one could say I hadn't tried. I had tried to lighten the mood, tried to show the others that the encounter with the Germans wouldn't break me. In fact, my nerves had hardened to a steely confidence. Confidence in Shpresa and that someone would arrive tomorrow to take the prisoners, dead and alive, and us, further north.

I put away the cards, and we lay circled around the fire as usual. The stars poked in and out of the smoke and twinkled with the rise and fall of the waves below.

There had been nights in the past year and a half that I'd hardly slept, from fear or hunger or cold. Then, after Ana, I tossed and turned with guilt. Rolling, gasping as much for air as for rest. On a better night, like tonight, with imminent danger pushed to an edge and sleep knocking, I began my meditation. I visualized layers of relaxation, like a pan full of baklava. In the first few flaky layers, I made an effort to breathe away the day. Next, I imagined my body shrinking and sinking into the more dense layers, the ones where the chopped walnuts lay. This is when my feet felt as if they were being melded together. Then my knees, then my hips. I imagined myself so small that half a walnut was a comforting pillow under my head. By the time I was deep enough to be in the sugar syrup at the bottom of the pan, I mouthed a lullaby my mother sang to us.

The sunrise was bright and open, forgiving yesterday of its broodiness.

I was eager to get up from the night's stiff sleep, but none of us were in any hurry to rise to no breakfast. I made a version of tea with crinkly and dormant bits of berry bushes I had noticed the day before.

"So, Boss, that's the cave down there? That's what we really came here for, right?" Kosta said. He pointed below the cliff, about a hundred yards in from the shoreline. The cave opening was almost wide enough for a fishing boat to moor sideways. "Looks very, very empty."

I suppose I had been nicknamed Boss because I was in charge of Shpresa. But if I was Boss, Major Prifti was *The* Boss.

We had driven to Saranda to see Prifti after Harris left us and my feet had healed. Our truck was reassigned, and we were directed to the headquarters building. We stood outside his office to await orders. A short conversation inside made its way through an open window. Before I could knock, I heard the words:

"They got her. My wife."

At the time, I didn't know Prifti's voice from the other one, but when he came outside a minute later, his eyes were damp and bloodshot. The other man's eyes were not. Prifti's hair was gray and short, swept over to one side to hide one of his widow's peaks. His thin mustache curved down around his upper lip in a most unpopular fashion.

Prifti's need for revenge and my disgust for the world at large turned out to be an efficient team. I was eager for it all to be over, and he was on a rampage. Frantic and harsh, at first. Later, more recently, he had been more controlled. Each time I saw him, his body seemed more stiff and contained. He was aiming to please the eye of the proper Communist Party.

"Maybe that's where these Nazis were, down in that cave, and they only made it this far. Before they got distracted," Kosta said.

"*Hajde*," I said.

Kosta put his hands up in teasing self-defense. "Okay, fine, let's see if they left anything behind," he agreed.

"Oh, maybe pirates left some treasure, too." Kosta, the fearless one.

"But then Prifti can claim it as his," Xhevi said as she smothered the small morning fire with dirt.

"Ha!" I blurted.

I had to admit, despite my thorough bitterness, that our sturdy uniforms could withstand crawling over rocks and the wild blackberry thickets that criss-crossed the steep path. And *path* was a charitable word for it.

At the bottom of the hill, we walked toward the cave. How did we get to this point, that we were looking for foreign enemies rather than walking back to our towels after a swim?

The Ionian Sea was known for its pebble beaches, opposite its sandy Adriatic neighbor up north. The sea rushed toward the shore, raring and happy under the sunshine. Then it sank back, making way, acquiescing, but not without rattling and pulling the lightest of stones over the heavier ones. The song it sang was both a ballad and a scream.

Endri bent over and picked up a worm shell and put it in his pocket.

I smiled. As it happened, Endri and I were ahead and out of earshot of the other two.

"What will you bet Kosta was the one pulling pranks as a kid?" Endri said.

"And the baby of the family, so he never had to grow up," I replied. "But there's hope. He's good with a gun, and that counts, for now. He's quick, he's charming; he'll find a wife and a job without a problem after all this is finished."

Endri sidestepped away from me. "Well, well. That's the most domestic, and the most positive, thing I have ever heard you say."

I shrugged and looked over my shoulder again, obsessively, as if other Germans would appear at the top of the hill.

"Right. Okay, Endri," I retied my ponytail. "Let's see what this is about."

We stepped into the cave. The temperature shift was considerable.

"So? Any skeletons or swords?" Kosta yelled ahead to us. "A fortune-teller with a glass ball, by chance?"

"One way in and out, backs against the wall," Endri assessed, mumbling.

Backs against the wall, my heart repeated. *Why here?*

Secret supply drop, my head said. *Recon, hideout. Just like us.*

"Nothing here," I said. "Let's go home."

I didn't see the land mine, and that's the point. Endri didn't see it, either ... oh God, Endri.

I blinked once and closed my eyes again, begrudgingly returning to consciousness. I tried to stretch my fingers, as they felt stuck in wet concrete. My tongue told me I was surrounded by dirt and smoke.

Surely there was a boulder under my spine. My legs, immobile. I felt as if I had been buried in the cold, crumbling ground.

Then, I screamed. The shout came from my throat, from my very soul, but was lost in a vacuum. I tried again. I should've heard my own voice. Instead, I heard only a piercing and constant ringing.

I lay still as a rabbit, perking all my other senses. I rolled my eyes in every direction in hopes someone would see me. The air around me was hazy and diluted, like a watercolor landscape. I slowly closed my hand around a fistful of earth and opened it over my chest. Again and again, my fingers found their strength and clenched more grit. Again, and this time, I aimed my fist to open deliberately over my belt buckle. I felt the pitter-patter and the sand in my fingernails but didn't hear it.

Leave me for dead, I thought.

I pictured my parents just before I passed out. *They will understand. They don't understand how I let their baby be taken, but this, yes. They will nod their heads as they are told their older daughter was part of the collateral damage. My mother will then fall to her knees and beg for mercy from every saint, priest, and the Prince of Peace Himself. My father will keep nodding his head, brush the back of his hand against his mustache, and wipe his brow. Over and over again.*

When I returned to consciousness, Kosta, bleeding from his arm, and Xhevi stood over me. Kosta pressed his lips into a solemn line.

At the sight of Xhevi crying, the voice in my heart said, *Ana.*

My head, my voice of reason, was helpless, wordless.

I sat up on one elbow and moved my lips in the form of a question. I put a hand to my right ear, then left ear. They felt warm and wet—blood covered my fingers. I looked at my hands, then at my friends. The tears turned to a sob and I slammed my fists into the sand.

I sank back down into the debris.

My heart begged Mother Earth on my behalf, *Swallow me.*

Dita

Dita fell silent, wondering and worried, as they drove back to Tirana. Ilir rolled down his window an inch or two, creating more noise than fresh air. He fell into the rhythm of the club music right away. Even with her phone in her hands, Dita barely heard the ring. She waved at Ilir to put up the window.

"Mami?" she said. She pressed a finger into her other ear.

"Hey, sweetie, um," she said. "We won't be home when you get home. We're at the hospital. Nana's had a stroke."

Chills rippled over Dita's body. "No, no, no, no, no."

"Yeah, they're going …" Lena paused, her exhale crackling in Dita's ear. "They're going to keep her overnight. We'll stay until they close us out. Do you want to come here, or …?" Lena left the question suspended between them.

"Of course. I'll be there in an hour. The hospital on the *Unaza*?"

"Yes."

"Okay. How is she now?"

"She's … she's …" Her mother sniffed and cleared her throat. "See you soon," she managed.

Dita hung up and looked at Ilir through her tears. He'd heard enough that she didn't need to repeat. He shifted to fifth gear and held her hand.

Nana. Love—an invincible fortress.

Ilir double-parked by the front door of the hospital and kept the engine running. "Do you want me to come in?"

"No, it's okay," Dita said quietly. It felt like a whole day had passed in the car. They leaned toward each other for a kiss, a gentle one. Dita opened the car door and silently questioned if the ground would hold her up.

Ilir retrieved her bag from the trunk. "Call me?" he said, handing it to her.

"Sure." She tightened her grip around her bag's strap and hustled up the steps as Ilir drove away.

Nana's assigned room on the third floor was as clean as it was stark. At the first sight of Nana, Dita teared up and blubbered and reached for her parents, hugging them three times over. To see her mother so upset was enough for Dita to make a deal with the devil.

"They don't think she'll recover any motor control of her left side," her mother said between shuddering inhales. Murat gestured to the two chairs; he stood and crossed his arms.

"How did it happen? When?" Dita said, keeping her eyes on Nana, asleep with her hands by her sides.

Lena folded and unfolded her tissue and raised her eyebrows to explain. "She had taken up her crochet hook with the blue yarn. 'Don't tell Dita,' she had said. She was going to make you something. I went to the balcony to hang clothes. When I came back in, the left side of ...'"

She looked Dita straight in the eyes. "The left side of her face was falling, like, like, candle wax. Oh, God!"

Dita wrapped her mother in a big hug.

The three of them sat and waited. The doctor had already gone home. When a nurse came to check on Nana, she told them visiting hours were over. Lena's hands gripped Murat and Dita's elbows, depending on them for strength.

At home, they picked at leftovers warmed in the microwave. Dita felt cleaned out, fresh from all the crying. The sense of loss was taking up most of the space in the room; the shock of the stroke sat in Nana's place on the sofa.

"Dita, did you call to tell me something earlier? The connection was terrible," Lena said.

"Oh yeah, we found a piece of gold at Rodoni. That's all."

Her parents looked at each other, then at her.

"A bracelet," Dita added.

"Really? Where?" her dad asked.

She told them about the storm and the loose brick. With Nana in the hospital, it didn't seem the time to celebrate an archeological discovery.

"We'd love to see it," Murat said.

Dita got it from her bag and laid it on the dining table. All three of them stared at the nugget, almost expecting it to say something. It was in every way extraordinary. Extraordinary to have remained hidden at all, for it to be gold and not silver, or bronze, even. It caught the overhead light and took Dita's breath away.

"It would be really nice if Sofia could hold it. Only for a bit, you know, before you take it to work," Murat said.

Dita looked at him, surprised. "Of course. I brought it back for her, not for work. As soon as she comes home."

"The stories it holds, right?" Lena said, reeling in awe.

"Exactly," Dita said.

"And sitting there in the wall. Huh. I should have given her more credit."

"Mami, it's okay."

When Nana came home, Dita tied the gold bracelet on Nana's left wrist.

Talk as if she can hear everything, the doctors had told them. "Gold at Rodoni," Dita encouraged. Nana's bursting effervescence had fizzled into a flattened form of what she was. She placed Nana's right fingers over the nugget, to feel it, to know it was there.

Nana shook unsteadily. Her mouth struggled to smile, but Dita saw her intention. Nana leaned forward and they pressed their foreheads together. It was another one of Nana's standards, all grandmothers, actually—to bring their head to the forehead of one of their babies, the way a ram headbutts another ram. But, dearly.

"Gold at Rodoni," Dita repeated.

"Gold," Nana said.

Dita didn't try to hold back her tears; she wept at the sound of her voice. She could not leave this for Rome. Though it meant going back on her word, she would not leave this for Rome. Everything she needed was right here.

In the morning, she sent a letter to the Etruscan Museum declining the fellowship.

The next two months of life continued almost as it had before the stroke. The weather had turned to winter, so Lena and Dita kept Nana in thick socks and fuzzy slippers. Sweatpants replaced her classic skirts. Before work each day, Dita checked that Nana was comfortable in her cozy spot and said goodbye the same way: "Nana, your hook is in your right hand. The blue yarn is in your lap. And the gold from Rodoni is … here." Dita gently tapped the bracelet on Nana's left hand. "Gold, from Rodoni, like you said."

The festive spirit of New Year's was in the air. Dita and Murat arrived at the airport minutes before Nora was due to land. In that time, the crowd of waiting, excited families pressed around the two of them. The cigarette smoke being exhaled by every man in the crowd exacerbated Dita's need for space and air.

"Let's go wait in the back," she said.

She relaxed when they worked their way out of the throng of people. "Whew. It'll be harder to see her, I suppose, but …" Dita said.

"Next time we're here," Murat began. "You will be leaving, too."

Dita sighed. "Babi …"

Passengers began to come out of the automatic doors, wearing puffy coats and pulling luggage on wheels. The volume of cheers and greetings took over the entire airport, dissolving the opportunity to tell Murat that she wasn't going to go to Rome.

Dita craned her neck, shifting from one leg to the other to see through the doors when they opened every other minute. Slowly but surely, the crowd thinned. The stale smoke remained.

"There she is!" Dita said, already walking to her, opening her arms wide. It wasn't until she saw Nora that Dita realized how much she had missed her.

"*Motra!*" Nora hugged with one arm. The other arm held a wrapped package. They hugged and swayed. The faux fur around Nora's jacket stuck to Dita's lip balm.

"Mmm, I'm so glad to see you," Nora said.

"Okay, okay, my turn," their dad said. "Hey, sweetie." A hug and a kiss on each cheek. He took her red suitcase.

"You brought that big thing for four days?" Dita asked, nodding to the luggage. Dita knew it was full of trendy Italian clothing. She decided not to tease Nora that the same stores were in Albania as well. Instead, Dita remarked on another observation. "You thinned your eyebrows."

"Yeah. It's a thing. You know, they were too, too … much."

"What's in the wrapping paper?" Dita asked.

"An espresso machine!"

The surprise of it stirred a laugh in all three of them. Dita and Nora linked arms and walked ahead to the parking lot.

"Easy flight?" Dita looked over her sister, searching for other, little changes.

"Of course. The train to the airport, though, whoa, I almost didn't get my suitcase on! Everyone and their presents, you know. But the vibe was happy, so whatever."

They shrugged it off, both of them, as sisters do.

Dita smelled roasted chestnuts, sugar syrup, cheese and chicken broth from the third floor. It soothed the comic task of getting the wobbly-wheeled luggage up the five flights of stairs. The apartment felt warm and snug, as if Lena had sprinkled some sort of welcoming magic throughout the rooms.

"Welcome home, sweetie." Lena squeezed Nora amid the tangle of coats and scarves.

From the foyer, Nora called out to Nana like she was a toddler playing hide and seek. "Nana!"

Dita and her parents followed Nora into the living room. In an instant, Nora's smile fell away and her hands cupped her cheeks. She looked to Dita, Lena, then Murat. She tiptoed like a dancer, in front of Nana's line of vision, then sat beside her.

"Hi, Nana," she said. "It's Nora." She lightly pressed her head to Nana's.

"Come on, lunch is ready," Lena said. She couldn't stop for too long. *Women—can't stop, won't stop.*

"Tell me it's soup, please," Nora said. "I need extra space for all the eating we'll be doing."

"You're in luck. Chicken soup," Lena replied with a smile. "You don't have to eat, you know."

"Ha! Words never before spoken by an Albanian mother," Nora replied.

Nora and Dita helped Nana stand and walk to the table. She looked at each of the sisters. She ruffled her lips. They sat down, elbow to elbow.

"Okay," Nana said matter-of-factly.

"Nana." Dita put her hand over Nana's, eager for any chance to question her. "Can you hear me? Nana, how did you know about the gold?" she asked out of desperation, wanting so much to avenge the stroke and everything it took: the jokes, the laughs, Nana's storytelling of legends and heroes. Dita asked out of anger at the stroke—surely Nana had more stories to tell, happy ones, funny ones even. If Dita was honest, she was disappointed in herself. She hadn't asked when she was younger because she didn't care. Now she cared, and now, it was too late. "How did you know about the gold?"

"Okay." Nana smacked her lips and looked down at her empty bowl.

"Right," Lena said, using the lip-smacking cue to fill everyone's bowl to the rim.

Within those first few hours, Nora was the energy they all needed. On the back side of Nora's cuddles and anecdotes about the Italian way of life, Dita saw Nora watching their mother. One glance between them told Dita that Nora could see it, too. After that initial welcome hug, Lena's smile was a little harder to find. The caretaking and all the moments of inadequacy were printed on Lena's face. She squinted her eyes and turned down her mouth.

Together, and without a word, the sisters took Lena by the elbows and plunked her in a dining chair. Nora put a basket full of walnuts in front of her.

"There, now, don't move," Dita said.

"But—"

"Just. Sit."

"Girls, I'm fine."

"Great. Then you can sit and crack the nuts," Nora said. "We can't have a new year without *baklava*."

Dita prepared *picaiola*, breaded pork chops baked in a tomato and red wine sauce, for dinner. The deep and rich aroma permeated the apartment. Nora boiled the veggies and pasta for Russian salad. The traditional New Year's side dish would need to chill in the fridge overnight.

The next day, New Year's Eve Day, was a continuation of the same, but more. More jovial, more food preparation, more smells inextricably linked to the New Year for Dita: butter, sugar, bay leaves, parsley, more parsley, sweet carrots, and the ever-loving garlic. Live concerts sang from the television all day and into the night, keeping them entertained while they worked wrist-deep in flour and olive oil. Even Lena and Murat sang along to the folk songs they knew, opening their arms like opera singers. Nana looked on from her perch, with one eyebrow cocked. She looked mischievous, as if she had a joke to share. Her hands fiddled with her hook and yarn.

Finally, it was time for the New Year's Eve meal. A golden turkey surrounded by roasted vegetables took center stage. Murat stood when everyone was seated in fancier-than-usual clothing.

"To a happy year, a healthy year, a joyful year." He said it so sweetly, taking the time to look at each of them. Dita placed all her hopes in his words. The five of them clinked their glasses and savored every bite.

After everyone had eaten more than they thought possible, they felt the need to loosen their belts. Yet, the platters held plenty of leftovers.

"Let's go out to the balcony and watch the fireworks," Nora suggested. Dita glanced at Lena.

"Let's try," her mother said.

Dita rose and retrieved Nana's heaviest coat, one of her handmade scarves, and a hat. When Dita came back into the living room, Lena's shoulders relaxed.

"Thanks," she said.

"Of course."

Once bundled, they opened the balcony door. Kids and adults alike stood in the courtyard below, throwing down little snaps that went *pop! pop! pop!* as they slammed into the concrete. The damp chill brought Dita and her family back inside quickly. Together they sat and watched the concert on TV, beautifully staged with poinsettias and gold curtains.

"Are you packed, Dita?" Nora said.

"Um ..."

"Wow!" Murat interrupted. "It's almost twelve!"

"Already?" Dita exclaimed.

Nora hurried to the kitchen and grabbed the bottle of champagne. "Ready!"

The fireworks lit the sky all over town for twenty minutes. Dita felt content to have her family together and a future full of intrigue and history rolled out in front of her.

Before falling asleep, she checked her phone. Disappointment seeped into her heart despite the enchanting evening. Maybe she should have called him?

Dita slipped into her room after breakfast the next morning to call Ilir.

"Good morning," he answered. "Sorry I didn't call."

"No, it's okay. Happy New Year." Dita smiled through the phone.

"Happy New Year to you, too."

"What did you do?" she asked, stalling.

He laughed. "The usual. Ate a lot. My uncles, aunts and cousins came unexpectedly, so there's people everywhere."

"Right. Nora's here. It's nice. She got us an espresso machine and ... it's good."

"Of course it is," Ilir said. "The *xhezve* takes forever."

Dita fingered her sheer, floor-length curtains. "Hey, so, you know, Rome? The museum fellowship?"

"Yes," he said, dragging out the 's'.

"I'm not going to go."

"Oh." A dash of surprise. "Okay." Easy acceptance.

"Yeah, so. Can't get rid of me yet!" She needed a punchline. Everyone she knew was better at those than she was. "But really, I can't leave Nana." As if there would ever be a good time to leave her. Or for Nana to leave her. "I want to figure out this bracelet. I think it will be as good for my career as the fellowship. There's a history behind the bracelet, and I have to find out what it means to her."

"I get it."

"See you at Bar Grand tomorrow? Nora leaves in the morning."

"Sure, see you then."

"Okay."

"Dita?" Ilir said.

"Yeah?"

"I'm glad you're staying."

"Thanks, me too."

Lena took charge of the *byrek me lek* for lunch. The person who received the piece of spinach pie with a coin inside would have good luck for the year. The fates smiled on Dita. Throughout the rest of the day and into the early evening, family friends came to visit and wished them a happy new year. They washed and rewashed the set of dainty crystal glasses from the glass curio cabinet. Nora poured the rounds of sherry. Dita scooped a generous helping of cherry preserves into silver dishes. Murat led every toast with "*Gëzuar!*"

Nora was happy to talk about Italy. Every one of the women commented on how far away it was and that it must be hard to be gone. Dita, on the other hand, understood her sister was a bird and meant to fly. Nora politely brushed it off and told them it was her duty to contribute to the global society, not merely locally.

When the opportunity presented itself, Dita casually asked older neighbors and friends if they knew anything about the Cape of Rodoni during Communism.

"It's beautiful," a few said. But no stories to tell.

"What's this all about?" Nora asked Dita when their next-door neighbors left.

"I'll tell you later. Want to go out?"

"Definitely. I need to walk off all those preserves," Nora replied, rubbing her belly.

The sisters changed clothes and said goodbye to the older adults. Linked arm in arm, Nora talked about the friends she would introduce her to.

"But, now, tell me more about this Ilir guy. You've only told me his name, that's all I know."

Dita could not help but smile. "Ilir? Ilir is ... Ilir is in business. He wants to make it to the top. He's full-steam ahead, all the time." Dita shrugged. "He makes me laugh."

On their walk back home, arm in arm again, Dita finally found the nerve to tell Nora.

"Nora, I've decided not to take the fellowship. I'm not coming. I'm going to stay here, at the museum, and stay here with Nana." She laid out the words gently like a picnic blanket. Disappointment was less harsh when displayed prettily.

Nora stopped walking. "But ... really? Wouldn't this internship be good for you, for your career?"

Dita scrunched her lips to a pucker. "The fellowship? I mean, yes, but ... I can't let go of this gold bracelet."

Dita recounted the moments when Nana had changed her trajectory. Relief at explaining her decision out loud, and to Nora, washed over her. Nora wasn't mad.

"But"—Nora unlinked her arm from Dita's—"we were going to have so much fun. You don't want to get away from all this? It's so heavy here." Nora squashed a piece of litter, then pushed it away with the tip of her shoe. "My friends and I don't eat at expensive places. We grab a bottle of wine, some bread and hang out at Monti's. It's a fountain. One of many. I mean, not every night, but, on the weekends, sometimes. Everyone wants to have fun, that's all."

"It's not the money," Dita said.

"But Roman history is even older."

Dita slightly shook her head. "It's not. And, we're not from there. You know?"

"Is it Ilir? You want to stay for him?"

"No, it's not Ilir. Truly, it's the bracelet. And actually, I like it here. I like this." She waved her arm in the air. "Mostly." She didn't agree with the fast life her generation wanted, now that the world was accessible and affordable. Maybe she should have been her mother's sister instead of her mother's daughter. "I like what I'm doing. I can't leave Nana's gold story. And all the other stories, too, you know? All the yesterdays."

Nora's face was hard to read in the street lights. "It does sound interesting. But not fun." She ribbed Dita with her elbow.

Nora didn't have to like it; Dita only hoped she understood.

"Sounds like there's nothing else I can say."

They waited for a swath of cars to pass before crossing.

"I'll be honest, the traffic's the same: terrible." Nora laughed. She had a knack for lightening the mood, for bringing light to the night.

The sisters stuffed their hands into their coat pockets. They walked the rest of the way without talking, the silence between them buffered by party music and car engines revving in and out of lanes.

Dita took Nora to the airport early the next morning. The air still smelled of fireworks and beer.

"So. No hard feelings? You'll call me?" Dita asked, anxious for everything to be okay, like it was before, between the two of them.

"Of course. If anyone can figure out this bracelet, it's you."

They hugged.

"That's kind of you to say." Dita tucked her chin into Nora's chunky red scarf.

They stepped back and wiped their cold and wind-chapped cheeks. "Take care of Nana," Nora said and adjusted her beanie. "And Mami and Babi."

"I will."

They hugged again. Dita watched her walk into the airport with her rickety suitcase.

The new year's fireworks fizzled quickly into a complacency compounded by the near-constant drizzle and cloudiness. A nagging attitude hung on Dita for days, questioning her decision to stay.

"How's the weather there?" Dita asked as soon as Nora answered her phone one desperate morning.

"Going on day four of rain, mud and smog, even," Nora replied.

"Here, too."

"Having second thoughts?" Nora asked.

"Maybe, I don't know."

"Chin up, head down in the books, or whichever phrase works. Get to work."

"You're right. Thanks. Love you." It gets damp and dreary everywhere; Dita knew that.

"Love you, *ciao*!"

Later, Dita popped open her black umbrella and hurried down the museum steps. Despite the downpour, she and Ilir had agreed to meet at their café. Not a memorable place, but a convenient meeting point between their jobs. She was glad she had chosen a pair of platform sneakers instead of ballet flats.

A gray car barreled through a pothole and sent a splash of street rain toward Dita. She scrunched her body smaller and cowered toward a travel agency's storefront. Its windows were plastered with faded posters of Big Ben and a Turkish beach resort.

When Dita turned the corner, she ran into Ilir.

"Hey!" They lightly kissed to greet each other: right cheek, left cheek, right again. Dita rested her cheek on his a moment longer to smell his shampoo and cologne. "You came more than halfway," she said.

"I wasn't sure you had an umbrella," Ilir said with a shrug and dimples. She closed her umbrella to consolidate under his. Ilir, fitting trimly into his black jacket, draped his arm over her shoulders. Together they navigated the puddles, trash bins and other pedestrians rushing to arrive at their indoor destinations.

"The coffee's worth it, right?" he asked over the growl of the rain.

"Oh, totally," she replied.

The cafe door's hinges squeaked from decades of open, close, open, close. Inside, spoons clattered on saucers. Cigarette smoke hung low and stale, in a space not much larger than Dita's family's living room. The muted television that hung in the corner above the bar caught her eye. An ad played in which a muscular man carried a silver platter of chocolate cookies. A woman with sultry red lips took one and slowly bit into it. Dita looked away easily; she was a bitter and savory kind of girl. The barman, on the other hand, stood mesmerized by the cookies and lips. When the ad was over, he returned to his coffee reality.

The lone waiter, dressed in a thin white shirt, stood ready to follow them to their table of choice and take their order. Instead, before they sat, Ilir held up two fingers, the universal sign for two espressos. The waiter relayed the order to the barman not more than ten feet away.

"So? Still glad you didn't go?" Ilir asked, shaking the wet chill from his shoulders.

"Huh? Oh! To Rome." Dita squeezed her coily hair, a frizz ball from the humidity. She let out a deep exhale. "Yes."

The waiter arrived and they sat back for him to place not only the demitasses but also two glasses of water, a clean ashtray, and a box of sugar packets. Finally, he placed a shot glass stuffed with the bill next to the sugar.

"Enjoy," he said with a bow. Ilir sat forward, ready, as if he were seated for a steak feast. He caught her eye and smiled. It was only three tablespoons, if even that much, of coffee. Not all that much to enjoy, but it was the sentiment behind it that mattered.

Dita watched the dark brew thicken to a shiny syrup when she added sugar. Mmm, yes, it was worth the run in the rain.

"And, your grandma, how is she?" he asked.

Dita sputtered a bit of espresso at such a turn in conversation. "She's …" She put up a hand toward him to stop the tears from flowing. Futile. Love, it's true, is a broken floodgate, rushing without restraint.

Ilir threaded his fingers in hers and rubbed her palms with his thumbs.

She looked at him and powered through. "Same. Stares out the window. Sometimes she'll say two words as clear as day … I don't know. She's stopped asking for her cup of mint tea, but we make it anyway. My mother and I take turns putting on her Nivea cream every morning. We're making more and more little assumptions, you know?"

Dita looked up at the television to distract herself. The commercials ended and the music videos' flashy lights and incessant dancing continued for another twenty-minute segment. The last of her tears released stubbornly onto the tottering, veneered table. She folded a few napkins and stuffed them under a table leg. Dita took another breath and looked at Ilir straight and strong.

"And you? Anything exciting?"

"I've almost sealed a deal with that Turkish candy company."

"Liri, that's great!"

"Yeah, sure. More candy from Turkey." He brushed his hands against his pants. "I want bigger clients, like Toyota or Mercedes, you know? They have factories there."

"You will. You've only been there for what, three years? Maybe you have to wait for someone to cash in on their pension."

"I don't know."

She looked down at the exposed coffee grounds in the bottom of her cup. Time to get back to work.

A few Saturdays later, Dita found her mother in the kitchen packing leftover *gjell*, cheese, a loaf of bread, olives, and a round of salami into a cooler.

"Mami?"

"Oh! Good morning! Let's go to Elbasan. Picnic, sightsee, have a coffee. Weather looks clear. Get Nana out of the house," Lena said.

"You mean get *you* out of the house."

Her mother replied by bobbing her head this way and that, to say no, but mostly yes. If she'd had the opportunity, she should have been an attorney instead of their assistant.

Nana sat at the table, her breakfast cleared, patiently waiting and staring at nothing. Maybe waiting to remember what to do next, waiting for someone to help her, or waiting for the memory of Dita's *gjyshi* to pass.

"Come on, Nana. We should get you fancy today. Want to?" Dita said.

Dita helped Nana to the bathroom and then to her bedroom to get dressed. Dita kept her foot firmly on the flimsy rug in the hall. Ever since the stroke, Dita had become more protective of anything that might confuse or bother her, like tripping on a rug.

Safely in the room, Dita felt peace wash over her. What spell did her grandmother conjure that, for anyone who entered this small space, the outside world was forgotten? The cool walnut dresser and the matching bed frame were part of the calming package. It was a beautiful museum, demanding its visitors come in, slow down and absorb. As museums do.

Dita led Nana to the edge of her bed and shimmied a pair of knee-highs around Nana's feet, then up her calves. Nana instinctively reached for the hose with her right hand.

A few classic basics hung in her slim wardrobe. "How about blue and silver, Nana?" Dita pulled out a navy blue polyester skirt and a silver-white acrylic sweater. "They go well with your hair, too."

Nana stood shakily and held on to Dita's shoulders to change her clothes. Dita tugged Nana's left sleeve over the Rodoni bracelet. The morning sun illuminated Nana's face. Dita saw her own silhouette in Nana's glassy eyes. The freckles on the bridge of Nana's nose fluttered across her cheekbones like wings. Dita was captivated.

At her antique vanity, Dita brushed Nana's hair, following the curls with the comb lightly, creating spaces from the comb's teeth.

A neighbor's piano playing wafted through the barely open window. Dita breathed in and out steadily. Behind the peace was the ever-present fear that one day Nana wouldn't be here.

Dita retrieved the rarely opened jewelry box on the vanity sitting below the walnut mirror. The box was a birthday gift from the four of them, the first year Nana moved in. Dita brushed her fingers over two birds carved from a darker wood, inlaid in the blond pine lid. She opened it with caution despite its sturdy craftsmanship and sporadic use. Inside lay a pair of irregularly shaped pearl earrings, a set of cubic zirconia studs, and a simple pair of silver hoops.

Dita chose the pearls.

She had never given any attention to the golden knob at the base of the box, like a tiny, spherical button. Dita pinched it with two fingers. It was a necklace drawer.

Dita pulled slightly.

"Nana?" she called over her shoulder. Nana Sofia, ever patiently waiting. "Nana, do you have a special necklace in here you want to wear today?"

Dita pulled the shallow drawer as far as it could go.

The jewelry box slipped out of her hands at what she saw lying in the drawer. For a moment, Dita saw herself from a bird-eye's view, free falling in slow motion.

"Ah!" Dita fell to her knees and caught the box before it could shatter and splinter on the cool terrazzo floor.

When the cry in her throat cleared and her breathing resumed unobstructed, Dita crawled over to place the mini chest next to Nana. She opened her grandmother's curled hand, and in it, she placed a bracelet. In the center of the dark leather cord lay a gold nugget, secured by rounds and rounds of thin wire.

"Nana, where did you get this? Please, Nana."

"Gold." Nana fingered the bracelet on her wrist. "Rodoni."

"I know, Nana." Her voice trembled. "But who gave this one to you?" Dita waved the newest find in the air.

She pulled up Nana's sleeve and pointed to the matching bracelet. "Can I take these to work? Just for a few days?" Dita slipped the bracelet off Nana's wrist and held them both in her hand.

Nana tried to smile.

"How did you know about these?"

Nana looked into Dita's eyes, searching. The two women began to cry.

Dita laid her head on Nana's lap and patted her arm. "It's okay. I'll find out, I'll find out."

Mira

The next day, finally, Rezart lifted his hand and led us into the trees off the dirt road into a forest above the Drin River and Rragam. We dismounted, barely breathing for fear of giving ourselves away, and created a circle of animals and men. We lost any refreshing breeze but gained all the shade.

This area was uncharted territory for most of us. Our men were seasoned fighters, I learned during campfire conversations, but not this far south. More than once in the past few years, the men were simultaneously fighting the Ottomans and the Serbs, against land theft and pillaging, against seeing them install their own rule. Power is a form of greed. Greed, with force, is power.

Rezart handed Plak's reins to Ymer. "Stay here," he said, motioning to the rest of our band. In a strained, thirsty voice, he called for Azmir. "Where are you? *Hajde!*" The young man emerged between two horses. "Pejani, you too. Follow me."

Without looking, he held his hand out for me. Like a wind finding the treetops and singing, my hand locked into his. "*Zemra*," he said.

Ten minutes of hiking got us to a lookout point, a cliff. It cut straight down to the Drin. From here, the river was so clear, I could see the stones sitting in its bed. It was wide enough to need the cover of night to cross. On the other side of the rushing water, dark-clad soldiers walked between a few outbuildings intended for smoking fish. The men's red *fez* caps bobbed between the stone huts and puny pine trees. It would be an exaggeration to call what we saw a town. Maybe there had been more to it, once.

"They'll see us," I whispered.

"They're not watching. They should be, but they're not." Rezart spoke in a whisper despite his confidence. A contingent of horses and wagons was organized on the far side of the buildings. "A general's here. Come on."

When we returned to our new site, the men opened the circle and closed us in. Again, Rezart gave the impression he had spent the last three days in the saddle, maneuvering everyone like a dance, determining every step.

"Genti, Deda, you two have your papers, so you should be able to pass by easily. Come morning, Pejani, you'll go with them to your father. In two nights, the moon will be full. When it is overhead, have him lead a dozen men to those buildings we saw. It's the general's headquarters. If anyone should try to stop you on your way …" He waved a hand in the air. He didn't need to finish his sentence. "Now then." He crouched over the ground and began to draw Rragam in the fertile soil.

The sweat from the hike began to cool on my belly, my neck.

Rezart turned his deep brown eyes to me. "Mira, you and Azmir will come from the south," he said.

My jaw fell open, incredulous Rezart would place that trust in me. He cleared his throat and looked back at the map in the dirt. I felt wide eyes on me, but when I looked around they quickly returned to Rezart and his plan.

"Except for those staying with the horses, I will lead everyone else over here." He pointed to the opposite end of the outbuildings. "We'll come from the north and take the general who arrived from Constantinople yesterday." He looked at our questioning faces. "Pejani sent word. He has men everywhere. Attacking soon after his arrival will be unexpected enough. He's no doubt assuming another round of talks. Then the general's camp will become our camp. Use your knives, if you can; keep it quiet."

Simple.

"You may get settled," Rezart instructed. "But don't get too comfortable."

A few men chuckled and clapped Rezart's back as they turned away.

When only Rezart and I remained, I stared at my hands, afraid that if I spoke my fear it would come true. I waited for him to read me.

"What is it?" He knelt down in front of me.

"How do you know I won't …"

"You are your father's daughter. You are a Zeka."

He took my hands in his and, God, I wished I didn't know him like I did. I wished I didn't want him like I did. I wished I could have seen a trace of hesitation. I wanted his daring, his fire to fight with his one and only life, to be what lifted me.

I looked away and relaxed my eyes to stare into nothing. I saw Revenge in the shape of a female ghost. The queen of my fears. But this time, I did not falter at the sight. Only slightly louder than silence and with the force of a flood, she found my easy ear and repeated their names.

"Luan. Bac. The men of Gralishte and Bujan. The families of Berishe."

I mumbled, my lips moving but voiceless, like praying the rosary, asking her, "But just them, and no one else will have to die, right?"

Did she stifle a laugh in front of me? "Would that make you feel better?"

A podgy form peeked from behind Revenge's skirt.

"Who's that?" I asked her, all while rubbing Rezart's knuckles.

"Oh, pay no mind." Revenge waved her hand flippantly. "Regret follows me like a shadow. What a bore."

It was my turn to stifle a laugh.

"What is it?" Rezart said, squeezing my hands to bring me back. "Mira?"

"Nothing," I said.

We didn't light a fire that night and ate only from our dried foods. With the knowledge of Pejani's additional men and the success of the previous missions, a camaraderie rippled through the camp. We were keen and more than willing.

By the grace of God, Azmir and I crept to the back of a building unnoticed. On the front side sat two soldiers. Azmir and I edged to opposite corners. Keeping my body against the wall, I looked in his direction and motioned to move forward. I crept around the corner and along the wall facing the river. My footsteps were absorbed by the soft soil. The soldier's knee was bent, displaying an easygoing attitude.

An instant, in a blink, I rounded the front corner. I bent my elbows at my hips and I kept my pulsing hands wrapped around my knife's grip. I bared my teeth. Another instant, in a silent fury, I thrust it, and the tip pierced the man's skin between the collarbone and that thick, jutting muscle attempting to turn to me.

Blood shot from his neck like a rainstorm's first drops on a dry, dusty earth.

I wiped my eyes and watched him slump. Azmir was equally successful. I looked for more. We skirted on our tiptoes to the only door. It was open slightly, loose on its hinges. Empty.

Ahead of us, men rounded the corner of the next building. They stopped when they saw us. The man in the middle wore a general's uniform.

In a fluid movement, I pulled my pistol from my waistband. I yelled. Azmir yelled. And from my right, there was more yelling.

I fired the first shot, effortlessly, thanks to Revenge. I struck the general's shoulder. He fell back, then sustained another shot from who knows where. Another and another and so much yelling.

The three bodies lay still.

The yelling stopped as suddenly as it began.

My mouth was dry and my teeth chattered. It was then I looked over and saw Rezart had arrived with our small, significant army. They stood, panting, some of them oblivious to the blood soaking into their black-on-white clothing.

As a whole, we were injured, but we were alive.

We sank to rest amid the trees before climbing the steep incline to camp. The decaying and regenerating earth was deceptively calm. It smelled rich and complex. The blood, the smell of anxiety exuding from our bodies, was heady. My hands lost their strength and my knife tumbled to the ground.

"They'll be mad as hell now," Ymer said proudly. "Come on, men, let's go."

"Azmir, go on." In his tone alone, Rezart acknowledged the young man's contribution. "Go and get some sleep."

Azmir's footsteps were silent, swallowed by the forest floor. Rezart never needed to speak twice.

"I was getting to you as quickly as I could," he said.

"I know."

"There were a few more than I expected."

He squatted behind me and put a hand at the base of my neck, a question. I fell a degree in his direction and in one motion his sure arms crossed in front of me. His body was a pillar against which I could rest.

He must have carried me back to our tent. I woke from light piercing through my eyelids. Rezart's form blocked the sunlight for a moment as he entered, and the tent flap shuttered behind him.

"Good morning." He lowered himself to kiss my lips, my cheekbone, and my lips again. I scrunched my face from his scratchy mustache, but my neck reached for more tenderness. He spoke with his mouth over mine, chills running wild over my skin. "You're the only one still in bed."

"Not anymore." I pulled him over me.

"Ah, well. I told everyone we would move to the buildings you conquered last night."

I pushed him to arm's length. My eyes narrowed, and with that, life was crystal clear again.

"Right."

Rragam became our main post for several weeks. Word spread of our tribes' location, consolidated outside of Scutari. It was no longer a game of us finding the Ottoman army or us hiding from them. No one was hiding anymore. For a while, there were small shows of retribution. But overall, the Ottomans sat on their hands, changed their minds three times a day, and seemed very unsure of what to do, like they were awaiting very specific instructions. Rezart said their orders came from a thousand miles away. It was a game of wits: who could keep their senses while talks began and failed, for the sorry illusion of diplomacy. Impatience raged within me like a hundred ant bites.

Natural leaders in the camp came forward: Vera, a woman who arrived from Koman, became head cook and therefore manager of the entire camp. Rinaj and Ymer took care of the animals and supplies. Pejani, Hasan's father, was a tall man, on edge but willing to listen and see reason. He and Rezart spent most days together. They attended the meetings with foreign representatives and other tribes. Equally important as Vera, Qazim set up a surgery in the outbuilding next to ours. His supplies consisted of a kettle for boiling water, a bottle of *raki* to act as sterilizer and pain chaser, and three sizes of knives. Rezart and I took one of the outbuildings as our home and as the central office.

Rations, doled out by international agencies, were sporadic and often only enough to feed the displaced children while feeding the adults to half-full.

"If these governments care enough to send cornmeal, why don't they end the war?" I had said.

"It's not that simple, *Zemra*. Pride is involved," was Rezart's steady reply.

During that time of back and forth, women, their children, and orphans arrived at our camp almost daily. I took to walking in the nearby forest with the children. I showed them wild mint and garlic whenever we came upon it. We foraged as much as we could fit in our hands and pockets, clearing our noses and filling the air with renewal. The children learned to add it to whatever was boiling in the kettle over our main campfire. Sometimes the contents were only a concoction of herbs in water. Truly, it was more like tea, but if Vera or another woman found an animal bone, we could call it soup and feel more full.

Our campfire, one of many surrounding Scutari, was large enough for at least twenty hungry, perpetually hungry, bodies to circle around. The youngest ones were fed first and fell asleep in the arms of a mother. It was then, with the fire stoked if not exactly blazing, we waited for a story to rise and warm us from the inside out.

Ymer, our resident storyteller, was one of the few who could grow a full beard. His *plis* stretched its maximum diameter to fit his head. He had one of those smiles that broke my heart. His voice was perfect for carrying stories over and through the fire smoke.

He strummed his one-string *lahuta* to quiet the already hushed conversations. "You all know the story of Muja and Baba Halil, the brave warriors undefeated by natural and supernatural foes. They were cunning and clever, and of course, they were the strongest of all warriors. Tonight, I will tell you the story of how Muja acquired his strength."

Rezart appeared at my side from a meeting with Pejani and a few other men. He scooted on the log to settle in, hip to hip. Everyone in the circle made eye contact with Rezart to greet him. A few men packed their pipes and lit them with a piece of wood from the fire. I sat with my elbows on my knees and fingered my rosary. Rezart crossed his ankles and lit his pipe, too.

"Muja," Ymer called out, as if summoning the man himself, "Muja, was a poor man. Poor in wealth but strong in spirit, because ..." Voices rallied at this, this *because* that everyone understood. Our destiny was to be part of the land and part of each other, not owned by faraway empires.

Ymer coughed. "Because we are! We are of the mountains!"

More verbal agreement.

He continued. "Muja's father sent his son to a landowner to earn money they desperately needed. The landowner made him a cowherd. He had other cowherds, but the landowner had many cows. Muja was happy to lead the cows to the green grass high in the mountains. The only thing that bothered him was the teasing he received from the other herdsmen for being so skinny and weak. But he kept his head down and took good care of the cows, to make his father proud.

"Unfortunately, one day he lost the cows. Gone! Naturally, Muja was beside himself. He searched and searched until the sun dipped behind the mountains. By then, it was too late to go back to the main house. What would he say, anyway? He couldn't face his boss and didn't want to subject himself to the others' ridicule.

"Muja was exhausted, of course. He lay down to sleep in a place much like this." Ymer motioned around us and the semi-circle of boulders enveloping us. "But, as soon as he laid his head on the cool grass, he heard crying. Helpless and infantile crying."

I was hanging on by a thread as it was. To hear mention of a distressed baby was enough to make me cry too. *Let this story be over soon*, I begged.

Ymer kept on. "There was no moon that night. He followed his ears to the crying and came upon two babies less than a year old. They were tied onto their narrow cribs that looked more like packs to carry on your back, and leaning against a boulder. Muja reflexively rocked them.

"Muja presumed they were twins, as they were the same size. As soon as the babies fell asleep, two lights glowed on the flat part of the rock, above his head.

"They were not just lights. They were *zana*, fairies of the forest, and they were grateful to Muja for putting the babies to sleep and keeping them safe."

Rezart kept his arms resting on his legs and studied the ground. *He knows this story.* In stories, the *zana* were sometimes tricky and always creative.

"'How can we thank you? Do you want riches? Land? Strength? Ask and you will receive your wish,' the *zana* said to Muja.

"Muja thought for a whole minute. 'Strength,' was his reply. If he had strength, he would show the cowherds who to make fun of.

"'Come here. You must have our milk,' said one of the *zana*. Not once but four times he drank from their full breasts. Then he had the strength to lift that very boulder and throw it into the Green Valley. And that is how the island in the Drin River was created, splitting the water to run on either side of it."

A story of equal parts longing, a pitch to inspire superhuman strength, and a creation story. Everyone had kept their ears, if not their eyes, open until the end. Now, with it told, exhausted bodies made their way to their bedrolls.

"Sleep?" Rezart asked me.

I smiled at him and nodded. He took my elbow and we made our way around the fire, with goodnights and handshakes to those still awake.

One day, more refugees came into camp, their jawlines cut hard against their dark coats and grayed headscarves. The blue sky overhead mocked them. Two were pale with fever. The lone toddler hacked a cough that, before, I had only heard from grown men, full of mucus.

I scooped up the little one and led them closer to the fire. "Vera, see that they get as much as they need."

I turned and ran to find Rezart.

"Put me out there, dammit! I cannot see any more children—" I bit my lip to find some control.

"We're here. We're doing it," he said.

"It's not enough!"

I regretted the ingratitude my words implied. "It's … it has to stop."

"We will. We have one more petty meeting, I—"

"Meetings! Meetings! Who are these meetings for? Who?"

"If they don't leave, we will begin on the edges of Scutari. You can come with us—me, Deda, and Pejani—to the meeting."

The meeting was that afternoon. I was in the same room as the enemy and the European delegates, whom I considered complicit by their inactivity. I didn't hear a word, not even my husband's demands and arguments. My attention was turned solely to the idea of my knife cutting their throats. A thin, clean sweep of red circling the room.

As we walked away from the fruitless meeting, Rezart placed himself between Deda and me.

"Deda," Rezart said, "I must take Mira somewhere. We will be gone for three days, maybe four."

I jumped. "What! What do you mean three days? What are you thinking?"

Rezart, endlessly undeterred.

Deda almost matched his brother-in-law: quiet, but without Rezart's confidence.

"You said we would take Scutari!" I argued.

"I said we would begin. Pejani said there are more men coming." His calm annoyed me.

"There are more women and children coming, too! Orphans, Rezart!"

"The Ottomans must be waiting on someone, or waiting for us to surrender. But we gave up nothing, and no one is leaving, either for their homes —"

"Homes? They have no homes!"

"They're not retreating. Yet. But they will, *Zemra*, they will." He took my hand and turned to Deda. "We'll leave before dawn. You'll stand in for me?"

In the last light, our faces were turning to varying shades of shadow. Deda glanced at me ever so briefly, then met Rezart's raised eyebrows, expectant.

"Of course."

I stormed into our hut. I only cornered myself. If there had been room to pace like a caged animal, I would have. Instead, I balled my hands in fists and looked for something to beat.

"*Zemra*," he whispered with hope. Did he know how his voice alone broke me? "I want to take you to Rodoni Castle. I want —"

"I want this over! I want my family back!" I turned to him, tears streaming. "I want them back! I want these children"—I waved my hand toward their general location outside—"to eat, dammit! I want them to have their fathers again!"

He held me around my waist and wiped my tears away. "I swear."

Even his whispers were doubtless and strong.

Val

My nose twitched. I smelled alcohol, white beans, strong Turkish coffee and wet stucco. My head felt split in half like a summer watermelon. I looked to my left. Kosta sat on a bed a couple of feet away. He smiled with closed lips, a smile full of pity and contrition. I rolled my head back to face the peeling ceiling. *Fall on me, whitewash and beams and stone. Cover me, please.*

Again, I slept.

I woke up again as dusk was falling, the room covered in watery black, and sad. My headache had waned enough to let me notice my hunger and thirst. I looked at a nurse standing across the room. Her smile oozed pity. Her red lips contrasted with her standard green uniform. A white scarf peeked from underneath her collar. Her hair was pinned in place under her green cap with the red star. I had stuffed my cap in my bag a while ago. My blue scarf kept my ears warmer.

She moved to help as I sat up with all the efforts of an old man, shaky but able. She offered me a serving of the humble beans. A piece of bread stood at attention in the bowl. I gripped it, afraid I would drop it with my new clumsy and weak body. I ate ravenously. My throat burned with each swallow, but I didn't leave a single drop or crumb behind.

Afterward, it occurred to me I had never heard the spoon scrape or clink against the bowl.

I bowed to her in gratitude. I didn't know what I must sound like and I was too scared to try. I doubted they would tell me I sounded different, but it mattered to me. I wanted to know. Friends to the end, but this was in between. Besides, I reasoned, I wouldn't be able to hear their response.

I held my hands up, palms to the sky to ask the nurse a question. So many questions. Where are Kosta and Xhevi? Endri? What do we need to do? Where are the Nazis? She held a finger up. *Just a moment.*

The nurse returned with a stained, bedraggled notebook small enough to fit inside my coat pocket. I flipped to an empty page and wrote in a flurry of desperation, beginning to panic about everything. I read her responses as she wrote concisely.

[My name is Nina. We're in Dhermi. Packing up and going home. Nazis gone.]

Again, she lifted her finger for me to wait.

I held onto the edge of the cot and made myself aware of my surroundings as best I could with the remaining daylight. This room, what would have been the main room of a normal house in normal times, led to a back bedroom. Through the doorless doorway, two men lay on cots like mine, covered by wool blankets up to their necks. One had his head wrapped in gauze. I watched each of their chests rise and fall and found myself breathing with them. I turned my head in the opposite direction, toward the front door. I saw things I could no longer hear: A driver and his truck arrived. He parked, got out, and closed the door. The driver shook hands with a comrade, whom I recognized. They clapped each other on the back. Another soldier carried boxes past the hospital and put them in the back of the truck.

I looked down at my boots. I shuffled my right foot, left. Nothing.

Deaf. God. I snapped my fingers. But the only senses that action occupied were my sight and touch. My finger slid off my thumb and landed on its pad. My eyes welled up, overwhelmed. God. Please.

I am so fragile that even whispering my name will break me. What am I?

Silence.

Yes, that was the riddle I would send the next time I had the opportunity.

Nina returned with Xhevi, followed by Kosta. My ribs tightened around my heart and lungs. I did not hug them so much as collapse my body of anguish into their arms.

Endri.

For a few minutes, we were a clutter of hugs, runny noses and firesmoke-soaked jackets. Xhevi waved her hands in front of my face, plastered a big smile, marched in place and saluted. I could not understand what she was attempting to tell me. I gave her my new-to-me notebook.

While she wrote, Kosta revealed an alert and innocent Shpresa from the crook of his arm.

I reached for her. Really, it was too much to ask one heart to bear. I curled her into my chest and laid my cheek against a wing and let my tears fall into her feathers.

Kosta cupped my elbow and led me to the back room. I hobbled and shuffled. The room was bathed in gradients of deep purple and sapphire blue. The sharpness of blood, of rusty iron, stung my nostrils. I felt the iron, too, like chains to my swollen ankles, dreading what Kosta wanted to show me.

Despite the bandaged head, I'd know those curly lashes and round cheeks anywhere. I flung myself and Shpresa onto Endri's chest. For a moment, I was blind as well as deaf. Blind with relief.

Endri flinched and I recoiled, afraid I had hurt him. His eyes fluttered and he fell back asleep. I dropped my shoulders in relief. I noticed his hands were bandaged, too.

Kosta lifted Endri's blanket to show the white sheet where his left leg should have been.

I motioned to ask if it was caused by the explosion or if it was amputated. Kosta lifted two fingers. I pointed to Endri's head. Kosta waved in a way to say it was not deep or detrimental, nothing to worry about.

I tottered out of the room—my feet felt like two tender nubs. Nina had lit an oil lamp. I walked toward it, despite the throbbing in every corner of my body. Here, I read what Xhevi had written.

[Prifti will be here in the morning. War is over! We're all going back to Tirana tomorrow. Germans are gone, in jail, or dead. You'll come with us.]

I wrote my reply without a moment's hesitation: [Not tomorrow, it's too soon, E isn't ready for the road. Needs rest. When you take E to Tirana, ask about Ana for me. I need to go home, I'll be waiting for her there.] My fingers cramped with frustration. Again, I wrote [Home] and circled and circled it, around and around.

Kosta towered over us and read my response. I looked at Xhevi and then up at him.

The look they exchanged said I had upset their master plan.

Xhevi forced a smile and wrote again. [Come to the fire. Talk more in the morning.]

I began to feel a bubble building ever so slightly up and around me. A glass bubble cutting me off from the world I knew.

The hospital house was flanked by houses built like my family's: simple and solid. More houses stacked like stairs up the hillside behind us. In front of the hospital, the road divided us from a flat clearing. The space was wide enough to be a parking lot, a campsite, and the place of tonight's bonfire. Beyond the fire, the land sloped and was full of brush all the way down to the sea. The same as the terrain surrounding the devastating cave. The cave. I bit my lip. My tears had yet to run dry.

Xhevi linked my arm in hers, and we made our way toward the crowd of soldiers. Enough wood had been gathered to create a bonfire as tall as I was, a little over five feet. Nonetheless, I tugged my coat more tightly against the wind. We sat on tree stumps, me between Kosta and Xhevi. More than one bottle of *raki* warmed everyone as it was passed around the fire. I took a deep breath and felt my sore ribs expand. Another deep breath, and I remembered Endri. He was young and I was confident he would heal, but not overnight.

Soldiers began to loosen up and let down their guard. I admit I cracked a smile when a soldier, cast in the fire's light and its shadows, clowned around by reenacting the past three years of the Italians, then the Germans, invading, retreating and surrendering. He ran around the fire with his knees high, elbows flailing, and with a comically scared face for more laughs. Everyone looked like they were laughing, anyway.

What the comedian omitted from his little play was the raw pain, the sheer fear, and delirious sleeplessness.

I stared into the blaze.

I fall over and over again, but never break.

I looked up to find the stars through the smoke. *Nightfall.* I would send that one, too. Soon, I hoped. A message from my pigeon contact would have been a glorious reprieve. I was skeptical they could fly this distance—we were forty kilometers from Tragjas and over one hundred from Elbasan, where the comrade was stationed. And then, a trembling panic: perhaps it was too far, but now, there was no reason for pigeon messages. I would never meet my comrade, my fellow riddle-master. I let the tears fall and fall and fall. I was done trying to build a dam.

Goodbye, friend.

The bonfire roared. This was not merely a celebration; it was also a farewell party. It was time to scatter, like bees leaving the hive each morning. I looked around and saw all the conversations I was missing.

Nina was on the other side of the fire, flirting brazenly. I watched Kosta's lips move, and my heart sank, again. Xhevi looked as if she would reply but caught my eye, and only smiled and nodded in response to Kosta.

How much do you want them to accommodate you? my Head said. *You want them to write everything down?*

Every damn word, I wanted to scream.

I tapped Kosta's arm and put cigarette fingers to my lips. He obliged without a second thought. I watched the cigarette smoke rise and crash into the bonfire's smoke. I smiled in spite of myself, thinking of my anonymous friend. Asking for his name didn't seem pertinent at the time, and it certainly wasn't safe.

She's not ready to think, my Heart told my Head.

But she has to, my Head insisted. *What are you going to do, dear? What's your plan?*

Not here, not now, I told them both.

My headache reared its ugly head again and, despite the *raki*, my stomach began to twist in a knot. I took one more drag and gave it back to Kosta with a nod of thanks. I showed Xhevi I wanted to sleep. I was ashamed to need them so much.

We stood to go.

My knees buckled over my bruised feet. Surely my right foot is broken, I complained inside. Xhevi held me up with one arm around my waist.

To put one foot in front of the other took all of my effort, but I didn't let go of Shpresa.

We made it to a clean, large room, in a house next to the hospital. The fireplace was filled and lit. I almost expected to see my father's cushion beside it. In between two cots was a small crate with a lantern on top. Xhevi must have been sleeping here upon our arrival.

Xhevi pointed to the cot next to hers. Shpresa's cage had been delivered to a stool at the end of my bed.

Good night, I thought to Shpresa as I put her inside.

My bag sat at the end of the bed as well. I took off my boots and stretched my wretched feet as far as the swelling allowed, too weary to wonder when I had last seen my toes, let alone bathed. Xhevi looked at me expectantly. I held her gaze for a moment before I covered myself with a blanket.

Xhevi rocked my shoulder as a wakeup call in the morning. *Rude*, I thought. *Besides, there's nothing to get up for; the mission's over.* Less than a week ago, it would have been me singing an obnoxious primary school song at Xhevi to rise and shine. I turned to face the wall. In response, bruises cried out from my shoulders to my feet.

Xhevi shook me again.

She did help get you here, after all, Head reminded me. As a courtesy to her, I flipped back the blanket, only to be met by decidedly winter air. So many mornings in the winter as a child, I wanted to stay in bed warm with my sister and our heavy sheepskin covers.

Xhevi waited for me against the back of the front door. Her cap squashed her dark curls. She had not tucked in her Partizan shirt. As I tied my boots, I felt that bubble enclosing me again. Like a transparent case rising from my feet and surrounding me, cutting me off from my own world. This should have been an easy moment. Any other day, we would have told each other about a wild dream, our prediction for breakfast, or briefed each other on the latest news. The difference was I couldn't hear, and it seemed an uncrossable chasm.

I threw a handful of seeds inside the cage to Shpresa and carefully put on my coat.

The sky was a cool gray, teasing the possibility of rain. We found a generous breakfast of bread, holy persimmons and stiff coffee, all of them treasures in and of themselves. Should I have been grateful? We were alive, we had food, and the war was over.

With each bite, I replayed a conversation I'd had with my mother under our own persimmon trees. "We'll put these in a cake, that's what we'll do," she had said. They were ripe, I had argued, and there was no need to adulterate them. I would never have a conversation like that, with my mother, again.

My tears fell onto my chunk of crusty bread. Damn, damn, damn it all.

Major Prifti appeared out of nowhere in front of us. All the buttons and bars on his uniform shone. He would do well for himself in the Party, I was certain.

Kosta and Xhevi stood and saluted.

I did not stand but gave him a half-hearted salute from my seat. Prifti looked at me and opened his mouth. Perhaps rumors about me were circulating around by now: Valentina Muskaj lost her hearing and she's going a little mad. When he shut his mouth, the extra flesh of his chin wobbled.

Kosta took a half step forward. He pointed to his own ears to explain my situation. The gossip was true, then. Prifti put his hand over his chest and bowed the traditional forty-five degrees. Then, he shifted toward them, not entirely, but enough to show I was no longer part of the conversation.

I focused on his mouth in an effort to read him. The mouth—a vessel for knowledge, folly, hate and affection. It makes space, it closes in, it shuts tight. The lips widen and reach for both ears to smile and affirm. Or, the lips close altogether, an enigma in and of themselves. The tongue is the powerhouse, able to reduce someone to nothing. It is able to heal. For Prifti, verbal communication was sharp and dramatic and abrupt. I had never noticed. Before.

Kosta turned to me and scribbled in the air. I pulled out my notebook, annoyed to use the essential paper to talk to Prifti. Kosta squatted down to me and wrote: [You'll come with us to Tirana, Prifti says.]

I flipped back to yesterday's quick conversation and circled my response three times: [I need to go home.] I added, [He has no command over me now. Ana. Ask.]

Kosta twisted his lips. His dark eyes were stern with concern, and wild, instead of comical and light-hearted. He pushed a lock of hair away and stood. Prifti's commanding demeanor changed when he read my response. His lips twitched as if weighing how much information he should share. He shook his head and he mumbled something that made Xhevi put her hands to her face.

Kosta wrote simply [Tragjas]. He held his hand over the notebook to write more. He looked at me, full of sorrow and remorse. My eyes widened, questioning Prifti. Panic cracked like ice over me. Prifti grabbed the notebook from Kosta and wrote, then shoved it in my hands. [Burned. I saw it.]

From the box I sat upon, I spun down on my hands and knees to the cold, hard ground and vomited. Even the precious persimmons.

I beat the earth with my fists. Xhevi put her hand on my back and offered her handkerchief. I pushed her away. My heart's cry rose from the deep. If only I could have heard it myself, then maybe I would know the Almighty heard it, too.

I wiped my mouth, my tears, my phlegm with my stiff sleeve, like a boxer and his gloves, ready to go another round.

Xhevi tried her luck with the notebook, the dull pencil and worried eyebrows: [We will take care of you in Tirana.]

I felt as strong and capable as jelly. With feeble hands, I held the notebook and wrote the one plan I could agree to: [Take Endri and find his mother. I'll ride as far as Tragjas. Drop me off at the end of the road. I love you all but I must go. If you want, write to me when the post resumes.]

My team seemed to attempt amends with Prifti. I closed my eyes and deflated my body over the munitions box. Everything was moving so fast, faster than the village children running out of the schoolhouse at the end of the day. The war was here and gone, my home was my hope, and gone, my very body as I knew it—here yet gone.

Xhevi and I walked in the direction of the morning sun back to the hospital. Nina had one extra bath towel not yet packed. She gave me a small bar of soap, then swiped her palms against each other and twinkled her fingers to say that was the last one. The last, precious bar of soap.

I undressed in a makeshift shower behind the hospital. The cold water in the bucket did not soothe me in the least, but I found scrubbing to be a painful catharsis. As I cleaned my wrinkly, warped toes, I wondered: What if I had been a mere five steps away? Ten? What if Kosta and Xhevi had been the first ones in? As I lathered my winter-pale legs covered in goosebumps: How long had the bomb been there? As I focused on the dirt in my grimy fingernails: What the hell am I going to do? A few bruises had turned from black to dark purple, some physical strength had returned, but my pride and my general will to live loomed in front of a large question mark.

My hair would have to stay dirty. It was too cold to walk around with a wet head. My final rinse felt incomplete. The lack of the combined cacophony of water falling, raining over me for a split second, then hitting the crude shower stones did not go unnoticed.

When I returned to my cot, I looked at Shpresa, back in her cage, thanks to Xhevi. Her beak parted. Cooing, possibly. She was a good bird in the war, not attracting attention with calls or flighty behavior. She must have avoided an untold number of mortars and shells and airplanes throughout her missions, making her as stubborn as me. One level above whispering, I began to pitch my plan to her, conscious anyone might walk in on me and my voice.

"We'll rebuild," I said. "That's the plan."

Shpresa's expression remained wide-eyed, curious, and cautious, not judging me and my strategy. I had to credit her for being consistent.

The next day, nearly everyone else cleared out in trucks heavy with leftover gear, radios, and victory. Nina, Xhevi, Kosta and I stood on the side of the road and waved goodbye. The air felt thick with diesel and waving arms and, I assumed from their open mouths, cheers. Most were headed north; a few drove south to Saranda. The feeling inside sat strange: I never wanted to be a part of this. Now, I felt like I needed everyone. And not because I couldn't hear. But because I had no one else.

Staying behind with the two injured men must have been part of yesterday's closing conversation with Prifti. I gathered the blanket on my bed, and Shpresa, before going to see Endri. He showed no fever or any other sign of infection, so I dared to hope.

The morning light poured into the room from the one southerly window. Endri was awake and cognizant. I wrapped my blanket around his back and over his arms, then rubbed his foot with my hands. Winter in the Mediterranean is mild, but we are weak to the dampness in the cold air.

I was too nervous to speak in front of him. His lips moved in shapes of words, but I, I was lost at sea.

Head was fed up with me. *You survived a bomb together! After all you guys have been through, why would this come between you two? What could scare him now?*

Heart came to my rescue. *Give her time.* My heart, my defense.

I gave him a big smile. He clapped his hand into a thumbs-up. I shook my head. He pointed to my ears and waved his index finger in a 'no' gesture, to show he understood what happened to me in the cave.

At that moment, a breeze swept through the room, as though the wind itself exhaled. Endri shivered. I tightened the blanket around him. He flapped his hands like wings, followed by a thumb up, then a thumb down.

Thumb up. Yes, Shpresa is well. *See?* I held her cage at arm's length to show him how healthy she was. He smiled as much as he could. He made a circle with his hand, then motioned his hand forward, the military signal for 'move out.'

I gave another thumb up. He closed his eyes. A tiring way to communicate.

Nina came in with breakfast for the boys—a simple bread and feta cheese mush, called *papare*, meaning 'without money.' She handed one bowl to me for Endri. She began to feed the other patient. I swirled the spoon around the bowl to cool it off a bit. It took an extraordinary effort on Endri's part to sit up enough to eat.

It was then he felt it. He yanked back the blanket covering what was left of his leg. Stunned, speechless—there's no other way to say it. I put down the bowl, scooted next to him and held him in my silent arms. *This is too much*, I told my Heart and my Head.

He pulled away and sank back against the wall. I insisted he eat. I sliced a bit of mushed bread, cold now, with the edge of the spoon and held it to his mouth. He took the bowl from me and fed himself, even with his wounded hands.

Afterward, he lay down. I took Shpresa out of her cage and tucked her into his elbow and ribs. He stroked her feathers and I ate my own serving of *papare* as the sun climbed above the window.

Kosta came in, holding out a cigarette for Endri. I bowed out of the room. Endri needed his cheer and goodwill. He needed to talk to someone. I could provide none of that. What I could do was be useful. I found Nina and Xhevi and offered them my open, helping hands. We spent the rest of the day packing up, leaving no trace we were ever there.

In the morning, we transferred the hay mattresses to the truck beds and settled the hobbling and dizzy young men. Nina would drive the wounded private. Xhevi would ride in a truck with other soldiers. Kosta would drive Endri and me. As much effort as the war was, the physical effort it took to leave it was stupidly simple. It was the other part that was so difficult. The sun will turn blue before goodbyes are not awkward and hard as hell. I tried to break past my newfound embarrassment to force a 'goodbye and thank you' to Nina. My dry lips only succeeded in twisting my face.

I climbed in the front seat. Shpresa and her cage sat on my lap. I kept my eyes forward to meet Prifti's truth or my family. Hope is dim, but its flame is eternal.

On the road, Kosta's mood felt jovial but stilted. His dark stubble gave him an air of mystique.

Dirt. Let's be honest, nobody's bathed, Head interrupted.

We kept our eyes on the sea as we worked through its dark December moods. The sun was trying so hard to break through the clouds.

Kosta's concentration turned to the road as we began our ascent up the Llogara Pass. What the truck lacked in insulation or any sort of comfort, it made up for in power. I could feel the rumble, its strength as Kosta switched gears to accelerate. We gained almost a thousand meters in altitude in fourteen kilometers of bare, paintless switchbacks. At the top, the wind was much stronger, but it had met its match with Kosta. Stability and fragility, all bundled and tangled in each of us. He remained focused and cool, and within minutes we were in the protection of the northern slope and its dense pine forests.

Kosta pulled over on the side of the road for a cigarette break. My bones continued to rattle from the rough ride. The driver of Xhevi's truck parked next to us. We got out to check on Endri. In the time it took for me to walk from my front seat to the back of the truck, I was blindsided by the thought that we didn't have to be afraid anymore. I held onto the side of the truck until that settled.

Once the cigarette was lit and shared, I pointed back and forth between the matches and myself. Kosta obliged and I hugged him as thanks. I had been able to pack a few persimmons, jerky, and a loaf of bread from Dhermi. I hoped it would be enough. I had no illusions: my parents would be on the brink of starvation after a lifetime of plenty. The river fish, the dried food in the storehouse, and my father's rabbit traps had kept us fed in the winter months my whole life. I doubted this year would be the same.

Endri sat up on his elbows to see us. To talk to Kosta. That globe of glass had come with us on the road, too. The divide between me and everyone else who had hearing was growing with each hour. Nonetheless, I was glad to see Endri's smile had returned, even that shimmer in his eyes.

As we began our descent, Kosta jumped an unforeseen rock on the road. Shpresa slid toward one side of her cage against her will. Kosta smiled, thrilled. We were no longer fighting a war, but we still needed release from its tension. With a side glance to Kosta's mischievous unpredictability, I kept my hand on the front dash for the rest of the way.

After another half hour that felt like a lifetime, I could see my road home, a southeast vein off this main, northwest artery. When the weather is balmy in the early summer, it's a three and a half hour hike from the coastal road to Tragjas.

[We'll come and see you soon] Xhevi wrote when we got out of the trucks at the intersection.

Xhevi. My friend, my almost sister, my fellow soldier. I bobbed my head with tear-blurry eyes. I squeezed her until I feared I would pop a rib. I composed myself and set my face to that of an older sister demeanor and motioned that she write to me. It was hard to believe any one of my letters finding them in the big city. A new life, an unimaginable life, was beginning for all of us now.

And then, Shpresa and I were alone.

The trees a stone's-throw away stood without a breeze. The birds may have been singing their prettiest song and the little insects that keep the fields alive may have been chatting. They were no longer part of my world.

No trucks, no grenades, no crashing waves, no rifles, no one to my right and my left, no conversation, let alone laughter. No reason to send a message with Shpresa.

I smelled the mugginess of the sea and burnt rubber. A thin canopy of sulfur's odor hung over us.

As far as I could see, I was the sole survivor of a world war.

Dita

Dita, her parents, and Nana drove south for over an hour, past dormant fields and salt flats, with their picnic lunch in tow. They stopped on a bluff overlooking the city of Elbasan. Not far from the parking lot was an abandoned train locomotive on a single piece of track.

When Dita got out of the car, a gust of wind pushed her from behind and swirled her hair in every direction. She pulled her coat more tightly around herself.

Dita opened Nana's door. "Careful, Nana, it's windy."

Lena bent down to offer her elbow to Nana. She made a grunting effort of it but stood tall, all five feet and nothing short of regal. She smiled at Dita. She was so precious it hurt.

"Welcome to Elbasan, the windy city," said Murat. "Blame it on being built in a valley, I guess." He tilted his head.

From where they stood, the earthy, dusty colors seemed to be richly saturated, not crisp and spry for a day in January.

Her father walked ahead and stood in front of the memorial train and its signage. Evidently, the locomotive was immune to the elements, radiating as if the black paint had been reapplied yesterday.

"What do you think, Mami? Remember the trains?" Lena gently asked her mother.

193

"Nice train. I built a railroad. You and me and Gjyshi," Nana replied.

Dita's breath caught somewhere between her heart and her throat. She stole a look at her mom, then her dad. Three complete sentences. Was the change of scenery all Nana needed?

"I see," Lena said. They waited for a minute, to see if Nana would say anything else. When she didn't, Lena suggested she take Nana for a little walk.

Dita read the plaque: "This locomotive was in service from 1947 to 1987, given to the people of Albania from the people of the Soviet Union."

Dita turned to Murat. "They used the railroad for mining, I guess?"

His thick hands rested behind his back. His belly was becoming settled with his age, softening, catching up with his static eight-to-five job. His eyes were closed.

"Babi?" Dita said.

"Huh?" He peeked one eye open.

"Are you okay?" This was as close to daydreaming as she had ever seen him.

He rubbed the back of his head, then folded his arms over his chest. Another wind smothered them anew in the pungent air. "Me? Yes. We were the only country in World War II without an extensive rail system, without *any* system. Did you know that? You probably knew that."

Dita remained quiet. She could tell there was more he wanted to say.

He continued. "I'm sorry you never had the chance to meet her, my Aunt Val. After she died, there was no reason to visit." He cleared his throat. "I was imagining what she must have experienced near a train."

"You mean, because she couldn't hear?"

"Yeah, you know, the steam hissing, whistle blowing, clicking and clattering over the ties, chains rattling."

"Tell me something else about her."

He opened his eyes and looked at Dita. "I was young and she didn't talk much, you know. It was an effort, like, she wasn't completely comfortable … but, her smile."

The wind brought tears to Dita's eyes.

"I remember because her smiles were so … *good*. Not, 'Oh, she has a nice smile,' but … it was like they turned the world over, everything new again."

Dita's tears kept coming despite the breeze. "Babi. That's the most beautiful thing you've …" She was too choked up to finish.

"I should have told you and your sister more. I'm sorry," he said.

"Like you said, you were little. And, we have the notebook. 'Home' is circled a million times."

"Yeah. She never came to us in Tirana. We always went to see her. Visited in the summer, on the beach in Orikum. Once I was older, I could see how lovingly she and her husband, Zamir, interacted. No, that's not right." He looked for Lena, walking around with Nana. Dita saw his shoulders relax. "Val and Zamir … they breathed each other. You know what I mean? He was the inhale and she was the exhale. Does that make sense? Maybe I need lunch."

"It's beautiful, Babi."

"Anyway, ask me anything. I'll try to make up for it."

The sun broke through the patchy clouds, raining down warmth and bright light.

"It's okay, come on," Dita bumped his elbow.

They drove further down the road to the Orthodox Monastery and Church of Saint John Vladimir. The dilapidated structure had all but succumbed to its fate. An older man crossed the sparse front yard. He wore a beige coat and a dark ivy cap. He stopped and waited when he saw their car park.

"Hello!" Murat called out and extended his hand.

The women approached and met the man as if he were family. He introduced himself as Bajo. He looked at each of them from under his cap and raised his eyebrows rather than attempt to straighten any part of his gently bent spine. Liver spots dotted one side of his face.

Lena told him of their plans to picnic. "Are you the groundskeeper?"

Bajo didn't commit to a yes. He grinned, though, and revealed an incredible set of healthy teeth. He gestured to a rustic table. A tree trunk, split down the middle, turned right side up, and coated with a thin veneer, made the benches. Dita's parents and grandmother walked in that direction.

Dita turned to face the church. She felt a tingling, similar to a sugar rush from too many frappés in one afternoon. The archeologist in her begged to ask Bajo questions. Her heart pulsed in her throat from fear of not knowing what to ask, or if she would have enough time to ask them. She really ought to start a questionnaire, to be ready to ask whomever, wherever, whenever.

"Do you know when this was built? Originally?" Dita matched Bajo's pace and led him closer to the church.

"Late thirteenth century."

"Thirteenth?"

"Monastery from the beginning. It's endured a lot. You know Shpataraku?"

"Eighteenth century. The beheaded painter."

"Well, the painter, before he was beheaded ..."

Bajo caught Dita by surprise, and she laughed so much he jumped.

"Anyways, yes," he continued, "he painted the frescoes inside. Most of the relics are in Tirana. There's a festival in honor of Saint John Vladimir every June. *Vladimir*, mind you, Saint John Vladimir, not Saint John. Big difference."

"Of course," Dita murmured.

"Huge fire in 1944, but, miraculously, the frescoes survived. I don't know how. If you want to believe in the faith, start with that." He waved a finger at her, then folded his hands behind his back, like any other old man out for a stroll.

"Right. You sound like you've said this before."

"Some people, like you, maybe, want to know the history. And I want to tell them. Others, well, I tell them even if they don't want to know."

They laughed again, together.

"Anyway, what else would I do? Watch my sheep eat?" He pointed to an olive grove.

Dita's eyes adjusted to the distance. Now that she was looking for them, she saw the off-white animals under the trees and among the still-green grass.

"I'm sure you deserve your time to sit and relax."

"You try it. Boring as hell," he said with a wink.

Dita couldn't help but touch the walls. In some areas, the exterior looked haphazard and rough. In other spots, the local limestone and mortar had been smoothed to perfection so even a toddler could trail their hand along it. A centuries-old monastery certainly carried its share of wailing. Even the ground she walked on soaked up the sobbing, right along with the blood of soldiers and innocents.

"How did the fire start in the war?"

Bajo shrugged. "Plenty of ways to start a fire." He was a simple, logical man. Dita estimated his age and did the math.

"Sir, were you here when the fire happened, when it was destroyed?"

"It was destroyed twice in my lifetime. So, this, even without a door and without a roof, is more complete than it has been for most of my life. But, you mean during the war? Yes, I was here. I was a boy. A lucky boy."

He encouraged her with a nod of his chin. "You can go inside. No problem."

Dita looked back at her family. Lena waved to her to say, "Go ahead." Without any front doors to open, she simply walked through the arched doorway. The groundskeeper followed her.

The floor was a recipe for a twisted ankle. Dita noticed not a speck of trash to be found. He was diligent, too, this Bajo.

The stillness inside was the textbook definition of perfect. Around her, Dita sensed an aura, still present, of steely resolve. In her mind's eye, photos from the museum's exhibit and the tranquil feeling of Nana's bedroom flooded and collided in this sanctuary. Chills rushed over Dita's skin. She felt clammy; small pinpricks of black obstructed her vision. The church began to spin. She reached out to a wooden pew to steady herself, sat down, and put her head between her knees. The three-hundred-year-old art works would have to wait.

Bajo stood next to her and waited. "Miss, do you need anything?"

"No, but thank you. I'll be okay. It's just … a lot."

In time, Dita slowly raised herself. She zipped her coat, feeling cold from the sudden sweat. She placed her elbow on the back of the pew, resting her head in her hand.

"That's better. Sorry."

He waved her words away. Dita pulled out her sketchbook and began to draw the altar. Rather, where the altar should be.

"Did anybody use the monastery during the war?"

He sighed. "Everyone wanted to use it, given its location and supposed neutrality. But the Allies held it most of the time. I guess you would say they used it as a communication headquarters."

Bajo squatted to sit on a red plastic stool opposite her. He put his elbows on his knees, and Dita understood this was a shape he made often. The stool contrasted with the time and location, yet, now that Dita had calmed down from the initial encounter of the holy place, she saw that the stool complemented the paintings behind him, bold in crimson and tattered gold.

The unofficial groundskeeper coughed. "I remember one man, a soldier, I mean, and how he would talk to the pigeons. I asked him once what he was talking to them about, but he wouldn't answer. Lots of unanswered questions then. He was nice, quiet, sort of serious. Not so serious as … burdened. Yet, full of *shprese*." Hope.

He *tsk*ed at the resurfaced story and rubbed his chin with his thumb. "You could see in his eyes that, when he smiled … he was the salt of the earth, that's what he was. You know that phrase?"

Dita nodded. "I know." She thought of her Aunt Val, certain she was a good person, too, without ever knowing her. "I don't suppose you remember a woman named Valentina Muskaj?"

"Here?"

"No, she was in Tragjas."

"Oh, no. I've never left."

"Right."

He looked up to the sky ceiling overhead. "We're still trying to raise money for a roof. It would keep the pigeons off the frescoes."

Dita put away her sketchbook and took out her wallet. "Thank you, sir. Thank you so much," she whispered.

"Oh. You're welcome."

She handed him a ten thousand *leke* bill. Not much, but it was all she had. "For the roof."

He held up his hands. "Please, there's a box by the door."

Dita and her family stopped at a café on the way home. The espresso proved worthless against the lull of the drive. Within minutes, Dita faded to dreamland.

On Monday, Dita took the stairs to the lab in rhythm. Getting her hands onto pieces of history, like Nana's jewelry box bracelet, helped to keep the gloomy doubts at bay. Gloomy like today's early February sky. And doubts, with a capital D, that she would ever figure out the bracelets' origins—her holy grail.

She hung her bag over her chair and sat down. She looked at Agon expectedly, waiting with the question written all over her face.

"Nothing." He threw his hands up in the air.

Dita squeezed her eyes shut to release the expectation. She exhaled deeply. "It's okay. I mean, I know. There are so many holes in our story."

"You didn't see anything else there?" Agon said.

"At Rodoni? I didn't really look, you know? I looked over my shoulder a lot, afraid we'd get caught. It's not that big of a place. But nothing else stuffed in the secret hole, no. And,"—she dug into her bag and pulled out the satchel—"this happened over the weekend." Dita tilted the pouch and the two bracelets slid out.

"A second one?" Agon picked them up with every care in the world. "They're so similar," he said.

"Basically identical. Effort was made, for sure, for the nuggets to be the same size. The leather cord. Couldn't that tell us something?"

"We could carbon-date them, but …"

"But it doesn't tell us why or where they came from, or how or who," Dita finished for him. "The mines near Elbasan, they're not gold mines, are they?"

Agon bobbled his head side to side. "I don't think so. I know there is one east of Elbasan, but not close to the city."

"And far, far away from Rodoni."

He ruffled his hair and adjusted his glasses. "I'll call a couple local historians I know and see what they can tell me."

"Thanks. I'll take the measurements. Any luck with those books?" She put Nana's bracelet back in the pouch, and back in her purse.

"Rulers, kings, queens, war, and politics. But I'm not done yet." He looked down at his desk and the layers of papers and literature.

Dita sighed, determined not to show Agon how discouraged she felt. "I know. There are other projects, too. I'll read. You can talk to your people." She winked. "Let me know if you find out about other books that may be helpful. Maybe they'd boost our case to Raco."

"Are you going to tell him about the second bracelet?"

Dita shook her head. "It's personal."

"Right." He looked at her with such understanding, she had to turn away.

"But if we have," she cleared her throat, "other, solid evidence. Or if one of your buddies has any clout, to push Raco, then I'd talk to him again."

"We."

"Thanks, Agon."

He scooted forward to his desk and dove back into his work.

Dita entered all of the information she knew of the first Rodoni bracelet into the green ledger in the corner. They measured one and a half centimeters by one centimeter, give or take a millimeter. She was out of reasons to keep it at home, now that Nana had her bracelet from her jewelry box once again.

She carried the Rodoni bracelet across the room to the wide filing cabinet. A label read 'Incomplete' on the drawer third from the top. Inside, the drawer was divided into nine, identical square compartments. It was full to bursting with objects either lacking important information or damaged beyond repair. She laid it gently in an open box containing some dangle earrings.

She wondered aloud. "Maybe I *should* put them both in this drawer. Let them stay in the drawer with the others? They could be drawer friends." She took the books from Agon's desk.

"Cop out," he said. "We'll get it, this mystery of yours." He pushed his hands ahead, pressing on some invisible brakes. "We'll get it, okay?" He smiled.

Dita put the jewelry box bracelet in her bag. She had promised Nana she would give it back to her.

Late that night, when everyone else in the house slept, Dita sat up in bed listening to the city. The street sweepers, with their ancient twig brooms, kicked as much dust into the air as they collected into their bins. Cats fought in the alley below.

Dita and Ilir had met their friends again at Bar Grand earlier in the evening. She replayed it over and over in her head: Ilir sat with the guys and had 'guy' conversations; that's how things worked. *Tonight was no different*, she told herself. *And Valentine's Day is at the end of the week.* But still, a feeling she could not shake sat on her shoulder, tapping at the side of her head. Ilir never looked over to wink at her, as a way of checking on her; he had not asked if she wanted another drink. He hadn't put his arm around her, not once. Something was off.

Dita snuggled in bed and closed her eyes. In her imagination, she turned the pages of great-grandma Mira's flower book. Dita settled on a pocket holding a pressed purple aster. She held onto the feeling of faith it invoked and sought soothing dreams.

Mira

Rezart sat up and whispered to get dressed. His knives and pistols clinked against the buttons of his vest. I hurried to match him.

When he opened the door, the sky was turning from black to broken blue and gray. Rezart mumbled in a tenor reserved for Plak as I mounted. We went west and south, keeping a steady pace so as to not arouse suspicion. As the land flattened and spread open before us, Rezart urged Plak faster and faster. I was so aware of our vulnerability, my back spasmed from fear of being shot.

I didn't speak. My trepidations jostled and landed each time Plak's hooves hit the ground.

We stopped long enough for Plak to rest and drink from the river. I unwrapped a small loaf of cornbread and Rezart found some passed-over berries along the bank.

The sun was near high the next day when I first heard a rushing, a steady *shh,* heightening, then quieting. I smelled salt. Salt. We ambled up a cliff and looked down at the sea below and before us. This was the sea. A blue, a green; there was no likeness in my mountains. Perhaps if the summer sky fell into the glass-clear river—that was the closest I could describe it.

It yelled at us with each wave's crash and hushed on its return to the endless water. "Leave me," then "come back, I beg you," it said.

The remains of a fortress consisted of an outer wall, an arch, and a tower burrowed into a steep, narrow peninsula. The top of the cylindrical tower was overgrown with unruly brush. It was so unattended and exclusive, I felt as if the two of us equaled an army of invaders. Rocks tumbled to the beach as we navigated the steep path with Plak. The scrubby bushes caught me more than once. On the sand, I walked to the water transfixed. Delighted, afraid to delight, afraid of its power.

The sun warmed my hair, and the salt cleared my nose. I knelt and laid my fingers open for the water to reach me. It tickled and teased.

I looked to share the joy with Rezart. He tied Plak to a bush in the shade. He was gazing at me with a rare smile.

"Incredible, right?"

I nodded. I had been so mad at him for stalling our offensive, but here, everything around us dazzled. The reflection from the water lightened the castle, even Rezart's face, as if a mirror was held under his chin. I smiled so much my cheeks hurt.

I motioned with my eyes to the outer wall. "Shall we see about it?"

Rezart opened his arm with a sweep. He took my hand in his, and I saw he carried a weight. A burden I hadn't seen before. I looked over my shoulder for Revenge. I didn't see her. Rezart and I walked forward together.

The castle was a mix of beige and gray stone, some layers older than others. The outer wall was divided in seven sections. Each was built around a lookout hole, allowing a slightly different view of the cerulean water. We stepped in one, and right away, my scalp prickled as it cooled out of the sun.

I closed my eyes and I felt around for my husband, to touch his hand as I rested. Instead, I felt his lips press against mine, urgent and strong. I opened my eyes in surprise. His brows were rumpled.

"What is it?" I searched for an answer in the corners of his eyes, in a twitch of his lips. I kissed him again.

He pulled back enough to remove his vest.

Later, the whisper of a wind ran a chill down my half-covered back and woke me. I pressed my hand against Rezart's chest and sat up. *We ought to go.*

"Are you all right?" he said and painted his fingers along my skin.

My stomach growled as much as the waves on the other side of the wall. "Yes."

He sat up and rubbed his eyes. For a moment, I could picture him as a child, waking from a midday nap, groggy and puffy, eyes like a fawn.

He tucked in his shirt while still on his knees. I stood and he watched me dress.

He held out his hand for mine. "Please."

I knelt in front of him, less than an arm's reach from the wall. "Rezart? What is it?"

Rezart skimmed his fingers along the stones, gripping every other one. "I don't think I ever told you; I come from a long line of pirates and merchants. They weren't bloodthirsty like me."

"You're not bloodthirsty."

He continued searching. "Surely, I can find one," he said.

My stomach fluttered. I squeezed his other hand.

He found a loose stone about shoulder height from where we kneeled and wiggled the brick until it came free.

From a pocket, only large enough for two fingers, on the inside of his waistband, Rezart retrieved two bracelets. In the center of each was a chunk of gold, the size of my fifth fingernail, wrapped with a dark thread. The gold found traces of sunlight and gleamed, proud. He pinched the bracelets in his beautiful, scarred fingers and held them up between us. The cords swayed in the air.

"I haven't given you anything, and for that I am sorry."

"That's not true," I said, aching to understand him.

"You have given me so much. Will you wear one?" He reached for my hand without waiting for a reply. He traced the veins on the underside of my wrist before tying it. "You wear one, and if I don't—." He pursed his lips, but not before I heard the lump in his throat.

"Stop."

He shook the other bracelet in the air, but he looked down at the sand. Not since our wedding night had I felt him cry. I held his face in my hands. He rubbed my fingers over his lips.

"Come back for this," he whispered over the waves' lazy yawns. "It should be enough, if you find yourself in need. From here, you can take a boat to Italy, where you'll be safe." He sniffed, gave it one last shake in the air and tucked it into the cavity. He placed the yellow-gray brick back in its place and held my hands.

"I can't breathe without you," he said.

Sometimes, there are sufficient words. Even more rarely, there are words that are true and bright. Barring these gems of voice, a kiss is the most right, the most acute way to say everything which needs to be said.

We rode into camp the next night, bone-tired yet alive in the mind. *Now, it will begin.*

Genti and Deda were on guard and met us.

"Pejani is ready. Everyone is ready. The day after tomorrow, following the prayer at dawn. As they leave the mosque," Genti said.

"Good, good," Rezart said.

"Come. There is something we must show you," Genti said.

Rezart glanced at me and put his hand on my back. My nerves jumped to an edge, a new cliff of anxiety.

Genti opened the door to the outbuilding Rezart and I slept in. Genti held his torch in the doorframe. There, under a blanket on our pallet, sleeping like dormice, lay three children. They looked like a staircase, with distinct heights despite lying down. The tallest, a girl on the left, then a boy, then a toddler. All three had dark hair.

"Their parents?" I whispered.

Genti closed the door and shrugged behind the fire in his hand. "They showed up yesterday. On their own, the oldest told us. Tringa is her name, Gjoni is the boy, and Sofia is the little one. Other than that, not a word."

The heart inside me, what was left of it, kicked and screamed.

Rezart held his arm around my waist. "We'll stay with them for the night. It will be dawn soon enough."

We said good night to Genti and reentered the room. I laid my head on my arm on the dirt floor. Rezart curled in front of me, closer to the door. I was too tired to sort worries, too tired to despair more, too tired to imagine the hell we would bring.

The sun had begun to rise when Rezart laid his hand on my hip. I sat up and saw what he saw: three sleep-swollen faces staring at us from across the room. Mouths agape, dark eyes unflinching.

I rose to my knees, then put one foot down to stand. Tringa and Gjoni cowered. I paused and I put my hands in front of me to calm them. "No parents?"

Tringa shook her head.

"Where are you from?" I begged God I would never have to ask these questions again.

I couldn't hear Tringa's whispered response. I didn't insist.

"We," I pointed to myself and Rezart, "will take care of you. I will introduce you to our people. Okay?"

Tringa bobbed her head once.

The children continued to stare at us as Rezart and I tied on our waistbands and filled them with life-saving, and life-taking, contraband.

"Come on, let's find some food," I said.

I led them toward the center of camp. A pot sat over a low fire. It was big enough to feed six people, but here and now, it fed dozens throughout the day. Women and children stopped and met the three siblings. In happier times, the mothers would have kissed them and coaxed their own kids to play with Gjoni and Sofia. But they had lost the willpower. Any remaining strength was reserved for fighting off disease and bullets.

I left the children under Vera's care and found the circle of warriors, including men from other northern tribes.

"Mira, when you clear this," Rezart drew lines in the sand, creating a corridor from the bazaar and from the mayor's building. "You—"

"We will come to you," I said.

"Like hell you will. Come back here. We cannot lose our camp." He looked back at his makeshift map, then at me. "Come back to the children. I will meet you here."

I brought myself to my full height, my weight even between both feet, and rested my hands on my pistols. "Swear it."

I heard other feet shift on the dirt around us. Someone coughed.

Rezart tossed his knife onto the ground. He stood and met my eyes. His breath put chills on my throat. In a low voice, and his hand over his chest, he said, "*Besa.*"

I acknowledged him with the slightest of nods. I pretended to look more interested in his plan in the sand. Anything to ignore the weight crushing my heart.

Late that night, when the children slept, Rezart gathered me and our leadership to the campfire. Though the blaze inside burned for justice, I was becoming dull to planning and talking. "I've asked Qazim to write this up. If you would bear witness ..." He looked carefully at each of his men: Qazim, Genti, Deda, Ymer, Rinaj, Azmir. "It makes it official

that the children Tringa, Gjoni and little Sofia are,"—he looked at me
—"ours."

I sank to my knees. Winning Scutari for Rezart wouldn't be enough.
Giving him the whole world wouldn't be enough.

Rezart took the south of Scutari with half of Pejani's men, a dozen of his
own, and the newcomers who had joined us in Rragam. Pejani attacked
from the north. I led my brothers and the rest of Rezart's men to the
eastern side of the city, a straight line from our camp.

Indeed, we rained hell and its fury. Fire and screaming and bullets
and blood and raw anguish, in every way. My lips were parched from
panting and yelling. My hand cramped from holding my knife within
the first hour. I chased down two Ottomans in our area. I screamed at
them to turn and face me. Two less for Rezart, two more whose blood I
wanted.

By early afternoon, we cleaned out our center aisle. One of my
eyelids was stuck shut with blood caked between my eyelashes. My
knuckles, split and bloodied. When I turned back to survey our losses,
something like a lightning bolt struck my hip. I crashed to my hands
and knees. I cried out but didn't recognize the voice as mine. I could
have been floating or flying; I had been disembodied. I felt for a bullet
hole through my pants—an entire cleaver knife, such was the pain.

Then, I heard shouting and I could feel the ground beneath my hands.
It shook from running feet. At once, my body was flipped upward and I
was blinded from a whiteness, a white sky.

A voice I knew as Deda's spoke near to my ear. His arms cradled me.
He might have said, "You're okay. We're going to camp, Qazim will
take care of you. Stay with me, Mira."

But perhaps that was a memory of what I wanted to hear. I felt myself
becoming delirious, screaming without ceasing. I didn't know up from
down, forward from backward.

I know what I saw when I passed out in Deda's arms. In those seconds of unconscious terror, I was falling into a bottomless pit at an uncontrollable speed. Images of faces flew past me. It was impossible to stop. That, I remember quite well.

When I revived, Pain made its presence known. It dug its rotten fingers into my hip, my spine. It walked on my legs, and each step lit a searing fire. My stomach felt inside out.

"What …" I mumbled through swollen lips. I was lying on my right side. "Where …"

A voice. Deda's voice again, like the river when it's calm in the autumn. "You were shot in the hip. Qazim was able to take it out. Mira, can you hear me?"

I slid my head up an inch or two to acknowledge the words, but it was too much, too fast. I vomited, bitter and putrid. It puddled around my cheek and nose before anyone could react. I heaved up whatever was left in my stomach. I couldn't remember when I last ate. My throat burned.

With nothing left to expel in my belly, my grief moved to my eyes. As Deda wiped me and laid another blanket under my head, I began to cry and cry and cry.

"Where …" I tried again.

"From the corner of the bazaar, we think."

I tilted my head into the cot to say *no, dammit*. "Rezart." That's what I'm asking.

I heard Deda's hard-working hands scrape together. He lowered his voice. "They're not back yet." He gripped my hand. "Mira."

I learned then the body has more tears than bile.

Val

Behind me, the Ionian Sea begged its way inland. Over the millenia, it had created the Bay of Vlora. It lay as calm as I wanted to feel.

My father had once taken a trip to the more northern city of Durrës. There, he said, the Adriatic Sea was dark and deep. Vlora, then, played hostess—it is where the briny, crystal-clear, take-your-breath-away Ionian Sea mingles and dances with the dark Adriatic.

The quiet hay fields on each side of me had long gone to seed and stood to be finished off by a rare frost. When the world was right side up, women and men cut with scythes soon after the harvest, filling donkey-driven carts to overflowing. Now, though, in the subdued sun, it looked like an ocean of scraggly, sick seaweed.

I pulled the jerky out of my sack and chewed and chewed. I imagined my return from Shpresa's soaring point. When I arrived at the arched entrance of Tragjas, I would look west to the Bay of Vlora, and it would be nothing short of glorious. I saw my reunion with my mother. Maybe she would turn around and see me walking up the road. Maybe old Fato and old Gani would look up from their game of dominoes and see me coming and yell for her. Maybe she'd drop the pot in her hand when she saw me in the doorway.

Secluded from any city, from any port, even from a road, Tragjas posed no strategic threat. Was it too much to ask that it be spared?

I hoped to cover the nine kilometers before the sun's last sigh. I looked down to see if my feet would move me forward. Once I got home, they would be able to heal from months of soggy, sweaty hikes and the explosion itself.

What will you only see once in your life?

Today.

I smiled at my own riddle. "Let's go," I told Shpresa.

A solitary hike, it turns out, is when the mind relives life's moments. One time, my brothers hid from my mother so well she was to the point of tears. Ana once dropped plums down the well. The water was even sweeter for several days afterward.

My legs, still shaky from the ride, were feeling the gradual rise in elevation. The cold air was a heavy force pushing from every direction, stinging my calves and cheeks alike. Shpresa's cage pulled at my shoulders and upper back.

"Really, you could say something, you know." I put my hand to my throat and felt the words vibrating. "Lighten the mood, give me some encouragement."

Remembering more stories became too taxing; I had to concentrate solely on breathing and moving forward and up. I stopped in the middle of the road to catch my breath. I had been too ambitious. I hadn't accounted for my injured body. Stupid. I was so tired. The all-over soreness from the blast was turning into piercing pain. My feet felt too swollen to take off my boots tonight, even if I tried.

In the nook of another curve was a tool shed. The door frame and its dark hinges seemed to be the most solid part. The roof was gone. It was enticing and sturdy enough for one night. I stopped in front of it and drank from my cool canteen. I pushed the door open with my shoulder and collapsed into a heap of deep sleep.

*

In the morning, my bruises felt stiff from the hard ground. I replayed the bits of the dream, the nightmare from which I awoke. Running, trees, hard breathing, dirt flying up to the cloudy sky.

Then, I remembered—I couldn't hear.

I sat up, and a creeping headache greeted me good morning. I relieved myself in the corner, then opened the door. I ate only enough breakfast to get me up the hill. Maybe, too, I was procrastinating. I was nervous. No, terrified.

An hour past the hut, I took another deep bend in the road. With the turn, the wind changed and blew tragedy into my face. I should have seen orange groves on both sides of me. Instead, the smell of sweet ashes flooded my nostrils, then my throat. Char tickled my tongue, and my chest tightened for air. The emptiness overpowered me.

Olive trees planted generations ago to welcome a weary traveler stood at the entrance of my Tragjas. As kids, we ran around them, weaving in and out of the musky branches. The memory of our laughter rang inside my head. I reached out for one to steady myself. It crumpled under my fingers.

What I saw was more than my heart was prepared for. My head— aghast, empty of reasoning, empty of explanation of how this destruction could be.

There was old Fato's house, right where it had been my whole life. Only this time the front door lay in shambles, and the walls were smoke-stained. The windows were framed with black burn instead of summer white. The roof, the damn roof, was mere kindling to a single German matchstick.

Our property was three plots beyond old Fato's. There was no door to open; I couldn't even recognize it in the ashes. As I stepped across the threshold, I sank to the floor and wept. Heart was still weeping back at the olive tree.

I felt like an old pot in which every last bit of food had been furiously scraped out, and now my very blood was next. And what did it matter? Take me too, go ahead.

Mice darted in the corner. I drained the last of my canteen, salivating for the last drops. I knew better than to add dehydration to my list of problems. I would need to go to the center of town to draw water. But first, I began to walk through the house.

Heart had caught up with me and Head. She couldn't leave me for too long.

Babi's seat cushion by the fireplace, where he sat and told us those old stories, was a mass of darkness. The sun shone through the kitchen window and illuminated a few of my mother's pots and pans, overturned onto the floor. Without thinking, I turned them upright, right on the ground, as there were no shelves to set them on anymore. My mother's walnut mixing bowl lay split in two, like an earthquake on a fault line, in the smooth wood.

Don't. Don't do it, Heart warned me.

But I did. I turned from the kitchen, toward the bay and away from the morning sun. My feet dragged the three steps it took to reach the bedroom where Sokol, Arberi, Ana and I slept every night of our childhood. There, under the front window, were Arberi's wedding shoes. He had shined them until we saw our reflection in them. I covered my mouth with both hands and sobbed, held up only by the blackened and crumbling door frame.

I didn't know what to do next. I didn't know what I *could* do next. I listened for wise words from Head and Heart, but they were as still as the forest after snowfall. The flaws and impossibilities of my dreams of rebuilding had blinded me of reality. How did I think I could rebuild a village by myself? With what materials? Why? For whom?

How can you make number one vanish?

Add a 'g' and it's gone.

Leave, Head urged me.

I grabbed my canteen and Shpresa. The poor thing had been caged for so long. I took a deep breath. For now, I would need water to drink, and a fire by nighttime. And, I would need something to cook over that fire.

My body knew where to go. It was one of the village children's chores to carry water home for cooking, and for our neighbors if need be. Drawing water was second nature.

I knelt at the well and saw the bucket was already lowered. Leaning back on my heels, I began to pull on the rope. Soon enough, the bucket was within arm's reach. Hallelujah. I set it on the ground and water overflowed.

I drank with care, then became desperate for more, gurgling, licking, sucking water from my cupped hands, inches from the bucket.

From the corner of my eye, Shpresa caught my attention. She began to toddle with excitement back and forth.

I sat back. "How about I let you out for a bit?" I asked her. She stopped pacing when she heard my voice. Shpresa tilted her head. The weak sunlight glared off her onyx eyes. I opened the cage door for her.

In an instant, she flew away. Gone, toward the sea.

"Not even a goodbye," I mumbled. I rested my arms on the rim of the well and laid down my head. "Please, come back," I whispered through my tears. "Please."

I felt the wailing in me and my shoulders, my ribs convulsed. Head and Heart were, again, silent. The well of hope was never dry. That was what Heart was supposed to tell me. Right?

I ... I don't know, she replied.

I raised my head, needing more air. My vision prickled with dots of light. When the smudge cleared, three Vlahs stood in front of me on the other side of the well.

Able-bodied men, Head remarked.

The men were dressed in white wool, black shoes, and hardened expressions. Each had a knife tucked into their waistband. The shortest had an old rifle slung over his shoulder. The one in front, with an over-grown mustache and the longest hair, spoke. With shaking hands, I indicated my hearing loss. He pointed to the well, then to his chest. I shook my head and pointed in the direction of my house, then to my chest. He understood, because I saw a shadow of regret, or remorse, flutter over his face like a cheesecloth. Their countenances changed, broke, as dry mud cracking off a boot. They didn't turn to leave as I expected. They looked at each other, then back at me.

Had they set up camp here? Were they blind to the desecration?

I focused on filling my canteen from the bucket. If I was honest with myself, I wanted to avoid every next minute. But, who wanted to be honest? It was too hard.

I found my legs had turned into pudding. With a deep inhale, I threw up my hands in the air. The leader motioned for me to follow them. They led me to the edge of town, on the backside of our hill, away from the bay. The Vlahs had moved into old Arberi's house. It was a smart location. The hill dropped sharply to the dried-up riverbed below, waiting for spring snowmelt. From this point, they were perched like eagles overlooking the road. The road I was on the day before. If anyone was crazy enough to approach Tragjas from the main entrance, the Vlahs' camp would remain unseen. They must have come after the Nazis torched my town.

The gypsies had hung sturdy canvases and animal hides over the main room, closest to the fireplace. The covers by no means closed off the entire room from the elements. But, if they slept close to the fire and to each other, it would be enough to shelter them from a winter rain. More canvases flapped a stone's throw away at Pellumb's house, that of old Arberi's son.

It didn't take long to catch the attention of the entire camp. The men and I stopped in front of a large campfire. More men and their women stood and formed a semi-circle. I counted four more men dressed like the others: layered white skirts over white pants cut at the knee, and hemmed with a black band. Their stockings met their pants, so that not an inch of leg showed, and even covered their leather boots. Their sleeves lay loose and uncuffed. The waistband around each of them was not a scarf or a belt like Baba Halil's. These were more of a pouch— to hold their firearms and hunting knives.

Of the nine women, two with babes in arms, three wore layer upon layer of black. Gold embroidered shawls were laid over their shoulders and tucked into their skirts. Red, yellow and green trim edged their aprons.

The other six women wore a commotion of color and jewelry from head to toe. Their shirts were striped vertically, their waistbands horizontally. Their apron trim was more elaborate than the others', weaving red and black with gold and white. Medallion-heavy necklaces laid on their chests.

How strange to not hear them jingle and jangle, Head said.

They wore headscarves, most of them plain white, and they slipped a bit with each turn of the head. Their hair was parted down the middle and pulled back into a tight bun. They looked welcoming, but I read the confusion on their faces. Who was I, and where did I come from?

I repeated the same nonverbal explanation as I had at the well, with all the grace of a frantic chicken. Of course, the lead man spoke faster. He pointed in the general direction of my house. Everyone looked from me to him and back again with solemn nods. Then, smiles. I probably imagined smiles from the men. More likely, they merely grunted. I'll never know, but the women were who I needed. I was accepted. The clan opened their formation and the women beckoned me to the fire. I clutched my stomach and hoped there was any sort of food in the pot sitting on a grill over the flames.

They acted as though gesturing and motioning was common and not at all limiting. They seemed to say everything with a nod of the chin, a wave of the hand or a bobbing of the head to mean no and yes. This was familiar.

I removed Nina's notebook and pencil from my coat. My fingers paused on the page holding the conversation with Xhevi and Kosta. The circles around "home" were dark and grooved, like tire tracks in mud. I lifted the notebook but stopped mid-air. The women stared at me. I slid the book back into my pocket and considered the challenging collision of illiteracy and deafness.

Food. That needed no words. Foraged greens boiled with wild garlic, and from a smaller pot, a bit of corn mush. Yes, please, and thank You, God. At this time of year, preserved food was eaten in careful quantities. As welcoming as they were, hunger showed in their cheekbones, and for a split second I saw a look of despondence pass over one plump lady's eyes as she scooped a ladleful for me. We locked eyes and she started laughing. She handed me the bowl, and I checked myself. Isolated as they were, mostly self-imposed, perhaps they fared better than I assumed.

Being alive, having some food, doesn't mean they haven't lost anything, Heart assured me. As if I didn't know.

My legs grew warmer from the fire. For the first time in a long time, I wasn't on the run, moving on, hiding, or freezing. Instead, I was free-falling. I wondered how I could stay here. And how could I not. Home, the one place I wanted to be, and it was all ash.

Is it? Head said. *Is this still home?*

The Vlahs didn't need one more mouth to feed. Doubtless, they would move on with their own sheep and their fresh lambs come Easter.

I had been so confident in my future, obnoxiously so. But, in the here and now, the opposite was true.

My belly was full, but my legs felt cramped. I needed to breathe clean air, fresh air without any smoke. I stood, put my hand to my heart and nodded in thanks. All the women rose and bowed their heads in response.

They know they will see you again, Heart said. After all, how far could one woman go without her ears? Again, I looked at my feet to see if they would move me. As if I had words of encouragement.

You could go to Eliza's house. Remember climbing the grape vines over her front door as a kid? Head suggested.

Go to the teqe, Heart said.

I'll go everywhere, I reassured them both. I'll walk my whole life over again.

But first, I walked back to the well. I picked up Shpresa's cage, then set it back down again so it would be in the same place for her if she returned. When.

I walked on and in and out of the burn, the char, the cold, gray stone homes. No matter which way the breeze blew, humidity, decay, soot, and smoke inundated me. There were the foundations for the houses of the Dakollaris, the Alushis, bless them, and their crazy lot of goats. Where is everybody? Every body? Only in my friend Lila's house did I find the remains of a body. *God.* I could only hope—I had a little left to spare, that some neighbors had time to flee before the Germans came.

My body was cracking, creaking from the grief, but I continued to wander. The sun stood overhead now, but I was cold from the inside out.

I did not enter the *teqe*. Instead, I walked around the back to the cemetery. I counted fifteen mounds without any dead grass, fresh plots marking the bodies' earthly claim: we are here. Other mounds had become one with the land, sinking to fit in. Some were child-size, between larger graves.

The west wind pushed against me, but I put my head down and rounded the front of the *teqe*. It was bare and holy, arguably holier than the grandest of mosques. Baba Halil's voice seemed to reverberate between the walls.

Nothing short of a miracle, there was one candle, down to the nub, still in the holder that could hold two dozen.

One candle, for everyone I had ever known.

Kosta's matches, Head said. Heart was still numb from the cemetery.

Desperate to do something, anything, I searched my pockets for Kosta's packet. A match caught on the first strike. There in the single flame, I envisioned my sister, my brothers, my mother and my father. I heard their voices over my father's baritone songs. Without taking my eyes off of it, off of them, I knelt and took a deep, shaky breath. Then another.

Then another and I'm running out the door, away from the *teqe*, as if a swarm of hornets was chasing me. Running off the bruises and pains, running past the ghosts, begging, praying the Nazis had left it alone.

No one in my tiny, silent world will be hurt. No one else is going to die. Hell no. No one else would starve through winter. A tall order, I knew, but, inside of resolve is love, and inside of love, we breathe.

Behind Auntie Juna's house, and low to the ground, was the village storage cellar.

It was still locked. I pulled at the iron rod, I bashed the latch with a rock. My hands shook, my thighs quivered, my throat rattled to be free from the bottled up rage.

The door opened and seemed to say, *I've been waiting for you.*

With a shudder, I stepped inside the dark room, and all the sounds inside me released in a frenzy. I laughed at the Axis's laziness to forsake this cold room. I screamed for my mother. I growled for the innocent days torn from the village children. I pounded my fist against the hard wall for arriving too late.

Mucus ran out of my nose. I blew dripping snot onto the floor and wiped my eyes.

Now go, Heart said with a stern voice, fully present now.

I wasted no more time on myself. I picked up a basket of beets and stacked it on top of a crate of onions. A tray of dried fish. A bottle of *raki,* divine. I was a shell of who I once was and ten pounds lighter, a portion of the sorrow lifted by compassion and action.

I closed the door.

I have no recollection of the walk back across town. But I remember the wide eyes and grateful hands as I set the food before the women at the fire. I looked around at all their shimmering eyes. At least I could see the tears, the sniffing, the men setting their jaws and wrinkling their noses.

At least I could see.

That night, they invited me to stay with them instead of alone in the skeleton of my house. I removed my boots and felt the men and women suck in their breath, shocked by my feet. They were getting wrinkled and discolored but not yet to full-blown immersion foot again.

To say I slept well after that catharsis of grief in the form of giving, is an overstatement. My body lay immobile by the fear of nightmares. I believed if I didn't move and kept my eyes closed, the Bringer of Nightmares, Epiales, would pass over me, pass over all of us. I would make a deal with him if I could: I will hold my breath, too.

The next day, we buried exposed bodies—the men had come upon others I had not seen. We gathered firewood and found mushrooms in the forest beyond the storage cellar.

I missed Shpresa. She was my friend, who had seen so much and appeared so unaffected, so steady. Until she wasn't and flew off. I needed her. I needed to know what my voice sounded like, and, although she would never be able to tell me, talking to her, even for a few moments, gave me some confidence.

The fire filled the makeshift space at night. The Vlah leader played the *çifteli* as the others took turns singing. I wish I could have heard them, but I didn't need to—I could see them pouring their hearts out like warm honey on a summer day. Life coursed through the leader's fingers, tearing down the floodgates of my eyes, first with a solitary tear, then with a blubbering bottom lip. I quickly lay on my side and half-covered my face with my blanket. I didn't want to be rude, but they must have been annoyed at seeing me cry so much. We've all been through Hell.

In the morning, my left jaw felt beaten and dislocated. My arm lay over my head and a thousand needles jabbed at me from the inside out. As if I was still rolling in the brambles in my dream. My left side prickled and ached, prickled and ached.

You slept hard, Heart said.

With extraordinary patience, I reminded her of the nightmare and its dry taste in my mouth. In my sleep, I was hiking in a lush, undisturbed forest. I climbed hill upon hill with ease. I came to a crest and suddenly, down, down, down, I tumbled. The forest became briars and vines of barbs and prickly weeds. I came to a stop in a tangle, cut and stinging. I looked to the ridgetop from which I had fallen and saw a pair of shoes, empty and the size of a grown man.

I sat up and stretched my legs, stiff as driftwood. The sun rose in degrees of dainty roses and fresh lemonade, dappling through the east window beside the fireplace. It crept along the floor, almost reaching my shins. I knew I was the last to wake up because I was alone.

I looked around for Shpresa. A panic gripped me around my ribs and my stomach. With a cold, quick inhale, I was awake and alert and remembered she left me two days ago, scared off by the men.

From where I sat, I could not see out the windows. The idea of waiting until someone checked on me was embarrassing, but my body refused to rise without a very worthy cause. I was still lost. My God, I was alive, and still, I was lost.

Like I said, you need a plan. You needed a plan before you left every-one you knew. Head, concise and logical. Then, Head went and hid in a corner to work out a defense against the nightmares. A paranoia was beginning to seep into Head's space that the nightmares were here to stay.

Heart ignored Head and looked me in the eyes. *Where is the Val we knew? The one who led her team through death and unthinkable cir-cumstances?*

She's back at that house on the cliff, the one overlooking the sea and overlooking the cave, playing cards and eating fish with her friends.

No. Where is the Val who told her superior she was going home and not following his orders?

He was no longer my superior. We were all but dismissed.

Excuses, and you know it! She's right here, wallowing. Yes, there, your beloved Heart said it. You're wallowing. Get up! Put a roof over your head.

I didn't have the courage to start rebuilding my own house. I would start at the front of the village, at old Fato's, by the welcome arch. I would need a hammer and nails and a saw. And wood not burnt to a crisp.

With a sigh, I stood up. Could I build a house with an inkling of stupid persistence, a fragile heart and healing legs?

I stepped outside, into the orange sunlight, to find breakfast and tools before I could talk myself out of it. I could spin myself in circles, in spirals toward insanity, and no one would be around to stop me.

The cooking fire smelled wet from wood the men must have chopped between storms. I was sure they had used up my neighbors' stores of logs and kindling. I smiled with gratitude and weakness, and nodded 'good morning' to everyone in the circle. The faint aroma of wildflower tea rose with the steam from an iron kettle. One of the women offered me a plate of hot, soupy cornmeal. I bowed.

It was uncomfortable, to be sure, not being able to communicate with ease. They seemed cheerful in each other's company. Their hand motions and clapping one another on the back suggested they teased each other often.

Like you and Xhevi teased Kosta and Endri, Heart said. A dagger twisted in my heart.

After the tea and mush, my belly felt warm and satisfied. I rinsed the plate in the pot of hot water, then turned it upside down on a log to dry.

I stood in front of everyone, waiting. They turned their attention to me and I pointed into the fire at the logs. I moved my arms in a chopping motion, then pretended to move one end of a two-person saw. I would need beams and planks. On them I would lay the salvageable slate roof tiles strewn about the village remains. Then, I put my hands over my head as a roof. The men, all holding hot tea, waited a minute, then bobbed their heads.

The men and women had a conversation, involving more enthusiastic arms waving in the air, and then several of them pointed to the forest east of Tragjas. The forest I had traveled with Ana and Xhevi.

The men nodded and stood. I fell in line behind them, to the north of town. I hoped it led to a roof and a door. They led me to our blacksmith's shed. Of course. We found some saws and even a couple of axes.

These might have been useful to the Nazis, Head commented.

Little forethought, those guys, Heart said.

Five men and I made our way down the hill, then up another one. Winter among bare trees is eerie enough, anytime, even more so without sound. It was disorienting.

We cut and hacked and trimmed pine trunks into rough planks for a new roof for old Fato's place. For me.

We walked home at the end of the day. No one had the strength to carry planks; we would return in the morning. I went to sleep pleased with the work we had done for the house. My limbs ached in a feel-good way. I felt like I was growing, reaching, making space for more muscle.

The well-deserved sleep was short-lived. The brambles and thorns came for me again. When I sat up, the room was bathed in diluted black, the embers at their dimmest, and everyone else still slept. I shivered from the sweat across my collarbones, under my arms and in the folds of my belly. I crawled on my hands and knees and added more logs to the fire. I encouraged it with a gentle breath until the twigs and logs caught, helpless in resisting. It was a magical, horrifying element. Its power was almost limitless. Only water stood as a valiant opponent. I couldn't get away from either of them. They were integral to my being and my world.

In the morning, I sat up and stretched to reach my toes. Every part of me was sore. I was the last to wake, again. The men would be ready to get to work. My excuse for my laziness was that the minutes of sleep almost equaled the number of minutes I spent in nightmare after nightmare.

I stepped outside to clean air and a cheery sun. If it could take human form this morning, it would be a little boy running, laughing until he collapsed in a pile of hiccups.

I saw straight away all the Vlah men standing in a semi-circle, near the campfire. The men's arms remained wrapped around their torsos. They were not involved in a tense conversation. There wasn't any gesticulation of the arms or any pacing back and forth. An argument would have been incongruous with the weather anyhow. I smelled tobacco. More than one wisp of smoke took flight and got lost in the bright, blue sky.

I walked closer, about ten feet from two of the men who had found me at the well. On the other side of this ring of black pants and white shirts stood a man in green, Partizan fatigues.

Dita

Valentine's Day fell on a Saturday. Dita and her family dared to defy the chilly weather and ate their eggs-and-toast breakfast on the balcony. With sweaters, the eastern sun, and Nana, there was nowhere else Dita wanted to be.

All four of them jumped when her phone buzzed on the table.

"Hey! Want to go out? Walk around?" Ilir sounded more enthusiastic than usual. She tipped her head to the side in confusion.

Dita stood and stepped to the edge of the balcony. "Good morning." She clipped her tone, sharp and questioning. Given his cold attitude the last time they were together, she didn't expect to hear from him. "When were you thinking?" It was just a bump in their road on their journey, no doubt.

"Whenever. We could walk in the park? Unless. You wanted to go somewhere for the night?"

Dita glanced at Nana, then rubbed her finger along the rail. "Hm. Let's start with the park."

"Sure, yeah."

"Are you … okay? You sound excited about something. The other night …" What she wouldn't do for an ounce of great-grandmother Mira's courage.

Ilir fake-coughed. "Me? It's Valentine's Day!"

"Okay, well, I'll call you when I'm ready," Dita said.

By the time she hurried down the building's stairs, she had settled her unsettling feelings. She left her misgivings at home with Nana and her parents.

Her heart fluttered when she saw Ilir holding a beautiful arrangement of flowers wrapped in green crepe paper. Purples, reds, pinks, orange even, and every texture, too.

Dita reached for them, hungry for the colors and the sentiment. "Thank you."

He wrapped an arm around her waist and kissed her with a Hollywood kiss. She slid her hand to the small of his back underneath his jacket.

"Hi," she said, giddy and overwhelmed. Intuition be damned.

"Hi." He kissed her forehead and his hands matted down her tight curls. "So." When he exhaled his nostrils flared.

"So?"

"Before we go, I have to tell you …" He slipped his hands over her shoulders then down her arms. "I accepted the job in the Istanbul office."

"The job? What job?"

Tears came hot and fast. Shock drowned out the hum of the cars and their honking at stoplights. It drowned out the smell of the oily puddles in the cracked asphalt. Her hands, the ones that fell away from his jacket and almost dropped the bouquet, grew hot and at the same time tingled like a numbing cold.

Behind the shock was a deafening hurt, silencing the questions screaming in her head.

He saw her face and paused. He patted her cheek and tried again, with a more tempered voice. "It's a bit of an advancement, with a pay raise, and it's in Istanbul. Istanbul! There's so much to do there. Don't you think? We'll walk the bazaars every weekend, we'll find an apartment on the Bosphorus, we'll—"

Her heart and soul were battling it out against his logic, leaving her speechless. Two against one.

Dita shook her head. She didn't want to galavant around the world—she had barely seen her homeland. She wasn't looking for brighter and bigger. And, Dita didn't want a fling. She wanted something deep, a tucked-away treasure kind of love.

"I thought ..." he started.

Finally. "This is my home," she managed.

Then, a slice of anger rose, belly-crawling on its elbows to be heard from the top of the hill. "I didn't even take the fellowship in Rome, with my sister. How could ... I ... I ... can't ... How ..." She couldn't. She couldn't finish her sentence. She couldn't run away with him.

"Bye, Ilir."

"You don't want to think about it?" he said to her back.

She turned around halfway. "No."

In high school art class, Dita once made paper from scratch. The process began with tearing paper-like material to bits, then mashing, mashing, mashing the shreds in a gooey liquid before straining it. Her ribs might have been the sieve, her heart the pulp, and her heart's beat the fist. Pound, pound, pound, squeeze, strain, strain. Let dry.

When Dita got upstairs, she tossed the bouquet on the dining table and flopped on the sofa. Dita's gaze fell on the flower book in the curio cabinet, and behind it, her great-Aunt Val's notebook. She retrieved it and sat beside Nana. Dita turned the pages carefully. Dita stopped at the one most familiar to her. The page with the word *Home*. It had been traced and retraced, written over and over, and circled a half dozen times.

She wiped her tears and smiled widely. Yes, this was it. Her home was here, not in Istanbul, and not with Ilir. Dita held her grandmother's hand and followed her blue veins and bones, strong and reflexive under her sun-stained skin. This was her story, her dig site, her treasure. She felt so lucky to have found it.

On Monday, there was no doubt in Dita's mind she had made the right decision. Even still, she ached a little.

"Morning," Agon said, not a whisper, not an attention-grabbing shout, but just right.

"Morning," Dita replied. She needed busy work, something that wouldn't take any effort. She flicked on the lamp in the corner of her desk and stared at the beige lamp shade. She studied the texture, the thinnest of threads woven together to create the blandest color known to the human race. The most interesting thing to her in that moment was how textiles were dyed. Someone ought to research that, in regards to Albanian imports and exports.

Imports. Exports. Ilir.

Agon snapped her out of it. "Review the Scutari coins."

"You finished them. I'm sure they're flawless."

"Re–" he said.

His voice made her think of trees. A rush of winter wind through pine trees.

"Sure. Right. Review. On it."

Dita felt his eyes on her when she crossed the room to the wall of oak and glass cabinets. First, by era. Bronze. Then, by location. Central Mountains. Size: One to two inches. Material: Gold.

Again, gold.

"Everything checked out, Agon. I told you."

Dita opened the Incomplete drawer like a glutton for punishment. Her eyes glazed over, not focusing on anything. It was a drawer without any leads. A broken necklace, a pair of earrings missing their gems, the Rodoni bracelet, a single link of a necklace.

Dita closed the drawer. On her return to her desk, she perused a slim bookcase among the thick and deep shelves.

The voice of reason in her head encouraged her. *Yes, that's it. Do that.*

Rather than pull her hair out staring at the ancient puzzle pieces, Dita worked through a thin book on clothing of the eighteenth century in the Balkans (someone's thesis, was a safe assumption), a helpful yet dull book on trade routes (yet no specifics on Rodoni). The lovely book of maps that started it all remained, albeit hidden, on her desk as a constant companion.

The door at the top of the stairs opened. Raco and his darting eyes descended.

"Good day," he said. He didn't have a commanding presence like Meta, but all eyes were on him.

"I've come to tell you all that, part of my duty as Director of Cave Artifacts is to look at the finances." He pursed his lips.

"And, I have done this. Effective immediately, the Cave Artifacts Department is dissolved. We will focus our efforts and our *limited* resources on Apollonia, Butrinti, Ali Pasha's castle, and other, larger, more obvious"—he looked directly at Dita—"sites."

Dita's jaw dropped. "But—"

Raco raised an eyebrow at her.

"Ms. Arbani, if there are any unfinished projects already in our possession here, you're to *finish* those now."

A dead-end task. Dita lowered herself into her chair and turned her back to Raco.

Agon stood. "Sir, we have evidence that people lived in Rodoni Castle. In my opinion, it would be worth the effort. We could make it larger; we could make it an attraction."

Raco stuck out his bottom lip. "You could, I suppose. But not on my watch. I expect with your expertise, A–"

"Agon." Agon's knuckles brushed the top of his desk.

"With your expertise, you ought to expect a leadership position at the Apollonia site."

What Dita wouldn't do to slip away. She was a little embarrassed to be called out in front of her colleagues. But mostly, she wanted to get away from Raco and his lack of respect for history. Which, really, was a lack of respect for the future. The fire of anger and purpose rose in her chest and reddened the skin under her blouse. She knew the ins and outs of this room, but now, when she needed them most, she couldn't find any tissues.

"Sir," Agon began again.

"Unless you'd like to help Dita with her projects." Raco waved his hands in the air to finish the conversation. He hustled up the stairs, back to his office and number-crunching. Agon sat down.

Dita laid her forehead in her left hand, feeling sorry for herself. She wanted to act like Raco's dismantling of her department was not a big deal. She knew she should believe there was still important work to be done.

"I'm sorry," Agon said.

"What? No, don't be," she said. She couldn't raise her eyes to meet his.

"Ah! I see now!" Agon said, keeping his voice low, trying so hard to get her to smile. "It's just as well he did that to you. You're not a historian. You are a natural-born actor."

He crumbled her defense. She looked at him from under her hand and a smile crept across her mouth.

And he doesn't even know about Ilir.

What would she tell her parents? And Nana? One bracelet buried in a wall, with no leads, was worthless. She might as well put it back in the castle. No one would know the difference. In fact, she would be quite happy to spend the rest of her career in the lab without a single promotion. Or, she would be happy to fulfill the crazy idea of hacking away at the castle until she found all the bracelets. Who knows how many there might be?

Dita made it to the end of the day, but barely.

The sky was somber when she opened the museum's front door. Her chest felt hollowed out and her feet seemed almost as heavy as her heart.

"Not today," she said to the gallant fighters overhead in the mural on the museum's face, a mural of billions of pieces of tile and stone. She couldn't bear to look at them to say good night like she sometimes did. They were not concerned with her feelings—how could they be concerned? They were larger than life, brave beyond comprehension, and impossible to ignore. They embodied The Resistance. It seemed natural that anyone would resist a foreign power's invasion. What did she know about fighting? Her emotional state turned embarrassing as she compared it to the lives they had led.

The surrounding cityscape took on the shadows of the setting sun— blue and black and bruised. In the daylight, the government buildings stood in their sturdy red and buttery yellow paint. Without the sun, the buildings simply took up space without a defined function. Dita could almost laugh at the similarity.

Kitchen lights and peals of conversation poured out of slightly open windows. The traffic's exhaust pressed on her. Her nose tickled with dust, canned tomatoes, and onions. Not for the first time, the frantic rush-hour drivers weaving in and out of nonexistent lanes annoyed her. Today, every annoyance clawed at her, amplified.

Dita's phone buzzed in her pocket. The lump in her throat stifled her. Silence and the mopeds' whiny acceleration greeted Agon in place of her voice.

"Hey," Agon said, exactly as he had in the lab that morning.

Dita tried her best to sound casual, "Hey."

"Hey, I wanted to say ... I don't know. He's an idiot, that's for sure. It's all politics, you know?"

Dita wiggled her nose and bobbed her head into the phone, "Yeah, yeah, I know."

"Do you want to meet up for a drink or something? If you're not, I mean, I guess you'll see Ilir, sorry ..." Agon said.

"Uh, yeah no, we're not. We're not together." Anger to add to the hurt. Salt *and* lemon juice to the open wound.

"Oh. I'm sorry. Again," he said. It proved too difficult for either of them to come up with a quip after that, so the quiet filled the void.

One short "Ha!"—a cough-laugh burst out of Dita before she could prevent it. She laughed at the twistedness of a path that was once, and not very long ago, so straight and narrow and clear. "Thanks. I'm going to go home."

"Sure. See you tomorrow?"

"Yeah, okay."

Dita spent a week in self-pity, subjecting everyone around her to frowns and minimal conversation. She spent another week in self-indulgence, starting with that handbag in a store window she passed every day, twice a day. She didn't need it, and worse, would probably never use it. Two ice creams and two Nescafé frappés in one day? You only live once.

Mira

I kept my eyes on the path into camp.

Our men hobbled in at dusk. Rezart was not in front where he belonged. At first, I didn't even see Plak, head and shoulders above the rest.

Despite my hip, the depth of my panic propelled me ahead. I broke into a pathetic, supernatural walk-shuffle. Qazim called after me. My body threatened to vomit from the pain with every other step.

"Rinaj! Where's Rezart? Where's Rezart?" I shoved the poor man toward the campfire. "Hey!" Not one of them lifted their eyes to me. No one replied.

I couldn't find enough air. And still, a rattling howl came from my throat, from my spine.

Pulling up the rear, Ymer led Plak. With a click of his tongue, he brought the weary horse to a stop. I grazed my fingers the length of the grayed coat, black from blood.

The men had harnessed a crude stretcher to be pulled by Plak, and on it lay Rezart. I knew the shape of him, even covered by their vests and sheep hides and torn coats. They had covered his face.

"Hey!" I coughed, fighting to breathe through my bloody, snot-filled nose. I kicked the edge of the stretcher with the bottom of my

234

foot. I stumbled back and my vision went double. The vest that had been placed over his head slid to his shoulders. I choked at the sight of his purple, graying face.

"Hey!" The pleading rose from my belly and scraped the edges of my throat. "Rezart! Look at me!"

I don't know when I began crying. The day I met him, I suppose.

His hair was crusty with blood and his bottom lip cut wide open and swollen. With my bad leg outstretched and the other bent on the stretcher, I straddled it and pressed my fingertips into his slack, gummy jaw.

"Open your eyes, dammit! You promised! You hear me? You swore to *me*!" My tears and spit splattered onto his nose. "You ..." —I cupped his face and stroked his eyebrows with my thumbs— "*promised*," I said through clenched teeth. I lowered my head next to his, cheek to cheek, my lips to his ear.

All I could do was fall in line beside him. The wooden branches of the stretcher squeaked as I positioned my body around his. Plak readjusted to accommodate my weight. I sniffed and wiped my nose on my grimy shirt. Ymer clicked his tongue again and we set off.

When he stopped Plak in front of our shelter, I rolled off the stretcher and stood, dumb. I was in a tunnel and far off, but not far at all. People shouted questions, and others were already wailing. The men carried Rezart's body inside. We had slept there the night before, or a lifetime ago, with the three children. Our three, adopted children.

I limped behind the men, and once inside, I put out my arm for the nearest wall to support me. I pressed my hands flat and slid to the cool, dirt floor.

When I woke, everything in my narrow line of sight lay behind a veil of gray, as if a layer of tattered muslin covered my eyes. The light was unchangingly dim. The room in which I lay had a dirt floor and stone walls. There was no furniture, save a single chair with three legs. In front of me, the wall opened up for a fireplace. I could not recall seeing it the night before. A fire had dimmed to embers. My fingers grazed the rough edges of two blankets. I could not recall those from the night before, either. I drew them up over my shoulders and shivered.

With a snail's speed, I turned onto my back, despite the lights shooting across my eyes. My body swelled with nausea.

"Rezart," I whispered. I closed my eyes and begged the sick sea in me to go away.

I became aware of snoring coming from behind my head. I was sure that, if I could lift my arm overhead, I could touch whoever it was.

"Hello?" My voice came out garbled and weak. I tried again and again.

"Mira?" A sleepy, groggy someone.

"Genti? Is that you?"

With a shuffle, he was next to me. He ruffled, then patted my hair. "Deda and I are in here with you. We moved you into a house in town. We captured it. Do you remember us carrying you?"

"Rezart, Genti. Rezart …"

"I know. I know."

What could he know?

"Rinaj, Pejani, all of us, we prepared his body. We're waiting for you before we begin the cry."

"I can't … I can't." I reached for his arm, his shirt, something to hold. His hand was warm over mine.

"Mira." His tone said it all. That there was no choice, that it would be done whether I was there or not, that women are not ever considered, that I was a leader and everyone still expected me to be that. But my soul had left the night before and it was out wandering, looking for him.

236

"I can't walk."

My heart was so desperate to breathe.

"I will carry you. It's my turn." He smiled, but the beginning of sunrise caught the tears welling in his eyes. "I'll go and get some breakfast and tell them you're awake."

"God," I moaned. Both a plea and a question.

Vera bustled in with the aroma of cornbread and wild garlic, doubtless in the form of broth. I did not converse, I did not argue; I was numb.

Before I knew it, the fireplace was roaring with flames. Tringa carried in a pot full of water. A bit sloshed out with each step and created splatters of mud. As Vera hung the pot over the fire, I realized they meant to clean me. I could not protest this; the scalding water might be a balm.

After the scrubbing, Vera combed my hair with her fingers and braided it from one temple and down across the base of my head. It was a lovely gesture, but it was for naught. Nothing mattered now.

When I was decent, my brothers came in to collect me. Deda held the door open for Genti and my lame body. Even if I had had the strength to walk, I would have crumpled in the doorway at the sight of inert, shattered Love. I screamed and threw my head back and beat Genti's chest with my fist. He faltered but kept me in his strong arms.

Rezart's body lay straight ahead. As if he had been waiting for me to get dressed and ready, too. I was a dressed ghost and not ready for anything.

He no longer looked gray and pathetic. They had presented him in full regalia and pride. The small, silver buttons of his undercoat gleamed from his collar to his waistband. My band matched his—the one with sequins along the edges and brown triangles made of beads evenly spaced in the center. His leather shoes had been cleaned and shined. His *plis* sat perfectly, and perfectly clean, on his head. The pistols and knives had been left behind.

Genti set me down on the left side of the circle. He had found a drum. I took it from him to beat out the sounds in the valleys of my heart.

I began the cry. I was delirious. I was in love.

In mourning, the primary expectation in the mountains is to remain in an ever-present state of sadness. Too easy. Those left in the land of the living are not to leave their house for forty days. Doubled, I would not know the difference.

After the cry and the burial, Genti brought me back to the house with the fireplace and laid me on the straw pallet. He said something about leaving in the next couple of days. My backside warmed from the fire, and I couldn't stop shivering. I faced the window. It didn't matter who entered or left. Through the window, the one with the broken glass, the rising sun arrived the next morning as it pleased, in its unerring fortitude and pervasiveness. It pierced my eyes.

I watched it come: first, a spoonful of light, then a ribbon, then a confident stride across the floor until it met my pieces of charcoal. Deda had pulled them out of the ashes yesterday and put them in front of me without a word. They were bits of hope; his effort to keep me on this side of madness.

But Revenge was a bitch, never satiated, and eager to see me fall. She sat on the windowsill and picked her nails clean.

"Didn't you get what you wanted?" she asked. "You wanted … what was it? … You wanted their blood."

I rose up on my elbow. "You can keep it all! I don't want them!" I screamed back to her. To no one. It was too late and she knew it, and she laughed and cackled to no end.

I drew to spite her.

The sun was a better artist than me, broadening Rezart's forehead with its light and adding color to his cheeks. It even created the damn *luster* in his eyes that appeared when he saw me. I merely hovered over to contribute the tears to make a mess of the black dust, to smudge his hairline and the crease of his nose.

I drew to remember him.

The clear pictures in my mind's eye of Rezart distracted me from the sickening, paralyzing pain shooting down my leg. Rezart in command, assigning positions, greeting another commander or one of my brothers with a smile. His absolute contentment when he recited poetry to me at night. Rezart and me in the forest, wandering instead of sleeping. Rezart unbraiding my hair over my vulnerable, tingling skin, as if it was the deepest of meditations. Rezart and me under our layers of wool and capes, his legs curled behind mine and his hand laid across my long thigh. His thumb brushed my skin, back and forth, back and forth.

"Is it a lullabye to you, stroking my leg?" I asked him once when he was on the cusp of sleep.

I felt him swallow before he answered. "You don't know what it is to touch you," he whispered. He pulled himself closer and spoke to my vertebrae, sending shivers to my toes. "It's impossible to me that you are real. I do it because if I die in my sleep, I am already halfway to heaven."

My thirst was interminable; another gift from Revenge, I'm certain. Tringa came often, but not often enough, and without a word, to give me water. The water seemed out of reach, all the time. Everyone still assumed I was ambitious. I recalled a young woman who yelled for a chance to fight against the Ottomans. She seemed to have moved on to another body, in another world.

A little while ago, Deda and Qazim came into the room.

My brother squatted in front of me and bounced on his toes. "It's time to go home, Mira." His level of anticipation was foreign to me.

Qazim quietly inspected my wound through the split seam in my pants.

"My leg. It's not healing, Deda."

"It will, Mira, it will." I shook my head, knowing otherwise.

"Is that what I'm smelling, my hip? Qazim, tell me."

"Yes," he whispered.

"My whole body is giving up, Deda. I can feel it. Take the kids home. Take them to the mountains. You will, won't you? Deda?"

"Yes," he said. So much anguish in such a small word.

"Tell Tringa to come here," I replied. "And please, may I have some water?"

Tringa sat near my knees. She tried to smile, and it took my breath away. Her big, dark hair and her square jaw and the endlessness of her eyes. I reached for her hand and she took it. My sleeve cinched up my arm to reveal my wrist.

"Untie this." I shook my hand in hers a bit.

Tringa bent over to find the knot of the bracelet. Her face was bathed in the sun, highlighting the freckles over her nose and her cheeks.

"I won't make it home," I said. "Our army will take you to my home. Listen to Mindi and Musine. They live in my house now. Listen to my brothers. This bracelet is for you and Gjoni and Sofia. It is valuable, do you understand? When you are old enough, go to Rodoni Castle and find the matching one, if you need it. It is hidden inside the outer wall. There, also, you will see the water. God, Tringa, the sea is so beautiful." A tear fell from my eye and another pooled on the bridge of my nose. "Never let anyone take this from you, understand?"

Silently, she agreed.

"Go and help Vera, please. Go."

Val

The Partizan stood tall and confident in his broad shoulders. His skin was as caramel as his hair poking out from under his green cap. I surmised he was telling a story. His eyebrows, at the moment, furrowed like two arrows shooting and crashing into one another. His eyes sat dark in the shadows of his cap. The sun kissed his chin. I never knew there could be such a thing as a perfect nose, but there it was.

He finished speaking. He smiled with closed lips as he listened to the Vlahs. A dimple formed in his cheek. He was, in a word, handsome.

And in his arms, Shpresa tilted her head and blinked at me.

I shrieked, unabashed by whatever the sound may or may not have been. The men parted, as surprised as I was. In an instant, I held Shpresa against my body. My surroundings fell away, only me and Shpresa and her smooth feathers and her static head twitches.

"Please don't ever leave me again," I whispered into the top of her head.

The man shuffled his feet and waited for me to finish my moment of reunion. His cracked boot blended sand and char underfoot.

Our eyes met and I saw peace. Peace incarnate.

Truth be told, eyes don't tell us anything. They don't change when they see love or hate, or show anger or surprise, remorse, or joy. No, not the eyes. It is the muscles around them that dissolve fears or convey disgust. Less romantic, but true. His eyes defied this science. They were the epitome of harmony, the color of surety and assurance, incapable of conceit or malice.

You could drown in that comfort, get lost in a serenity like that, Heart said.

He broke our gaze and looked at the men, then back at me. He pointed to his round, right ear. He asked me by raising his eyebrows and shaking his head. His lips moved. This time, with him, I kept my chin up and bobbed my head to confirm my deafness. He and the other men exchanged a short conversation that ended with everyone stepping away and taking seats around the cooking fire.

I stretched out my arms to look at Shpresa, to inspect her from head to toe. With a lowered voice, I used some strong words to reprimand her. She ducked her head. I interpreted that as an apology full of shame.

But no.

This is not Shpresa! Head yelled, on my side of a situation for the first time.

This one was missing Shpresa's black spot on her neck. My mouth opened, then shut, inhibited once more by my auditory deficiency.

The Vlahs put the Partizan in the middle, at the head of the circle. A few continued to stand, but others found a stump on which to sit. The herdsmen passed around a bottle of *raki*. Absurdly early in the morning, but to die is better than to have nothing to offer a guest.

I stood in front of him with tight lips, jaw locked with the deception. I opened my mouth, then shut it again. I walked between the men and sat against a rock, behind and close to my supposed comrade.

[This is not my pigeon!] I wrote in Nina's notebook.

I rapped his back with the notebook. He turned his fit rectangle of a body toward me and read.

242

The man agreed with a nod, stuck out his chest and pointed to himself.

[Mine] he wrote. I watched his mouth, his full lips, form the word, reiterating his written reply. He smiled. Again, that dimple. He handed me the notebook. He held my stare for a moment longer. He did not turn away from me but waited.

[Yours?! Why did you give her to me?] I thrust the book into his hand. Embarrassment crept up my throat at my hasty mistake. I examined his face while he read and replied. His jaw was chiseled from stone but softened at his chin, dipping into a cleft ever so slightly.

I clenched my hands into fists, released, clenched again.

Heart had a question of her own. *Can't he write any faster?*

He handed me the book. Before I read, I cut a glance at him and saw one corner of his mouth upturned. He returned to the conversation with the Vlahs.

[You took him from me. The more you take, the more you leave behind. What am I?]

A riddle. Only two people in the world have provoked me with riddles, and one of them was graying at the temples and rotund and quite likely dead. I kept a tight hold on not-Shpresa. Mute, and thrilling from head to toe, I stood. I wavered. I repositioned my feet. My scrappy existence, my immediate place in the world, was a blur.

Head sat back, dumbfounded. Heart squealed with delight. Delight.

The man looked over his shoulder at me. He stood.

I wrapped my free arm around him, hoping he understood that I understood. "You found me?" I whispered, weak in every way. "You found *me*?"

His cheeks formed like hearts underneath his eyes with his smile. He nodded, his turn to be speechless. He drew out the shape of a word; maybe he was saying 'yes,' dramatic and exaggerated.

I looked down at his riddle in the book. Now that I wasn't furious about not-Shpresa, I recognized the handwriting I had come to look forward to, to want too much.

He took the book from me and scribbled. [I need you.]

I laughed. It burst out of me, out of my control. The feeling of it lit and consumed every cell, alive and dancing. All you know are my terrible riddles, I wanted to say.

[How did you find me?]

[Tirana. I found your brigade. Kosta and Xhevi told me where I could find you. And it sounds like you're the only one with a pigeon down here. Where did yours go?]

Answers led to more questions.

Head chimed in, irritated. *Talk! He's going to come all this way and then leave because you don't like how you sound? You don't know how you sound!*

[What's your name?] I asked in the book.

[Zamir] He continued to write, turning the book toward me so I could read while he wrote. [Will you talk? Can you? I hope it is not painful.]

I took a step back and bit my bottom lip, not from apprehension but to rein in my fragile emotions.

Heart and Head were in agreement. A breeze, a whisper of the conviction I had lost with my hearing filled me.

[Not here. Tell the Vlahs we'll be back later.]

I led Zamir to old Fato's house. As we walked, he took off his cap and scratched his head. He kept the cap scrunched in his hand. His eyes turned to dark slits as he squinted from the sun. He looked around at the remains of everything I had ever known. Nothing kept him from walking forward.

Inside the house, my ankles felt the coolness of the ground.

"I am," I began. And the tears began, too. I combed through my hair. It held the sun's radiance. I cleared my throat and turned a full circle before trying again. "We are rebuilding. Starting here." I put my hands out, then let them fall to my sides.

He circled a finger around the one-room house and then pointed at me.

No, it is not my house. "No," formed in my lips, with my voice. I felt its singular vibration between my tongue and teeth. A simple word I had taken for granted and one I had not used enough. No, Ana, don't go to the trucks. No, Mami, Babi, no! No, Prifti, I am not going to Tirana. No, I cannot go on. No. I will not give up.

Heart nudged me.

"Where is your family?" I asked, too loudly, perhaps. But who would mind?

Exactly! Who will mind? Head declared.

Zamir shook his head and shrugged. Alone. God, everyone's alone.

I looked down at my hands and the medley across my knuckles of pallid white from the adrenaline and red from the cold air. I took a small step toward him, shaking from the inside out. I attempted a more quiet voice. "You are welcome to stay. You could help." I tilted my words at the end. I meant for it to sound like a question. I hoped.

In two strides across the dirt and burned floor, Zamir's fingertips pressed into the back of my head, tangled in my hair. The thick bases of his thumbs lay on either side of my nose, smashing the last tears. He tipped my head up. His eyes glanced at my mouth, then again into my eyes.

Yes, you can drown in peace like that, I agreed, in eyes like wild honey.

His lips healed mine, smooth and sweet. My legs buckled, weak with rapture. I felt encompassed, whole, inside his unerring hold, inside his lean, solid arms.

Zamir took a half step back and looked over me, from the neck up.

I'm going to need a week to recover from that, said dear, dear Heart.

He brushed dust from my hair and traced my eyebrows with his fingers.

Joy. That's what that face is saying, Heart said.

He seemed to be made of boundless strength. I was tempted to pour all my troubles into him. I doubted they could faze him. He kept me inside his arms and looked up to inspect our roofing progress.

He may be a builder. We won't know until you talk, Head said.

Zamir pointed to the sky, where a roof ought to be, and spun his finger in a circle.

"Yes, let's go," I managed, still soaring from his nonverbal answer. "We have the pieces, now they need to go up."

That night, we sought and surveyed each other under the new roof.

Every day, Zamir did the work of three men, cutting, hauling, and lifting. He and the Vlah men chopped trees and made planks for roofs. Some were cut smaller for shutters and some were nailed together to make doors.

I spent days collecting slate wherever I could find it, among debris and disaster. It was a test of my nerves, as much as planting a bomb, to walk into a house. Fear fed hungrily on me. Even in daylight, I feared I would find a body. Or, almost as terrible, a memory.

If I wasn't gathering slate, I foraged for edible roots, nuts, or late berries ignored or rejected by the forest animals. If I wasn't foraging, I stayed with the women. It was better to keep my body busy; all of me hurt less.

After we finished old Fato's house, we covered the Vlahs' house, even though they would leave soon enough. I hoped their herd would multiply in the spring. I hoped they knew they had a place to come back to, if they chose, in the fall.

Some days, we woke at dawn, and if the sky was clear, Zamir and I walked to the bay and set fish traps. A few weeks passed, filled with renewal, smiles, and lovemaking. Being in his company began to sew up the hole in my heart.

Still, my nightmares plagued me every other night. Monsters and empty shoes and Ana, running in the wind. Zamir understood and held me when my sweat turned cold.

One night, I curled my body into Zamir's. He stroked my hair, and I spoke into his chest. "I can't stand it anymore. We have to go." I felt him nod, he kissed my head, and that was that.

To the One Who Finds This—

If you are reading this it means two things: you were looking for something, and the world is in a better place. Nothing could be worse than what the Earth has managed to survive. If we deserve to survive is another matter. 'Survived' may not be the right word, anyway. 'We're still here' is more appropriate. Millions are not.

After the last nightmare in Tragjas, I couldn't stay. I thought maybe if we left, I'd stop seeing my little sister run toward me with goats chasing her. Maybe if we left, I wouldn't see my mother with her hands on her hips while she talked to her lifelong friends. This weight, the weight of my past and its ghosts, almost crushed me. I know we need voices and the sea, laughter, and a living, breathing community. Those of us still here need to dance, create, and love. These things are easier to write about than do, most days.

But, I couldn't go too far. I could not. What if my family came back, on the wings of a miracle? I am not strong enough to continue walking among the ghosts, but I can be their guardian from a distance. We're one hill closer to the sea, busy establishing Tragjas i Ri, or New Tragjas.

Zamir reconnected with a few comrades. It is a testament to their friendship and their confidence in Zamir to move here and build a new town. We've named ourselves the village council, as any proper village must have. And, a couple of residents of Tragjas returned recently. They had fled just in time. Together, the men are building houses.

Our two-room house faces north, uphill. Sweeping south, we've planted grapevines and corn. Here, the sea breeze plays with the white curtains all day and all night.

I dug out the roots of my mother's bougainvillea and planted them on our eastern edge, the side of our old Tragjas. I will let it grow untamed.

Ana is alive. She found me three months ago. How can I express the way my heart felt? It burst and healed in the same moment. What was dead and gone was in fact alive and well. She brought with her her husband and their baby boy, Murat.

After she was taken prisoner by the Germans, they handed her off to the Ballisti and she was transferred half a dozen times. She managed to escape in October 1944, one month before the liberation. She has a secure job with the Party and as such is building a life in Tirana. At the end of our reunion visit, I was grateful to not hear her say goodbye. It hurt enough to see her drive away.

I signed my name, Valentina Muskaj.

I folded the paper into thirds and placed it in a damn British munitions box, stamped *DN-81112* in yellow paint. I said goodbye to our rendezvous cave and walked through the woodland, back to Zamir in Tragjas i Ri.

Dita

Spring arrived early, urgent and determined after winter gave one last rainstorm.

Agon quietly attached himself to the Durrës Castle project. "It's close by. If you need anything ..." he had explained.

"No, it's okay. Really," Dita had said.

On the first Wednesday in March, Dita went upstairs to walk through the Independence exhibit one last time before it was dismantled and replaced with an art history exhibit.

She was afraid of the ultimate sin against the dead: to forget them. Raco had meant to embarrass her, but now it was a point of pride that Dita had been tasked with clearing the Incomplete drawer. She would tackle it and finish it as a thank-you gift to the women in her family, in her land. She wouldn't let them down; they would be remembered.

By the time she returned to the lab, everyone had cut out for the long weekend. On her desk lay a book she had never seen before. *The Music of Balkan Tribes under the Sultans* scrolled across the top. The beautiful cover displayed an Impressionist-like painting of women holding hands in a circle. They glowed in sunset's hues. Each had one leg lifted higher than the other, indicating a dance. On the first page was a note in rushed

handwriting, "Time, and music, heals all wounds. Happy Women's Day
— Agon"

She sat with a plop and chewed on her thumbnail.

Dita walked home that evening, mocking Raco's words from a few
weeks prior: "Ms. Arbani, you may work on the unfinished objects ..."
Precisely. Like the rest of her life—unfinished and incomplete.

"That's it!" Dita said aloud. Oh, very much out loud. "Unfinished!"
She spun around and broke into a jog. An uncomfortable jog with clogs
on her feet and friction between her thighs. The front doors were locked.
She caught her breath while she called Agon.

"Are you still close to work? Can you come back?"

Dita ran along the long side of the gigantic building, to the staff
entrance she had used a handful of times.

Locked. She shook the handle, just like characters in the thriller
movies.

"I'm coming!" a muffled voice called from the inside. One of the jani-
tors opened the door. "Thought I left it unlocked, I apologize."

"No, it's okay, it's okay. That's twice now you've saved me," Dita
said, flustered, and ran past him. "Thank you!"

"Incomplete, incomplete," over and over she mumbled to herself.
She came to an abrupt stop in front of the file cabinet containing the rid-
iculous drawer. Dita's teeth chattered from adrenaline.

She opened the Unfinished drawer. She knew what she was looking
for: back left compartment, a box containing the incomplete earrings
and the Rodoni bracelet. She lifted the box from its place and set it in
front of her.

"Hi!"

"Agh!" Dita held her hand to her heart. "Agon, don't scare me like
that."

"Sorry. What are you doing?"

"Come and see." Dita narrowed her eyes. She held the Rodoni gold between two fingers and hovered it over one of the earrings missing its stone.

"Dita," Agon whispered.

"You think it's a match?"

"Do you have the other one?"

"No, Nana has it. But the measurements are the same."

Nana. Her gold at Rodoni.

She looked at Agon and he didn't look away.

"Thank you for the book."

"You're welcome."

"I should get some gloves," she said.

"Yes, yes, you should," Agon said.

"I'll measure again, then place the gold in one of the earrings."

"Really?"

"It's the same as cleaning something, then replacing it, I figure, don't you think?"

"Yeah. Let's do it."

"Tell me what you know about Queen Teuta's suitors," Dita said. She set up a bare table with the jewelry, opened the toolbox full of calipers and monocles, turned on the table light and put on a pair of latex gloves.

"Oh, you got me there. Sounds like you know."

Dita spoke gently, keeping her concentration on the gold. "Who would have the guts to come to the court of the most successful pirate queen of her time? She probably laughed at the gifts she was given. I would. But they couldn't come empty-handed, either."

"They would bring jewelry fit for a queen."

"Exactly," Dita smiled.

The gold fit in the earring.

∞

Dita slept in the next morning, feeling she deserved it after yesterday's momentous discovery: Nana owned jewelry once owned by the pirate queen of Illyria.

Also, it was Women's Day. Not an excuse, but a reason to sleep in. She slept in for the mothers bleeding out and the women who disguised themselves as men in order to keep the family property. For the poverty-stricken; the ill females who get out of bed anyway and go about their daily labors; for the girls younger than she who would face society's pressure to be everything, all the time.

She chose her clothes as if it was the first day of school. A yellow scoop-neck top to match the weather and her best jeans that flared at the bottom. Her yellow lace bra gave her a little boost. Dita's studious frown lifted to a smile. The bra: a tool to trick the eye. Women are powerful magicians indeed.

On the television in the living room, the anchorman read the newspaper headlines aloud while the overhead camera showed the front page. Dita pulled the fourth espresso shot, one for each of them, from Nora's machine. It was becoming normal. "Let's go to Djati for lunch. My treat."

The restaurants on the western face of Mount Dajti boasted incredible views of the city. On a clear day, maybe a holiday such as today, when cars weren't clogging the roads and clogging the air, one could almost see the coast.

"Nonsense. *My* treat," Murat replied. "What kind of man would I be if you paid for us? And on Women's Day, of all days?" He smiled at her so she knew he hadn't forgotten the day's significance.

"Fine. But we'll go?" Dita looked from her father to her mother to

Nana. A round of the signature head bobbing in the form of an infinity symbol. Everyone except Nana.

Murat guided the car into the parking lot adjacent to the Restaurant Panorama. Even the cars had a great view. The road continued on past the establishment, up, up Mount Dajti to the row of antennas at the very top.

Upon entering Panorama, guests were greeted with a wall of windows overlooking Tirana. Green hills rose and fell on its outskirts like protective older brothers.

Inside, opposite the windows, along a solid white wall, was the restaurant bar, where the waiters lingered when they weren't taking orders or delivering food. The minimal decor consisted of a silver and white recessed ceiling and navy blue vases as tall as Dita's waist.

"Good afternoon," a waiter said with a nod of a greeting. He led them to a table set at a diagonal near the windows. The sun had begun to slide along the floor. Dita felt its warmth on her ankles and calves when she sat.

"What can I bring you to drink?" He clasped his hands behind his back, ready to memorize.

"Let's start with red," Dita replied. She ordered enough food to fill the table and then some.

With a quiet coolness and deftness of hand, the waiter poured the wine. He and his assistant returned soon after with two trays covered with platters of fries, a plate of cheese, three small plates of green salad, yogurt with olive oil, cornbread, a bowl of olives and mushroom-smothered steaks. The sting of the vinegar and onions in the salad, the bread covered in yogurt, and saltiness of the meat almost made Dita go cross-eyed.

Dita's phone rang halfway through their meal and easy conversation. She let it ring. Her parents questioned her with silent eyes.

"What? I'll call them back. If it's Nora, she'll call you next. I don't want to eat this cold." With her fork, she snagged two fries and dipped them in her sauce. "Right, Nana?"

Nana sent a half-smile around the table.

By the end of the meal, Dita was full to her ears. The sun had lowered enough to warm her hips and thighs through the glass wall. When the younger waiter whisked away the tray full of empty white ceramic dishes, the thinner, older waiter suggested dessert. "Coffee? Ice cream?"

After such a delightful meal, no one seemed capable of answering such complicated questions. Lena finally replied. "Yes, four espressos, but we'll have them outside, please. And four cups of vanilla ice cream. Right, Dita?"

"Yes, vanilla," she agreed and linked Nana's arm with hers. Outside, the sun bathed them from head to toe.

They sat on one side of a lounge chair, next to another chair. A table sat in between the chairs, perfect for their bowls and cups.

"Who did I miss?" Dita asked herself and pulled out her phone.

"Hey, Boss," Agon said as a greeting when he answered her return call. She rolled her eyes and smiled but didn't correct him.

"What's up? Did you mean to call?"

"Yes, I'm in Tragjas. You've got to come see this for yourself."

"What's there?" A chill ran down her spine, followed by a sigh—another place in her own tiny country she'd never visited. She played with the wafer triangle wedged into the ice cream.

"There's something here you have to see. But, it's not just that. You have to *feel* what it's like here."

Another chill.

"Are you staying there for the night?"

"Yeah, I figured, why not? You know? There's no place to stay here, exactly, so I'm staying in Vlora." He paused. "Will you come?"

"Yes, totally. But I won't be able to get there before dark, so I'll catch a minibus first thing in the morning."

"The bus station in Vlora is in the center of town. I'll meet you there."

Dita insisted her family come along, but her mother insisted more: no. Dita gathered from the shine in her eyes that Lena wanted to give her space and didn't feel like traveling with Nana right now.

It took half an hour to reach the edge of town. The city limits gave way to villages surrounded by fields. Fields and villages and blue skies for three more hours.

Dita and her bus drove into Vlora as the morning shifted to the shade of light blue jeans. The houses and apartment buildings presented visitors with uniformity: unity in their shutters, warm orange tile roofs, and white stucco exteriors. A few pedestrians strolled along the wide, tiled boulevard. Time for the mid-morning coffee. Others hustled with a fresh catch and a bag of groceries, stressed to have lunch ready by two o'clock. If they were anything like Lena.

The driver parked at the end of a line of buses, in front of a mini mart. A packaged ice cream price list hung in one of its windows, frozen in time, bleached from the overbearing sun. Posters of last summer's local concerts curled on billboards that popped up out of the sidewalk every fifty feet. On the other side of the bus, marble benches, palm trees and an Independence monument filled a long and wide meridian, splitting the directions of traffic. Come July, an available hotel room or empty cafe table would be hard to find.

The sea air reached for Dita's hair through the bus's open windows. The moisture would crown her with a halo of frizz within the hour. And the smell of fresh fish, well, one either loved it or hated it.

Agon was waiting for her.

"Hey." He pushed his glasses up his nose. "You made it."

"I did."

They greeted each other with a hug and a kiss, right side, left side, right again. Same as always, same as anyone.

"How many coffees did you have while you waited?"

"I'm always up for another," he said. "You?"

"That would be nice, but a quick one. You're keeping this mystery locked down tight. I can't wait."

"It's not going anywhere, don't worry."

Finding a cafe wasn't difficult, and neither was drinking the coffee in one gulp.

"Well, okay then, let's go," he said.

Being in Agon's car brought back the memory of finding the cobalt ring outside of Tirana. This time, he drove more carefully. The road followed the coast, slithering past hotels with yellow or blue awnings, built into the cliffs.

"That's it," Dita declared. "I'm coming here this summer for vacation, and I'm bringing my whole family. I'll plan it when my sister comes to visit."

"I don't blame you. It's amazing. Where did you go last summer?"

"Nowhere."

"Dita. You get vacation."

"I know." She had no excuse, not even a lame one.

Soon thereafter, Agon turned the car left and away from the sea, and began the incline. Plots of scraggly grass, neglected olive trees, and clump after large clump of wild berry bushes rose and fell on both sides of the unpaved road.

They passed a sign that read *Tragjas i Ri*, or New Tragjas, and a left arrow. They continued straight.

"Let me guess. Old Tragjas was destroyed in the war."

"You guessed it. It had quite a run. Since the fourth century BC."

"Quite a run," Dita echoed.

The road ended at the entrance of Old Tragjas. Dita got out of the car without taking her eyes off the ruins and wreckage. She walked forward, mesmerized. Agon was right; the aura here had a distinct *ping!* in the universe. For anyone willing to listen.

Dita felt awkward and exposed, like she was interrupting a close-knit community. She rolled her feet, heel toe, heel toe, over the fertile earth. In every direction, archaic foundations supported weeds and vines. No, not only weeds and vines. In the center of what might have been a house grew a healthy fig tree. Dita cupped her cheeks with her hands. The tree billowed and stretched, reaching for the neighbors' homes. A voice in her heart spoke to the presence of former countrymen. *It will feed you,* Dita begged the spirits. *Come back. It will nourish all of you with supple figs that fall into your hand at the slightest touch.*

Birdsong was the sole sound to break the silence. A silence not to be found in Tirana, not even at three in the morning.

"God," she breathed.

"What—"

"Agon!" Dita put her hands to her chest. "That's twice now you've scared me!"

"Where else would I be?"

"I didn't know where you were, exactly." Her mouth swept into a smile. "This is … truly incredible."

"But this isn't what I called about. It's a bit of a hike, when you're ready."

"Okay."

Dita and Agon walked through brush, short trees and boulders similar to the ones they had driven past in the car. Dita stopped at a flat part of the hill to catch her breath. She turned around and saw the green valley falling, running to the sea.

"Well, you're right"—Dita waved her hand out in front of her—

"about this, too." She should sketch this, but how? How do you draw sanctity and reverence?

"Yeah." He stuffed his hands in his pockets and looked out at the blue–dark blue expanse. "Come on, we're about halfway to the cave."

"A cave?"

"Yeah," he said. "It's our specialty, and don't you forget it."

Her heart could stay and listen to the serenity until forever. She ached to hear the rush of the sea that she could see from this vantage point. Dita swore to her heart she would hold this feeling tightly until she could return. With her family and Aunt Val's notebook.

The landscape changed to a forest of oaks and neglected olives. Boulders lay scattered everywhere, looking as if they had been pushed from the mountain's peak and tumbled until they ran out of steam.

"So, defensively," Agon began, "anyone in the cave would be pretty safe. Until they weren't, at which point, of course, they would have nowhere to run." Agon walked a step ahead, as if this were his backyard. He climbed like an agile billy goat, and Dita felt like a clumsy foal.

"You must've been one of those kids who played in the hills all the time," Dita said between breaths.

"Guilty as charged. Generations of my family, both sides, are from Gjirokaster. Cousins are still there and all. The houses are built into the mountainside."

"Right. Sorry, you were saying this cave would be a good place to hide out?"

"Great in the summer, not so much in the winter."

What it would be like to live in a cave for weeks, maybe months, as so many had over the centuries? Some had sought shelter during the war, narrowly escaping the Axis powers. In peacetime, a shepherd would spend nights in a cave with his herd. With or without bombs dropping overhead, a substantial number of people had thought the caves trustworthy to safeguard their valuables. Dita's job was evidence of this, that the caves were a refuge.

They stopped on top of a boulder, directly in front of such an opening in the rock.

"This is it?"

"This is it."

They stepped inside. The forest's melody morphed into a faraway hush. The stagnant air smelled like algae and tasted wet and ever so salty. Dita swallowed. The cave was tall enough for them to stand at their full height and then some. Their feet stepped over gravel and soft earth, reminding Dita of the salt scrub Nora gave her one year for New Year's.

Agon flipped on a flashlight and walked further in. The cave widened into the shape of an onion.

"So this." From an outcropping, he lifted a brown metal box, about the size of a shoebox, but longer. "This is it." Agon brushed some sand from the top. *DN-81112* was stamped on the front side in yellow paint.

"If you want," he said, "we could take it out and sit on top of the cave."

"On top?"

"Yeah, and the view is better. May I show you?"

"All right," she said. She might hear that *ping!* again.

Indeed, there was a narrow path, mostly hidden by bushes, next to the entrance. With the box under one arm, he held out his other steady, slim hand to her. She looked at him and then, without a word, took his hand.

Dita felt light, like she was walking in a dream—the view, the box, the breathlessness from the climb. She looked at Agon. Her smile broke into a small laugh, a laugh of incredulity at the beauty surrounding them. A laugh, admitting that she should have been going to the gym all this time, as Luljana suggested.

Agon smiled back and handed her the box. Then, his shyness broke their gaze. He ran his hands over his hair. She hugged the box to her chest. The whole world was on pause. There was no sadness or evil, just Earth's breath.

"Come on, sit down here," Agon said. "Open it."

"Is this too much suspense for you? Is this the first time someone other than you has opened a new piece? Did you already open it?" She pushed him with her shoulder in jest. His hand brushed her back.

"Maybe. Okay, yes, but only enough to know it's good. Really good. And it's not jewelry." A breeze pushed against his collar.

She looked at Agon once more before she opened the box. *It's been him all along. His is the heart you need.* She leaned toward him and kissed him. He kissed back sweetly, lips warm and confident.

"It's been you all along," she whispered, an inch from his mouth.

"Likewise," he said.

"I didn't see it. How long have you known?" she asked, as she moved her hand to find his arm. Every other part of her was frozen, on fire.

"A while. I was scared to hope. I'm sorry," he replied. His eyes took in her features now, up close, closer than the two of them had ever been. He tucked a corkscrew of her hair behind her ear.

"No, it's okay. I'm the one who's sorry." They smiled, lips grazing, and kissed again.

Glossary

Baba   a priest of the Bektashi order of Sufism

Babi   Father, in central Albania

Bac   Father, when addressing him directly. Northern Albanian dialect. To be grammatically correct, when speaking about and not directly to him, Bac is referred to as Baca. For clarity and consistency, the author kept Bac throughout the story.

Ballisti   Albanians within the Balli Kombëtar, a nationalist, anti-communist movement who aligned themselves with Nazi Germany.

Besa   an oath of honor of utmost importance

Çifteli   two-stringed instrument

Gëzuar   cheers

Gjyshi   Grandfather

Hajde   let's go

Kanun   The Canon by Lekë Dukagjini, a compilation of customary laws within the tribes of Albania, especially in northern Albania

Lahuta   single-stringed instrument usually accompanied by storytelling

Motra	Sister
Opinga	house slippers in northern Albania
Papare	a dish made from stale bread boiled in water. Pa pare – without money
Plis	men's dome-shaped woolen hat
Raki	a distilled spirit made from grapes
Shapka	house shoes, slippers
Shpirt	term of endearment meaning life-breath, implying shpirti im – my life breath, my spirit
Shpirtrat	plural for shpirt
Teqe	in Sufism, a place of worship
Unaza	lit., a ring. A term for the bus loop in central Tirana
Vlah	a person of the ethnic European group largely known for their nomadic way of life
Xhezve	small pot used to make Turkish coffee, from the Turkish word cezve
Xhubleta	traditional dress of northern Albania
Zana	fairies, common characters in Albanian folktales. Zana, singular
Zemra	a term of endearment meaning heart, implying zemra ime – my heart; from the word zemër, the heart – the organ in the body

Further Reading

Bailey, Roderick. *The Wildest Province.* London: Jonathan Cape, 2008

Durham, Edith. *Twenty Years of Balkan Tangle. London: Centre for Albanian Studies,*

Durham, Edith. *The Struggle of Scutari.* London: Centre for Albanian Studies, 2015

Hupchick, Dennis P. *The Balkans.* New York: Palgrave, 2001

Mangerich, Agnes Jensen. *Albanian Escape.* Lexington: The University Press of Kentucky, 1999.

Smiley, David. *Albanian Assignment.* Leeds: The Estate of David Smiley, 1984

Albanian Folktales and Legends, ed. Robert Elsie. London: Centre for Albanian Studies, 2015

Shote Galcia, en.wikipedia.org/wiki/Shote_Galica, Last modified July 24, 2023.

Acknowledgements

Thank you to my Furxhi family for lovingly sharing their insight and life experiences. Thank you to my Fitzgerald family for their encouragement and professional opinions. Thank you to the Ninja Writers community; I'm so glad to have met you. Thank you to my beta-readers and friends for their support and feedback. Thank you to Kamila Franz for her help with the maps. Thank you to the editors Pam Sourelis, Doreen Martens, and Julia Quay. Thank you to the cover designer, Richard Ljoenes, and the interior designer, Iram Allam. Thank you to the artists on my Desiderium playlist, including Freya Ridings, Dermot Kennedy, Niall Horan, Alban Skenderaj, and Fabrizio Paterlini—creatives who took me down low and deep with their work, then brought me up again. Thank you to Phillip Glass for *Glassworks 1*, performed by Signal—that piece was there from the very, very, *very* beginning. Thank you, shpirtrat e mamit, for being just that—*shpirtrat e mi*. Edhe per Zemrën time, thank you for your editorial help, your understanding, dhe dashurinë tënde çdo ditë. Jeta ime me ty është si një ëndërr.

About the Author

Julie Furxhi enjoys reading, sewing, and happy dance parties in the kitchen. She cannot be trusted near a fresh batch of oatmeal chocolate chip cookies. She lives with her family in Colorado. This is her debut novel.

Printed in the USA
CPSIA information can be obtained
at www.ICGtesting.com
CBHW020715310124
PP14852600001B/2